© nilitsu

ALFRIK GULLIVER

A warrior who managed to reach Level 5 despite being a prum. Together with his three younger brothers, bears the title Bringar.

HEDIN SELRAND

Puts his faith in Freya. An intelligent magic swordsman. His title is Hildsleif.

OTTAR

vel 7, the Labyrinth
ty's strongest. His
title is Warlord.

ALLEN FROMEL

A first-tier adventurer,
the Labyrinth City's fastest.
His title is Vana Freya.

HEGNI RAGNAR

A dark elf and
Hedin's old foe.
His title is Dáinsleif.

"...So she can smile like that, too?"

The oasis had already become the goddess's personal slice of paradise.

© nilitsu

Familia Chronicle

Episode FREYA

VOLUME 2

FUJINO OMORI

ILLUSTRATION BY
nilitsu

CHARACTER DESIGN BY
SUZUHITO YASUDA

NEW YORK

IS IT WRONG TO TRY TO PICK UP GIRLS IN A DUNGEON?
FAMILIA CHRONCLE: Episode Freya
FUJINO OMORI

Translation by Dale DeLucia
Cover art by nilitsu

This book is a work of fiction. Names, characters, places, and incidents are the product of the author's imagination or are used fictitiously. Any resemblance to actual events, locales, or persons, living or dead, is coincidental.

DUNGEON NI DEAI WO MOTOMERU NO WA MACHIGATTEIRUDAROUKA
FAMILIA CHRONICLE episode FREYA
Copyright © 2019 Fujino Omori
Illustrations copyright © 2019 nilitsu
Original Character Design © Suzuhito Yasuda
All rights reserved.
Original Japanese edition published in 2019 by SB Creative Corp.
This English edition is published by arrangement with SB Creative Corp., Tokyo in care of Tuttle-Mori Agency, Inc., Tokyo.

English translation © 2020 by Yen Press, LLC

Yen Press, LLC supports the right to free expression and the value of copyright. The purpose of copyright is to encourage writers and artists to produce the creative works that enrich our culture.

The scanning, uploading, and distribution of this book without permission is a theft of the author's intellectual property. If you would like permission to use material from the book (other than for review purposes), please contact the publisher. Thank you for your support of the author's rights.

Yen On
150 West 30th Street, 19th Floor
New York, NY 10001

Visit us at yenpress.com
facebook.com/yenpress
twitter.com/yenpress
yenpress.tumblr.com
instagram.com/yenpress

First Yen On Edition: October 2020

Yen On is an imprint of Yen Press, LLC.
The Yen On name and logo are trademarks of Yen Press, LLC.

The publisher is not responsible for websites (or their content) that are not owned by the publisher.

Library of Congress Cataloging-in-Publication Data
Names: Ōmori, Fujino, author. | Nilitsu, illustrator. | Yasuda, Suzuhito, designer. | DeLucia, Dale,translator.
Title: Is it wrong to try to pick up girls in a dungeon? familia chronicle episode Freya / Fujino Omori ; illustration by Nilitsu ; character design by Suzuhito Yasuda ; translation by Dale DeLucia.
Other titles: Dungeon ni deai wo motomeru no wa machigatteirudarouka familia chronicle episode Freya.
English | Episode Freya
Description: First Yen On edition. | New York : Yen On, June 2018.
Identifiers: LCCN 2018006599 | ISBN 9780316448253 (v. 1 : paperback) |
ISBN 9781975327552 (v. 2 : paperback)
Subjects: | CYAC: Fantasy. | Kidnapping—Fiction. | Adventure and adventurers—Fiction.
Classification: LCC PZ7.1.O54 It 2018 | DDC [Fic]—dc23
LC record available at https://lccn.loc.gov/2018006599

ISBNs: 978-1-9753-2755-2 (paperback)
978-1-9753-1825-3 (ebook)

1 3 5 7 9 10 8 6 4 2

LSC-C

Printed in the United States of America

VOLUME 2

FUJINO OMORI

ILLUSTRATION BY nilitsu

CHARACTER DESIGN BY SUZUHITO YASUDA

Ali and the 8 Followers

1

"I wonder where my Odr is."

—*Here we go again.*

Ottar was struck by an impulse to cover his face with his boulder-like hand.

"Hey, Ottar…"

"You mustn't."

"…I didn't even say anything yet."

"You cannot go."

In his usual overbearing way, Ottar admonished his patron goddess, Freya, who was pouting like a moody child.

They were on the top floor of Babel, the looming tower at the center of the Labyrinth City, Orario.

This one-of-a-kind space was a physical manifestation of the special privileges granted to the patron goddess of the familia that reigned at the top of the city. The giant, flawless glass window that looked out over the metropolis below; an entire wall devoted to elegant bookshelves that were filled to the brim; the plush carpet so thick that crossing feet sank into it; striking depictions of the sun and moon; a side table that tastefully evoked the image of an apple tree.

Compared to the conspicuous gaudiness of the avaricious wealthy, this room was furnished with relatively few items, but the craftsmanship visible in each and every item was enough to demonstrate the class of the room's owner.

It was here, in the beautiful goddess's private chambers, that Ottar was trying to talk some sense into Freya.

"You were about to say that it was time to search for your destiny again."

Freya was having another of her fits. The aforementioned Odr was the companion she was fated to be with one day, and she was planning to set off on an aimless journey to find them, wherever they were.

For Ottar and the rest of the familia, Freya was the sole object of their absolute loyalty, the one they offered all their respect, veneration, and love to. As far as they were concerned, the idea of her going on a journey alone was nothing short of sweat inducing. If even a single scratch were to mar their goddess's beauty, her followers would never forgive themselves. If such a thing ever happened, the members of Freya's familia were liable to take on extreme penances, like scarring themselves worse than anything their goddess suffered as an act of atonement.

In general, they were overly protective, but this attitude was emblematic of how devoted they were to their goddess and just how precious they considered her to be.

Ottar's response was a natural extension of those values.

Normally the shining example of a perfect retainer, Ottar's response smacked of a lecture. Freya, reclining in her regal armchair, took offense and elegantly raised an eyebrow.

"Ottar? When did you learn to speak to me like that?"

"Ordinarily, I would never take such a tone with you, Goddess. However, I only have your best interests in mind. As your vassals, it is our job to admonish you if it is necessary for your own safety."

". . ."

Beneath his almost excessively polite choice of words, Ottar was trying his best to communicate that Freya should restrain herself in light of her position as the patron goddess of what was arguably the city's most powerful familia. The lack of a rebuttal seemed to indicate that she found his argument persuasive.

Once in the past, Freya had gone for a stroll in Orario without bringing along any of her children. While she never went beyond its walls, she was still out on the streets of one of the world's largest metropolises, all alone. Ottar and the others had understandably panicked and turned the city upside down looking for her. Mistaking *Freya Familia*'s mobilization as the prelude to some major operation, *Loki Familia* had raised their alertness in response, which ultimately led to an accidental clash. This racked up tensions between the two factions and the dispute came very close to escalating into open warfare.

Incidentally, Freya had tried to play off that disaster with a cute smile and an "I'm sorry. ♪" (Given her demeanor at the time, it wouldn't have been strange if she had giggled and stuck her tongue out to boot.) For once, Ottar and the other members of *Freya Familia* could do nothing but watch as the goddess Loki delivered divine justice to Freya with an iron fist.

Returning back to the moment at hand, Freya understood that her current situation was liable to end in a similar fashion, so she reined herself in and opted to candidly express her displeasure instead. Her childish outburst was rather charming. This unexpected contrast was a perfect example of the "gap appeal" that many deities often spoke of. The sight of Freya pouting like a little girl was so bewitching that it wouldn't have been strange if Ottar fell to his knees on the spot.

However, he was certain that if a burly man such as himself openly reacted that way, he would be called out for being creepy. Fully aware of what was at stake, Ottar somehow managed to maintain control by sheer force of will.

"How is it that you can spend so much time by my side and still not understand how I feel?"

"…I hope you find it in yourself to forgive me. If you ask for anything else, we will gladly do it for you, even if it costs us our lives…"

"You're trying to keep me locked in a gilded cage, just like the foolish gods who tried to keep me cloistered up in the heavens."

She refused Ottar's attempts to placate her and completely abandoned her usual sublime bearing, behaving like a fickle sprite. Turning away from him, she swept a dismissive hand to the side.

"Leave me."

The enchanting goddess of beauty could never be satisfied with just one love. Not even countless loves could ever be enough. At a glance, her amorous nature appeared to simply be outrageous and immoral. However, that was merely by the standards of mortals. As a deity, there was probably nothing insincere about her feelings.

Ottar had a faint sense of what Freya truly wished for, which made things complicated for him. While he could understand what it was she wanted, he had to do whatever he could to stop her from behaving recklessly. His desire to respect Freya's will and his concern for her safety were at odds with each other.

"…"

At times like this, the expression that often crossed Ottar's face betrayed his utter loss at how to respond. If anyone watching were asked to share their impression of what this warrior was feeling, it would definitely be described as sorrow.

The young girls working as attendants were getting worked up in the corner of the room, looking to Ottar for cues on how to proceed.

One of the boar's ears on top of Ottar's head bent over, as if to drive home the fact that he had no idea what to do next.

Later that day, as the flood of light and the bustling chatter of the sleepless Labyrinth City filled the night air, several figures gathered around a giant round table. This meeting was not taking place on the top floor of Babel nor was it some nondescript bar on the outskirts of the city. It was inside *Freya Familia*'s home, Folkvangr, located in the city's fifth district. They were in a conference room where only the top members of the familia were allowed to enter.

"What's this about, Ottar?"

Allen Fromel, a cat person sitting at the table, was the first to open his mouth. Though he was only one hundred sixty celch tall, his gaze was piercing, so sharp that it caused others to shrink back. His very presence seemed violent, as if he might snap at any moment. The black fur and blue eyes he sported would have normally been considered quite handsome if not for how dangerous he seemed. He was a Level 6, a first-tier adventurer known as Vana Freya—Freya's Chariot, a paragon of Orario whose name rang out far beyond the confine of the city walls.

"How long has it been since the last emergency assembly?"

"The all-out war with the Evils, wasn't it?"

"Then this must be for a battlefield to match that."

"Should we ready our weapons?"

The same voice ringing out four different times came from the quadruplet prums sitting across from Allen. They were the Gulliver brothers, first-tier adventurers of *Freya Familia* often mentioned in the same breath as Vana Freya. The four of them were known collectively by the title Bringar, the Four Knights of the Golden Flame. As Level 5s, their teamwork was indisputably the best in the Labyrinth City, and they were powerful enough to overcome the physical disadvantage of being prums. Naturally, their features were identical. The only visible difference between them was the slightest variance in eye color. From the right, starting with the eldest, they were Alfrik, Dvalinn, Berling, and Grer.

"The harbinger is upon us, the horn of demise signaling the twilight of Orario…a great war embroiling all the familia comes…M-my arm trembles…Heh. Hee-hee-hee-hee-hee…"

"Don't force yourself to speak, Hegni."

The dark elf's lips twisted into an ominous grin marred by spasms that only aggravated his struggle to string words together. The one chiding him like this was a regular occurrence was a white elf. The elven duo, Hegni and Hedin, was often considered a pair even though they were not related by blood. Their full names were Hegni Ragnar and Hedin Selrand. The former had dark sable skin and silver hair that was almost a pale purple, while the latter had white, nearly translucent skin, and golden hair flowing down his back. They were both Level 6, first-tier adventurers, and they were both magic swordsmen who wielded powerful magic and their weapons with equal amounts of skill. The titles they were granted by the gods were Dáinsleif and Hildsleif respectively. Together, they were known as the black and white knights.

The people currently assembled at this round table were *Freya Familia*'s pride as well as their greatest assets in battle.

"The reason I summoned you all is…Lady Freya."

Looking around the table, Ottar's solemn voice rang out as he got right to the point and raised the topic at hand. In other words, how to control Freya's urge that had reared its head yet again.

"…So that's what it is."

Immediately, Allen and the others fell silent as everyone present assumed rather serious expressions.

"In that case, I understand why we were all called."

"It was fairly touch and go last time…We were right on the verge of a direct confrontation with *Loki Familia*."

"Yeah, we nearly killed Nine Hell."

"Wait, I thought the real issue was that we had pissed off all the elves, even the ones outside *Loki Familia*, and barely managed to escape their wrath."

"""Shut up, Alfrik."""

While the elder brother bore the full annoyance of the other three Gulliver brothers for pointing out an inconsistency in their stories, Allen glared at Ottar.

"I said it before, didn't I? We've given her far too much freedom. Who cares if she's passionate or whatever? We should force her to behave a bit more like a proper patron deity. Even if that means locking her away in a cage."

"—Watch your mouth, filthy cat."

"A stray like you has no right to infringe upon our goddess's freedom."

The Gulliver brothers had instantly put their bickering aside to confront Allen for his comment, but he refused to back down, spitting back with venom in response to the four sets of murderous eyes now trained on him.

"A bunch of nobody prums who can't do shit by themselves shouldn't be so cocky."

"Heh…Hee-hee…Now is the time for ones such as I, who have surpassed savage valor, to show their devotion…No one can match my zeal, and of course that includes you worthless rabble…"

"I said quit talking already, Hegni."

With even the dark elf Hegni joining in, the meeting was quickly spiraling out of control. Hedin's heavy sigh went unheard as the hostile atmosphere thickened around the round table. The leadership of *Freya Familia*, or rather all of Freya's children, did not have particularly good relations with one another. In fact, the majority was often at one another's throats. The only one they had sworn loyalty to was Freya. And the only thing they desired was her favor. The other followers with whom she had shared her ichor were nothing more than obstacles to be kicked aside. In order to demonstrate who was more deserving of her love, they held death matches masquerading as training every day.

Despite knowing that was happening, instead of putting a stop to it, Freya would simply smile and say, "You get along well, don't you?"

But that severe internal rivalry was the secret behind the dominance of the city's strongest faction. The ceaseless competition that cast aside cheap platitudes like "working together to grow and mature" was what enabled them to reach ever greater heights at a speed that no one else in the city could match. And they did all of it in order to court their goddess's love. Freya's charisma and divinity were what drove them.

Theirs was a strength born of refusing to pay any heed to their comrades, the polar opposite of *Loki Familia*, led by Braver and other adventurers who banded together to reach their true potential.

On one side was an assembly of powerful individuals who constantly probed one another to maintain their keen edge. On the other was an organization of like-minded allies who cooperated closely to cover one another's weaknesses. That was the most fitting description of the two familias at the top of all Orario.

"Starting another unsightly quarrel won't solve anything. Whatever we do, we should do it quickly…"

Hedin pointed out the meeting's lack of progress in the hopes of making some headway.

Unable to dispute the elf so handsome that even deities admired him for it, Allen and the others scoffed as Ottar nodded and returned to the original topic.

"Restraining Lady Freya…will not be an option this time, either.

Indeed, if we snatch away her freedom, it will only cause an even more severe outburst later. The best we can do is to protect her from the shadows."

Everyone's eyes lit up at Ottar's grave tone. They were all glaring, intent on keeping one another in check. The meeting had shifted to the next dispute on the docket: Of all the first-tier adventurers in the familia, who was best suited to protect Freya?

"I'll go with her. I'm her chariot." Allen was the first to speak up.

"Heh." One of the prums immediately sneered at his response.

"—Which of you assholes laughed?"

The cat person exploded with murderous rage in the blink of an eye as the Gulliver brothers openly ridiculed him.

"A cat pulling a chariot? Don't make me laugh."

"Hey, we won't get anywhere this way, so drop it, Dvalinn."

"Quit pulling chariots and just go plow the fields already, livestock."

"Listen to me, Berling."

"Filthy cat, rutting just because our goddess scratched your chin once or twice."

"I said stop already, Grer!"

""""This is why pets like you are so worthless!""""

"Stop this!!!"

—More accurately, only three of the Gulliver brothers were mocking Allen. The eldest was desperately trying to hold them back.

Alfrik Gulliver was the most worldly of the four brothers. Though he was older than his siblings by only a few moments, the role of reining in his unruly brothers often fell to him.

Even as it became clear that Alfrik was on the verge of tears from yelling, no one at the table seemed inclined to help. As far as the rest of them were concerned, they considered this business as usual.

The situation was deteriorating and only getting more explosive by the minute, which prompted Ottar to speak once more in a heavy tone.

"...As I suspected, I'm the one who should go with her."

""""Huh?""""

In an instant, the air around the table froze. As if they moved with the will of one mind, every single person around the table glared at Ottar.

"Know your place, boar. Bold of you to propose standing next to our goddess with that enormous head of yours."

"Besides, how exactly are you planning to sneak around with that huge body of yours, meathead?"

"You'll just make her uncomfortable, meathead."

"Have some shame, meathead."

"The only joke you should stick to is that ridiculous thing you call a body, meathead."

"Hee-hee-hee…M-meathead."

"You really are quite the disappointment, Hegni. That said, you *are* a meathead, Ottar."

"……"

Unsurprisingly, Allen and the rest were quite unhappy with the boaz adventurer entrusted with serving as Freya's retainer.

Ottar's face went blank as he fell silent, mercilessly berated from all sides by his heartless comrades. It wasn't because he was the head of the familia and believed that he should be where the buck stopped when the familia members complained. No, even Ottar could get angry and had limits to his patience. He wasn't that tolerant. However, he recognized that as a simple warrior, he could not win against them with his words. In other words, what he needed in order to silence them was—his fists.

He exchanged gazes with each and every one of them.

Even when empty, a first-tier adventurer's fist could easily be considered a lethal weapon, and Ottar's cracked as he clenched it. Right when it seemed like the tension was about to snap, Helen entered the room.

"Umm…Lady Freya has left behind a letter and gone out…"

""""What?!""""

Ottar and the others all swung around to focus on Freya's lady-in-waiting. They all froze, wide-eyed, like statues.

—This bunch is beyond help.

Helen's eyes stared off into the distance as that single thought crossed her mind.

"It should be fine as long as I don't cause a fuss inside Orario, right?" Freya, would-be queen, spoke to no one in particular as she stood outside the giant walls enclosing the Labyrinth City.

She realized her excuse was nothing but exploiting a technicality, but that was hardly enough to stop the capricious goddess from going where her whims took her.

Just a few scant hours ago, the goddess had quietly forced her way into the Guild chief's office. The head of operations, Royman Mardeel, was understandably flustered by her sudden appearance as she approached him with a seductive look. Once an enamored expression appeared on his face, Freya struck.

"—*You don't want me to tell Ouranos the secret you've been keeping, do you?*"

Royman turned deathly pale, and Freya smiled broadly as she whispered a proposition. "If you find it agreeable, we could just say that I enthralled you and made you let me out of the city."

As she stood there with a smile that would captivate any victim, she was without a doubt the epitome of an enchantress. She was like the wind itself, slipping through any and every crack in the city, and even the highest-ranking official's secrets were not safe.

The Guild chief customarily forbade familias from leaving the city, let alone their deities, but Freya's ultimatum left him little choice. In the end, he caved in to her request and allowed her to depart.

"It's rather refreshing to see the outside world like this..." She laughed to herself quietly. "...Or perhaps it's simply the building anticipation that I'm feeling."

A sea of grassland plains spread out before Freya. All along the road paved with white stone stretching into the distance like a bridge, the smell of fresh blossoms and flower petals dancing in the air seemed to greet her. Spring was in full swing. Freya was certain the goddess of this gentle season was surely in a good mood and blessing her trip.

"East, west, north, or south?...You there, which direction do you think would be best?" Freya called out to a group of people on their way to the city.

The goddess was sensibly wearing a robe with the hood pulled up to conceal her identity. Passing her by was a traveling merchant with a horse-drawn cart, some travelers in road-worn clothes, and a demi-human bard. Staggered by the goddess's beauty that was apparent even when obscured, they each pointed in the direction they recommended.

The Beor Mountain Range to the north.

"—If you pass through the rugged valleys, there is a hidden lake as beautiful as any in the Dungeon."

The saltwater lakes leading to the ocean to the west.

"—This time of year, you should be able to see a sight that can't be found anywhere else in the world: waterfalls rising up into the sky."

The stretch of land that led to the center of the continent to the east.

"—You will be greeted by the wondrous bazaars that have thrived from trade that spills out from the Silken Road."

The unexplored expanses that had not yet been fully mapped to the south.

"—The remnants and ruins lost to the passage of time will surely show you something that has never been seen in this lifetime."

Freya smiled faintly as the children of the mortal plane sung the praises of each respective direction, like odes in honor of a goddess. Her eyes narrowed bewitchingly as she looked out at the scene unfolding before her.

"Now then, where could my Odr be waiting for me?"

2

The ship flew over the "sea." There were two tall masts thrust into the air and large white sails opened wide to catch the westerly wind. The ship itself was a mix of wood and metal, large enough to easily carry more than fifty crew and passengers. This vessel cut a dauntless figure as it sailed, its prow slicing through the swells in its way.

However, the ship was not sailing across a blue ocean but atop a sea of sand.

"Crossing the desert on a ship seems more eccentric than ground-breaking," Freya commented as glaring sunlight beat down on her. Not even the hottest days Orario had ever seen were comparable.

She stood atop the deck of the ship, balancing herself against the railing and staring off into the vast expanse of the desert. To the average observer, there weren't many scenes odder than what looked like a proper seagoing vessel crossing the desert dunes instead.

"Still, it's certainly a part of this world that I didn't know about. Perhaps heading in this direction was the correct choice."

Freya smiled with her eyes as the bone-dry wind whipped past her. Her journey had started at Orario, once called the edge of the world for its location on the western fringes of the continent. After she departed from the city, she headed southeast in search of unknown lands she had never visited before. The first notable sight she encountered was an expanse of sand that reached past the horizon in every direction.

This was the Grand Sand Sea, which was as about as far removed from the deep blue as a place could be. It was also known as the Kaios Desert, an arid region located to the southwest of the center of the continent, where so many countries were clustered.

"Ottar and the others have brought back all sorts of items from Sand Land and the like, but…it really is another thing altogether to experience it myself."

Towering dunes spanned a great distance, like a mountain chain that continued for as far as the eye could see. A never-ending carpet of sand and wisps of gritty clouds wafting into the blue sky. Was the hamada swaying at the distant edges of her vision a mirage or just a product of heat haze? When she managed to put the oppressive temperature and desiccating atmosphere out of her mind, the sights were stunning. Looking out at the majestic world of sand from the view atop a ship was what let her smile at it.

An attendant with a veil covering the lower part of her face approached the goddess and suggested she retire to a room inside the ship, but Freya refused with a raised hand.

Seeing that, a man approached her.

"Is the desert cruise to your liking, Lady Freya?"

He was a stoutly built human. The arrangements for the trip aboard this ship were thanks to him.

"It's quite stimulating. Never before had I imagined something like this was awaiting me outside of Orario," she responded frankly.

"Splendid! It is an honor that a no-name merchant such as I, Bofman Fazoul, can be of service to a goddess! Should you desire anything during your journey, don't hesitate to let me know!" The merchant finished with a slick salesman smile.

His name and body shape were reminiscent of the Guild chief, Royman, but Bofman was taller and broader. The black beard and tanned skin combined with the turban atop his head gave him the air of a true resident of the desert.

"Truly, it is a blessing from the heavens to even meet the Lady Freya, whose power and jewellike beauty is praised throughout the mortal realm. A chance to accompany you like this cannot be anything but a stroke of good fortune! Surely the patron god of merchants smiles upon me!"

Perhaps he intended it as flattery, but Freya was struggling not to laugh at Bofman's bombastic, colorful speech. After all, when it came to gods in Orario who were most often associated with merchants, the first one who came to mind was Hermes with his shady grin. Moreover, Bofman called himself Freya's companion, but it was not like Freya had gone out of her way to employ him as a guide or anything. She had simply met him in a town right before crossing the Kaios Desert.

Upon entering a tavern, Bofman had noticed Freya's peerless beauty peeking out from beneath her hood and could barely contain his interest. Once she had revealed her identity, he leaped at the chance to volunteer himself as a guide for Freya's journey that had no specific location in mind, free of charge. Of all the merchants there who had offered their services, he had simply been the fastest.

All of that just so he could have the honor of assisting Freya on her travels, probably in the hope that he could earn a favor from *Freya Familia* while also making sure that *the* Goddess of Beauty, Freya, remembered his name. To a merchant, such an achievement was no different from earning an immense profit. Connections with a powerful familia were profitable in all sorts of situations, ranging from the obvious—like selling supplies, equipment, weapons, and the like—to being able to call upon them to deal with dangerous or difficult jobs. "Better to join hands with a powerful familia than weak royalty or nobles any day of the week" was a well-known saying among merchants. And when the familia in question happened to be arguably the most powerful faction in the city hailed as the center of the world, then the return from that connection might well be considered immeasurable.

The costs of an aimless journey were a cheap price to pay if it meant building a relationship with Freya. It was a sign of how far Freya's reputation had spread to the rest of the world when even a lowly merchant like Bofman flew into a frenzy at the sight of her.

"Bofman, I came here to escape boredom, and I chose you because of your talents. Since you've accepted the job, I expect you to provide an experience that can satisfy a goddess's ego."

"But of course, Lady Freya! Leave it to the great merchant Bofman, who has crossed this desert countless times!"

"First of all, I'd like to go someplace where the children gather."

"Leave it to me! Hee-ho-ho!"

Setting aside his penchant for boasts, Freya recognized that Bofman was actually a skilled merchant. That said, the way he spoke and laughed annoyed her from time to time.

But in any case, Freya allowed herself a bit of anticipation for what was to come. A smile unlike that of the queen of Orario crept across her face as she enjoyed the scenery of the desert without pretense. The goddess of beauty's smile, tinged with a hint of childlike innocence, left Bofman and the attendant beside Freya stunned, entrancing them both.

"That reminds me…Was this ship made in Altena?" Freya suddenly asked.

"Huh? Ah, yes, yes it was!" Bofman's voice was a whole pitch higher than normal as he snapped back to his senses. "It is called a desert ship! Altena recently started selling them here in the Kaios Desert!" He made the declaration proudly as the speeding ship raised sand clouds in its wake.

Alongside Orario, the magic country of Altena was considered another major global power and this ship was effectively a giant magic item that had been manufactured within its borders. Produced from the dedicated work of dozens of mages, it was the world's first desert-sailing ship.

"What powers the ship? With how many dunes there are, it can't possibly be driven by wind alone, yes?" Freya asked as the ship crested over another dune.

Unlike a normal ship that was propelled by wind and currents, this vessel had to operate on different principles. Bofman pointed down below the deck.

"It uses magic. Over thirty slaves are held at the bottom of the ship. The ship is able to sail thanks to the power they provide. Controlling a ship with magic is rather fitting for Altena, wouldn't you say?"

According to further explanation, there were apparently several crystal orbs positioned on the bottom of the ship that were designed to absorb magical energy when hands were placed on the orb. A magianaus—a magic ship rather than a military trireme powered by oars.

I see. That is rather like Altena, Freya thought.

Altena was a country with a fundamental belief in the supremacy of magic. They had an elitist bent toward mages and the like and the citizens of Altena could readily be seen saying "Magic is everything" with straight faces.

Between the thousands of people making a living thanks to magic, it was plausible a significant proportion of residents were elves—that was why they were hostile toward Orario and its powerful mages…

Those without magic are not qualified to control this ship. The voice of Altena's magic supremacy could almost be heard emanating from the ship.

"It seems we should be wary of Altena…"

Recently, the magic-stone-based items that were the pride of Orario's economy were being exported to the rest of the mortal realm. It was common knowledge that they were the most used tools due to their utility, but this desert ship was an amazing development as well. Because it could not operate without magic power, it was not a product that could be used by the masses, but at the very least it had the potential to power a new method of commerce in the desert regions. Altena and the other countries and cities around the continent were serious about not letting the Labyrinth City have a monopoly on all the good ideas.

However, for the slaves used to run it, life was just as harsh as ever. Even if a revolutionary new magic item was developed, even if they did not have to row the oars, they were still exploited and drained of magic in order to power the vessel.

"Does your firm also handle slaves?" Freya asked. She was a goddess, but she had no intention of declaring it inhumane.

"We do, though it would perhaps be most accurate to say that all of the Kaios Desert region does. Unlike Orario, where you've established your castle, this land is barren, a harsh world of sand where the institution of slavery is accepted," Bofman responded carefully, explaining the system of slavery they had developed, which was not present in Orario.

There were several areas in the mortal realm where slavery existed, even outside the Kaios Desert. In fact Orario, which was hailed as the capital of adventurers, was considered the exception for its complete lack of a slave market. While it was true that the Guild maintaining the familia system imposed more structure and regulations on its residents than other countries and cities did, the biggest reason for the lack of slavery surely lay in the intent of Ouranos and the other deities who worked with him. They were trying to build a promised land where a hero would be born, so they rejected what they considered to be a heretical system.

"I didn't really ask before, but your company is mostly a trading company, isn't it?"

"As expected, Lady Freya! I underestimated your all-seeing eyes! You are correct. We immediately purchased a desert ship when it became available and handle a portion of the trade routes that cross the desert!"

She had just asked on a whim, but that was all the encouragement Bofman needed to start a heated explanation.

"Even as large as the Kaios Desert is, the number of firms with a desert ship can be counted on one hand! The Fazoul Trading Company is truly the most suited for ensuring you the perfect journey!"

Freya could easily tell that Bofman was boasting as he rubbed his hands together enough to wear away his fingerprints, but she could also tell that it was not a lie, either. Even looking out into the distance, there was not another desert ship to be seen anywhere in the sand, which reached all the way to the horizon. A traveling merchant train on camels fading into a dot in the distance was all there was. Those who owned a desert ship like the one she was riding were surely rare. And when it came to trade, while a ship sailing the sand certainly evoked a certain sense of oddity, it was entirely reasonable when imagining the desert as a sea. Considering how valuable sea routes were for trade, and considering the fact that cargo ships able to carry large amounts of goods were often the most favored, it was reasonable that someone who owned a ship that could sail the sands would be successful. History told the tale of how important ships were to commerce, so a desert ship to cross the Great Sand Sea was certainly well suited for that task.

On that point, Bofman could certainly be called an influential merchant.

"And I must say, the clothes I prepared for your journey suit you quite well."

However, he talked too much, and his constant patronizing tone was also quite off-putting. Slightly fed up with him, Freya looked down at herself. She was wearing a short white dress, a red hood to avoid the sun, and a matching red waistcloth paired with a sheer black skirt that enticingly veiled her legs. All the pieces were decorated and held in place by various rings.

The outfit was sort of understandable for both dealing with the brutal sun beating down on them while staying cool, but she could just wear a cloak for that. And as an eternal, unchanging deity, getting sunburned was of no concern.

The new clothes she had acquired for the long journey had also been provided by Bofman. From the outset, members of the crew were constantly mesmerized by the alluring figure of the goddess atop the deck. That was to be expected to some extent, since it was the goddess Freya standing there after all, but she was still a little bit concerned that it might be impacting the ship's navigation.

"Gee-hee-hee…"

The other concern was Bofman, who could not restrain his lustful gaze. The merchant certainly appeared extremely rational and composed, but his sticky gaze crawled over every inch of Freya's body.

"Hee-hee! Lady Freya, considering how I'm contributing to this by bearing not insignificant expenses, in the event you are able to achieve your goal with this journey, I'd quite like to ask a favor, if it pleases you…"

"…"

The merchant was leering at the luscious, otherworldly legs peeking out from Freya's skirt. Perhaps because he was true to his desires, he was filled with motivation in anticipation of getting a little something for himself. Besides the commercial benefit of pleasing a deity, being invited to share a bed with a beautiful goddess was both the greatest privilege as well as the greatest pleasure possible in the world.

Even if it cost him everything, he wanted to experience that one night's dream. There was a never-ending supply of people with that same thought, though. To the goddesses of beauty, shallow people like that were the most boring of all, and they largely just ignored them. However…

Avaricious in addition to being lecherous. He has the worst sort of character, but there is no question he is extremely shrewd…In a way, he's the quintessential merchant.

When she saw right through Bofman with her divine sight, Freya felt the same sort of disinterest as every other goddess. Because she recognized the appeal of her own body, she did not feel overly unpleasant to be subjected to such lust-filled gazes. She observed it with detachment, merely thinking, *It's a good thing Ottar and the others aren't around.*

If the crusaders who worshipped at the altar of the Goddess Freya—namely her followers—had been present to see someone acting so impudently, they would have immediately crushed, pulverized, and blasted any who dared to gaze at their goddess with such impure thoughts. Truly, Bofman was lucky.

It was unknown how many times those who had been impolite to Freya had been discovered having suffered tragic accidents, and it would be safe to say that there were none left in Orario who would behave so insolently.

As a beautiful goddess, annoyance and discomfort were always with her. And also, other goddesses' jealousy, other goddesses' jealousy, and other goddesses' jealousy.

Because of that, Freya was well schooled in not letting minor irritations get to her and revealed no visible signs that she was dissatisfied with Bofman. She just naturally brushed her hair behind her ear, and then—

"I can hear something."

"Huh?"

"It's not a very pleasant sound, though," Freya said as she closed her eyes.

As Bofman stared at her in confusion, the strange noise that only the goddess could initially hear gradually approached. The roar of the surf and the cries of seabirds could not be heard on an ocean of sand. And there was no such thing as rough seas or whirling maelstroms. There was not even a sandstorm happening, so if there was a noise shattering the lonely calm of the desert, then it could only be—

"—GUOOOOOOOOOOOOOOOOOOOOOOOOOOOOO!"

—caused by monsters.

Right in front of the ship, a massive plume of sand blasted into the air like explosives going off. A giant worm burst out aboveground. Its skin was a sandy color, and its long body undulated in a way that evoked a visceral disgust. It did not have anything that could really be called a face, just a giant round mouth around where its head would be that was filled with hideous fangs. Raising its upper body off the ground, it was tall enough to match the desert ship.

"That's a…a sand worm?! And it's a big one!" Bofman exclaimed as he lost his composure and grabbed onto the side of the boat.

In the ancient times when monsters spread all across the surface world from the giant hole, their territory encompassed the land, sea, sky, and everywhere else in the mortal realm. The Kaios Desert was no exception.

Sand worms moved underground, and when they detected the presence of prey, they burst out from their hiding places. The abnormal sound that Freya had heard had been caused by the monster burrowing its hole.

"T-turn the ship arouuuuuuuuund! On the double!" Bofman shouted, spittle flying from his mouth.

The merchant train riding camels in the distance panicked and was already fleeing. The human guard on lookout on the deck turned pale and seemed to be getting ready to use the cannon the ship was equipped with, or perhaps some kind of magic, but it was already too late. In response to Bofman's command, the slaves poured in more magic in order to speed the ship up, but they wouldn't be in time, either.

It was a perfect surprise attack. Their guard had not been diligent enough. The monster was too close. The worm's giant mouth was about to tear into the ship's mast and smash against the side of the ship.

And while all this was going on—

"That's not necessary," the goddess announced matter-of-factly.

"What?!"

"Unfortunately…"

Freya's tone was not one of surrender. Instead, as if finishing her thought for her, the sand worm's head was blown backward.

"Gueeeee?!"

The cries it raised in the throes of death were drowned out by the sound of a large amount of blood spurting out. A sharp flash of silver reflected the sun's light. By the time that flash was visible, it was already over.

"............Huh?"

Time froze for Bofman and the rest of the crew. The monster slowly collapsed in a fountain of gore. Billions of grains of sand shuddered, unable to bear the load of the giant worm, and began billowing up into the air, causing a sandstorm as a thud echoed across the desert.

As Bofman and the others stood in shock, Freya finished her sentence with a smile.

"...it seems like they've already caught up to me."

Inside the swirl of sand, eight different figures were visible: four small prums, two elves, a warrior with a giant sword on his shoulder, and the catman who had sent the monster's head flying back with such blinding speed.

They were like the classic image of knights arriving to save a goddess from monsters, a fairy tale come to life.

"...!"

Bofman's face tensed up as he glanced over at Freya, who was calmly watching it all without any concern. The lust abruptly drained from his gaze as he started to tremble in trepidation. He apparently finally realized exactly who the deity before him was and just what kind of familia that Vanadis, the Goddess of Love and War, could call upon.

He broke into an intense, uneasy sweat, fearful of being condemned for the disrespect that he had perpetrated earlier. However, Freya simply said, "Shall we go?" to the many trembling gazes accompanying Bofman's.

She nudged the journey back into motion with a light tone. And as the sailors finally came back to their senses, their shoulders heaved while they quickly hurried to demonstrate their obedience to the goddess's divine will.

The ship left the monster's corpse in its wake and continued to sail the sea of sand.

"We finally caught up, huh?"

Allen's silver spear whistled through the air as he swung it down to remove the monster's sticky blood. He was wearing a hooded robe over his standard equipment. Audible annoyance at the free-spirited master who was always causing him trouble rose into the air, carried by the desiccated breeze.

"Let's go," Ottar said.

The Gulliver brothers, Hegni and Hedin, and Allen had already started running on their own, not waiting for his instructions. They moved so silently and so quickly they seemed to have been erased from the scene, leaving only footprints and the slightest trace of unsettled dust in their wake while the members of the merchant train that had just been starting to flee wondered whether they were seeing a mirage.

The goddess's followers chased the ship disappearing into the distance, determined not to let her escape again.

Freya and the desert ship arrived at the town of Leodo. A town built around an oasis praised for its clean, refreshing water, it felt almost like a small island situated in the middle of an endless sea.

A port specially designed for desert ships had been constructed in the south part of town. By following the three-meder-high wall surrounding the town that kept out monsters, they arrived at the port. Because it was a sea of sand, there was no lowering of anchors. The ship was instead fixed to a docking pillar with chains.

Down on the wharf, a scene similar to that of a seaport unfolded at the large desert port built of stone. Cargo was unloaded from the surrounding ships and carried away. Because desert ships were so expensive and rare, there were not many of them, but the mass of people moving around them did not seem particularly any less busy than what would be seen in an average port city. Most of the activity was done by well-built men, though there were many children who appeared to be pages rushing around, too. In terms of races, dwarves, who were well suited to heavy manual labor, were unsurprisingly well represented.

The main difference between this desert mooring and a normal seaport was the lack of a salt smell and the fact that most people were not showing much skin in order to avoid the intense sun. Nearly everyone was wearing clothes that were designed to be breathable and comfortable.

"It's a bit late to be commenting on how dry it is," Freya said as she climbed down the gangway lowered from the ship and set foot in the port.

Despite the fact that she was wearing a robe with a hood, there were still those who caught a glimpse of her and stopped moving, their attention stolen away by her beauty. Young and old, men and women alike. Accustomed to such occurrences, Freya easily led Bofman and his protégés, cutting through the center of the port.

"I'm sure Ottar and the rest have already slipped into the town..." Freya said to herself, the murmur drowned out by the bustling docks.

"Hmm? I'm sorry, did you say something, Lady Freya?" Bofman asked.

"It's nothing," Freya said, brushing it off.

Her followers had not shown themselves, but it was entirely impossible that they would have failed to track the ship, so logic dictated that they were somewhere nearby, hiding, positioned so they could immediately react if anything should happen to Freya. Since she had already gotten this far, and because they did not want to ruin their beloved mistress's mood, that was their sign to her that she should do as she pleases.

She could just imagine Ottar's brusque face silently nodding and Hedin closing his eyes and sighing. And Allen would be getting progressively more annoyed even as he made sure to stay closer to her than anyone else. Smiling to herself, Freya decided to not hold back anymore and just follow her whims.

"Bofman, tell me more about this town," Freya said.

"It could best be described as a merchant town. It is located in the country of Israfan. Israfan is a country that has grown quite prosperous from its trade, and Leodo is a town centered around an oasis close to the country's border," Bofman—who was carefully following two steps back and one to the side of the goddess—explained as they cut through a section of the warehouses that the Fazoul Trading Company owned.

The Kaios Desert was split into east and west by the giant Nire River running through it. And Israfan, the country of merchants, was located on the western side. In telling the history of the Kaios Desert, the closer to the great Nire River a country was, the more likely it was to flourish, and the farther it was, the smaller it was likely to be. Israfan was one of the latter countries. It was surrounded on all sides by several different countries in the middle of the western desert. And the town of Leodo was located near its northern border.

"The town itself is not particularly large, but thanks to the oasis, it is a place that is easy for people to gather. And on top of that, it is almost at the exact center of the western Kaios Desert, so it would not be hyperbole to say it is a crucial location for trade."

"So that's why its port is so well furbished, too?"

"That's it exactly. Both in terms of the logistics of moving goods around the surrounding countries and being able to observe the trends in nearby countries, this town is a crucial base for merchants, a place that is easy to live in without the risk of losing touch with the market trends."

Apparently there were several other towns like this one, but Leodo was the most convenient of the lot. It was safe and orderly and had limited exposure to monster attacks. In other words, it was a town that was blessed by geography and had become rich because of it.

Freya herself could tell that the town was thriving just by the fact that it had built a desert ship port. That they had recognized the utility of the Altena-made magic item that had not yet become the norm for the desert world and invested a significant sum in it made it clear that the town was an important hub for merchants, just like Bofman had said.

"And from here, we can easily reach any country in the western desert, so we should be able to find whatever you are looking for, Lady Freya—or at least, that was what one such as I was thinking!" Bofman finished decisively, still intent on earning her favor.

Incidentally, she had not told him anything about what she was searching for: her fated companion.

While Bofman was acting proud for no particularly obvious reason, Freya splendidly ignored him, moving forward like the unfettered breeze. As they emerged from the warehouse district adjacent to the port, the field of view dramatically opened up.

"Ooooh…a merchant town really is a fitting way to describe it."

What greeted Freya was the bazaar. It was probably the main street, since the wide avenue was filled to the brim with stalls. There were humans and demi-humans wearing the same kind of turban as Bofman, street merchants accepting valis coins and exchanging them for various products. Luxury goods like carpets and vases, clothes for crossing the desert, swords and guns and other weapons and gear, as well as oil and gunpowder. Any- and everything was being sold in a decidedly organic and unorganized fashion.

In terms of food, there were a variety of freshly made breads and dried beans as well as all sorts of dried meats. There were several different kinds of preserved fruits and dates shining like jewels. Burlap sacks and jars filled to the brim with spices imported from places outside the desert realm by merchants like Bofman were flying off the shelves.

There was a veiled elf taking orders, mixing the spices like a magic powder into a soup filled with dried meat; a prum trying to entice customers by raising a full ladle from a cooled water pitcher and sipping at it as if it were the most refreshing thing in the world; and a teenage beastman barbecuing a fresh fish. Most likely that was something bred in the giant oasis. As befitting a place called a merchant town, seemingly no expense had been spared in developing the local industries.

The ground was a copper color, hardened by the countless people constantly moving around over it. An Amazon on a camel pushed her way through the bustling crowd. The buildings on either side of the street made of sun-dried bricks likely belonged to this or that trading company. There were also many taverns. One of the round tables shoved out into the street a bit was surrounded by red-faced dwarves enjoying a hearty lunchtime drink. The busy street never seemed to rest.

Just like with the sun overhead, there was a different sort of energy in the air compared with Orario. It was more chaotic, more intense, and had a wilder, freer feeling to it. At least that was how it felt to Freya. As she walked along the street, she elegantly looked around, basking in the unique atmosphere of the desert country.

"The oasis is quite grand as well," she commented.

Looking straight ahead, the big oasis was visible up ahead at the center of the city. Beyond the bazaar, what looked like an emerald-blue lake was visible. On top of that, there was a great deal of greenery as trees that could usually only be found in the southern countries were growing around the oasis. And on the island at the center of the oasis that was connected by a bridge to the rest of the town, dozens of luxurious buildings lined the streets. Even the pavement of the roads was different.

And among all that splendor, the most eye-catching thing of all was surely the giant mansion featuring a majestic dome. It almost looked like a castle. Its magnificence easily blew any mid-tier familia's home out of the water. It was well within the realm of upper-tier familias' homes.

"The flow of people and goods is certainly lively. Always something fresh and interesting to see."

"Yes indeed, yes indeed!"

Bofman had settled comfortably into his role as guide, rubbing his hands, beside himself with excitement.

Upon further observation, there were many vendors dealing with magic-stone goods. The designs were a bit different, but there were stalls lined with dozens of lanterns with designs befitting the desert. Orario's magic-stone goods were leaving their mark even in the desert world.

The Guild must be proud, Freya thought without any particular emotion. And then her eyes suddenly narrowed.

But the atmosphere here stings.

The bazaar itself was booming, but something in the air was

on edge. Freya, with the all-seeing eyes of a goddess, had astutely noticed the mood of the town.

"As you can see, this is a town where many people and things are gathered," Bofman said as he held out his hand, gesturing to the surroundings, entirely unaware of Freya's observation. "Goods from other countries, of course. And slaves as well."

As if timed with his words, a different sort of stir spread through the bazaar.

"Ah, speak of the devil," Bofman said.

As the two of them turned around, a group emerged onto the main road from one of the side streets. Males and females of various races were paraded out, all wearing the same rags that could hardly be called clothes. Every face looked exhausted. Some were tinged with despair, others with disappointment. There were many with wounds covered by clotted black blood. They had iron manacles on both wrists to keep them from fighting back and collars around their necks connecting them to one another with rusted chains. Slaves.

"...Bofman, what are they doing with those slaves?"

"I imagine that's a fresh batch one the slave traders brought in, since this town has a slave market as well."

"That seemed like quite a few slaves. Do they go hunting for people like that often?"

Freya did not feel particularly shaken or disgusted, but she did feel a bit suspicious. That was too many slaves. Even at a glance, she could count more than a hundred of them, which was absurd. Just simple kidnapping or people selling themselves to pay off debts would not reach that sort of a number. That line looked more like someone had raided several villages and then sold everyone they captured into slavery.

"No, of course not! They would not under any circumstances disrupt the order in the countryside here! However..."

Freya could generally guess the answer Bofman had for her. The tense mood of the town and the large number of slaves. Those two taken together would mean—

"In the western half of Kaios, there is currently a war going on..."

That.

"A war, huh?"

"Yes. The country directly north of Israfan, a kingdom known as Shalzad, is being invaded by Warsa, which lies to the east."

Freya did not know much about the current state of affairs in the desert, but she did have a basic understanding of region. Every country established in the Kaios Desert was a kingdom. There were not any country-style familias influenced by a deity's divine will, and the majority of familias in the desert were generally managed as the military arms of kingdoms. It was common to see low-intensity conflicts, but full-scale wars for supremacy were rare—or at least they were supposed to be.

"There have been rumors in recent years that Warsa has been paying a powerful mercenary familia to support their military, and then they unilaterally declared war on their neighboring country, Shalzad..."

"And Shalzad was immediately defeated?"

"Yes. They were apparently incapable of resisting Warsa's military might. Their capital fell and the interior of their country is being overrun..."

"Hmmm...meaning their country has fallen into chaos, creating a convenient environment for hunting slaves."

"Indeed."

Soldiers drunk on blood and violence could easily become beasts. In the process of invading Shalzad, Warsa forces had surely attacked every settlement they encountered along the way. Innocent villagers and townspeople were brutalized, and those who just barely managed to escape would have been easy pickings for slave traders.

"That explains the heavy mood over the town."

It also explained all the weapons and gunpowder and the like in the bazaar. The merchants had caught the scent of war and were stocking up on items that would be crucial if more conflict broke out. Meanwhile, the residents of the town were feeling nervous at the signs of war.

"D-don't worry! The capital of Shalzad did fall, but the Shalzad army still has their prince, who managed to escape, and there is still a resistance movement rising up in every corner of the country! Warsa surely has their hands full with dealing with that, so there won't be any sparks flying in our direction!"

Meaning the invasion was an ongoing process. Even if the capital was taken, as long as the country's officials and soldiers continued to resist, the war would drag on, and they would not dare bring a third country into the mix. Bofman tried to assure Freya of the town's safety while carefully watching her face.

"A-anyway, the rumors say that Warsa's soldiers are even now rampaging through the towns and villages of Shalzad. The fleeing refugees are falling into slavery, but…that's not an uncommon sight in this desert realm."

"…"

It was a long procession of young and old, men and women, being forced to walk through the center of the bazaar. The crowds split to the sides to avoid them, whispering to one another as the people passed. Whether their whispers were filled with scorn or pity did not particularly interest Freya. However, with her ability to see the radiance of children's souls, as far as she was concerned, it was a boring spectacle. The souls of those who had been enslaved were all a dull, ashen gray. For Freya, who prized brilliant, gleaming souls, it was a spectacle that bordered on viscerally distasteful. Not many people would be pleased to see a mountain of sludge and waste. Even though it was another country's problem, the flames of war burning brightly would cause the scene before her eyes to occur again—the number of slaves would continue to grow. If that happened, she would not be able to search for her Odr in peace.

"L-Lady Freya, your clothes…!"

As even Freya looked on at the procession in discontent, the wind blew. Bofman became flustered because it had blown her hood down. He was concerned about the bazaar grinding to a halt if the people noticed the goddess of beauty's dazzling figure. After all, he himself had been captivated by her profile. Just as it seemed like the surroundings had been hit by a wave of murmurs, it quickly died back down.

Those who had noticed Freya stopped moving, their faces blank as if they were in a dream. The same was true for the slaves as well. They stopped walking, their eyes widened, and their mouths dropped open. Even in the midst of the despair that had caused them to close off their hearts, they just had encountered something entirely not of this world. No matter how much the slave traders pulled at the chains and cracked the whip, they could not break hold of the goddess's beauty.

The procession of slaves ground to a halt.

"—!!"

Something new had appeared. Freya's silver eyes noticed a glimmer. Hidden in the middle of the chaotic line, there was a girl who seemed to be hiding behind the others—as if concealed by the shadow of the countless stagnant souls. She had brown skin and disheveled black hair. Her eyes were a light purple. Her face was a bit dirty but exceedingly well proportioned. Her figure, hovering on the edge between young girl and adult, evoked the image of a not-quite-ripe fruit in Freya's eyes. She was probably fifteen or sixteen, wearing the same sort of rags as everyone else, while looking down at the ground as if trying to hide herself as much as possible.

"…!"

Seemingly noticing the goddess's eyes, she met Freya's gaze, and just like the other slaves, her eyes opened wide—and then she immediately looked away.

That was a shock to Freya. The girl had by her own will resisted the figure of a goddess alluring enough to entrance any mortal.

The girl was again pointedly looking at the ground, her face twisted by her predicament and yet still dignified. Her grim, sharp gaze had not faded yet. Like that of a tiger biding its time, waiting for the moment to strike. At least that was how it appeared to Freya.

As the slave merchants finally regained their senses and cracked their whips to get the procession moving again, the girl disappeared from Freya's sight in the press of slaves.

"Bofman, we're going."

"Yes, Lady Freya…? Wh-where did you want to go?"

Fixing her hood, Freya started walking like the wind as Bofman

© nilitsu

desperately tried to keep up with her. The goddess's lips curled into a crescent smile.

"Please take me to the slave market."

The slave market was near the very heart of the central district of Leodo, built along the southwest edge of the oasis. It was clear at a glance that several of the buildings had been constructed by skilled masons, with dedicated platforms for the slaves to stand on, so that those who visited the market could conveniently inspect the products. There were also tents scattered all around the plaza, and even some merchants who simply had the slaves lined up on a carpet laid on the ground.

Perhaps because of a need for manual labor, there was a preponderance of male animal people with good physiques. As for women, it was mostly human women who were capable of producing children with basically every race. Amazons were the least common at a glance. The most beautiful specimens were displayed at the front to garner the most attention. Most of them were beautiful girls with exotic darker skin, wearing almost entirely transparent veils. Probably to make it obvious at a glance that they had not been damaged.

To the right was a gorgeous oasis. And to the left was a garden filled with slaves whose resignation was pasted across their faces.

Not a bad display, Freya thought unironically.

If Hestia or Artemis or Astrea saw it, they would surely have pursed their lips in disgust. Well, Artemis would probably have pulled out her bow and arrow before going on a rampage to save all those who wanted to be saved.

"Welcome, welcome, milady! Welcome to our slave market! My name is Rozzo, the manager of this establishment."

Having reached the trading company she was looking for, Freya was greeted by a human similar to Bofman. He was middle-aged, average height, and average build. His face was not too shabby, and he had a beard. His attire was top class, so much so that even if all the other merchants nearby pooled their resources, they still would not match him. Put bluntly, he was arguably a superior version of Bofman.

"Hey, Rozzo, this is the Lady Freya, whose renown sends tremors through even the Labyrinth City. Carelessness won't be forgiven," Bofman said as he leaned forward to emphasize his point.

"Come now, Bofman. Just because your trading company lost out to mine...You remind me of that Far East saying: 'You're a tanuki trading on a tiger's reputation.' Or was it a fox?" Rozzo snickered a bit at him. "And this coming from a small little company that can't even afford to buy a building on the island. You might be a bit too green for this kind of conversation."

"Arghhhh! That's rich coming from the weakest of the big four!" Bofman's face turned red as he stomped the ground.

They seemed to have some kind of history, but Freya really could not care less. And honestly, the scene of a full-grown adult's flabby stomach jiggling in frustration was just hideous.

"There was a child among the slaves who were brought here that caught my interest. Would it be possible to see them?"

"But of course!—Hey, line 'em up!"

Even without Bofman saying anything, Rozzo had already found out about Freya. He did not hesitate to do as she asked, ordering one of his underlings line up the slaves he had just gotten in.

"...How revolting."

Freya looked around the surroundings again as the slaves were being readied. The only people who were lively were the merchants. The majority of the sea of slaves was hunched over, looking down at the ground like convicted criminals.

It was not like anyone who became a slave did it because they wanted to. If you looked hard enough, maybe you could find one or two hoping to be bought by a kind master or perhaps dreaming of a livelihood that was better than whatever they had left behind. But at least as far as Freya's eyes could see, everyone's spirit was clouded over.

Having lost their pride their dignity stripped from them, the despair stained not just their faces, but reached all the way to their souls. There was not even anyone begging for help. Nor was anyone praying to the gods. Freya coughed a little, as if the despair filling the air made it hard to breathe. It was almost a mournful sigh.

The eagle-eyed Bofman was the only one who seemed to notice, though, as he kept glancing over at her nervously, perhaps concerned about the goddess's mood.

"Sorry to have kept you waiting. Here are the items you requested. As you know, we only just received these products, so they have not received any training at all. However..."

Finally, the slaves were lined up in a single row under the brutal sun's rays. They had surely been walking for quite a long distance. Every last one of them looked exhausted. The elderly and youngest children looked like they might collapse at any moment. Rozzo alone had a grin on his face.

Freya started walking along the line. She completely ignored the pleading gazes and the eyes of those who had been charmed by her looks, simply confirming the faces of all the slaves in order.

And then she found her.

"...!"

The girl from before.

When the girl noticed the shadow had stopped in front of her, she looked up, and her breath caught. Freya put her finger under the girl's chin and made sure their eyes met.

"You, what is your name?"

"......Ali."

As if unable to defy the goddess's divine will, she whispered that and nothing more. Her voice was like a singing lyre that could be heard across the sands of the desert night. Her eyes narrowing, Freya released the girl and looked around again. Everyone was watching her, as if entranced by the goddess's each and every move.

"Hey, I've decided what I'm going to buy," Freya said.

"Ooooh! Really?!" Rozzo looked ecstatic at the goddess's words. "Very well then, which of them did you—"

Before the slave trader could finish his sentence, he was interrupted by the goddess's next words.

*   *   *

"All of them."

Time stood still.

"………Huh?"

Underneath that intense merciless sun, for just a second, the entire slave market fell silent. Everyone had the same reaction. The girl who called herself Ali, Bofman, and all the slaves nearby—none of them could move, not believing their ears. Rozzo, who was looking at the goddess, was the only one who managed to utter a sound.

"I said all of them. Every item you have in your inventory…and anything else for sale in this market. I'll take all of them."

She thrust her demand at the frozen slave merchant. As time stood still in the market, Freya smiled. It was the smile of an empress confident in her ability to do whatever tyrannical, irrational, or absurd thing she desired.

"This dull scenery is unpleasant, and this is a small town, so it is particularly eye-catching. Seeing slaves is unpleasant," Freya began speaking freely, without any inhibition. "After I'm gone, you may continue trading flesh to your hearts' content. However, while I am in this town, I insist you not show me anything that will ruin my mood."

And for that reason alone, she *bought all the slaves*. Not out of charity or compassion. Just because she wanted to change the scenery of the town for the few days she would be staying there.

"…M-milady! I'm honored, but if I may…our products all come at a price befitting their quality…T-to buy every…every one of the slaves in this market would be…!"

Managing to break free from his stasis, Rozzo's face started to twitch as he tried to point out as politely as he could what he was thinking: *There's no way you could possibly do that.* But Freya would not brook any back talk. Her smile widened as she asked the slave merchant before her a question.

"Who am I?"

"…Milady, you are the Goddess Freya."

"And what is my familia?"

"...*Freya Familia*, milady."

"And what is my familia's known for?"

"...For being the most beautiful and most powerful! They are the followers of the goddess who has amassed more fame and wealth than any in the world!"

The slave trader broke into a cold sweat.

And finally, Freya had one last question.

"I can have all of them, right?"

"—Yes, Goddess!"

Rozzo bowed, unable to do anything other than obey. At the sight of that, all the other slave traders turned pale and followed suit. The entire slave market was bowed before a single deity.

The next moment—

"*OOOOOOOOOOOOOOOOOOOOOOOOOOOOOOOOOOOOO OOOOOOOOOOOOOOOOOOOOOOOOOOOOOOOOOOOOO OOOOOOOOOOOOOOOOOOOOOOOOOOOOOOOOOOO!*"

—a staggering roar shattered the silence. Bofman and his attendants covered their ears to dampen the clamor. Men and women, young and old, people of every race. It was like the desert itself cheered. The cascade of voices sounded like a chorus of thundering waterfalls. There were those who cheered in joy. There were those who choked back tears. And there were those who dropped to their knees, clasped their hands together, and offered up a prayer of thanks to the goddess. The explosive swell of emotion coming from the slaves shook the entire market—no, the entire town.

The girl who was the goddess's true target stood there in shock as Freya turned away from her and calmly started walking away.

"Bofman, undo those children's bonds. My children do not need such accessories."

"R-right away, milady!"

Bofman's shoulders jolted as he called out to his trainees. Snatching the keys away from the merchants, they undid the restraints on the slaves one after the other. There was no way the number of employees he had there would be enough, so one was sent running to the Fazoul Trading Company's headquarters to gather every last person working there to help release all the slaves.

The slave market, filled with an unending stream of cheers, was about to become even busier. And, indifferent to everything going on around her, Freya walked briskly forward as Bofman desperately tried to keep up.

"L-Lady Freya! If I may, the money to pay the merchants...?"

"Just give me an advance on it. I'll give you a contract with the familia later to cover the costs."

Leaving Bofman aside as he went bug-eyed at the incendiary situation she was handing off to him, Freya added another item to her order.

"Also, ready something to transport those children."

"Those children" were, of course, the slaves she had just bought. She had paid for hundreds of them. Bofman was already in a cold sweat as he desperately tried to get his mouth to work.

"L-Lady Freya! Pardon me, but transport them where? My deepest apologies, but with the buildings my trading company has, housing all these slaves would be...!"

In response to Bofman's misgivings, Freya needed just a single finger to answer. The oasis in the middle of their field of view. She was pointing at the largest building in the town that looked almost like a castle with a dome, built in the middle of the island at the heart of the oasis.

"I'll buy that mansion as well."

This time, Bofman's jaw dropped as if it had come loose.

3

To the residents of the town, it was called the oasis mansion, and true to its name, it was built in the middle of the island at the heart of the oasis, its majestic dome bringing to mind a palace. It was constructed of a white stone that reflected the sun, inlaid with golden decorations to create a dazzling image. Surrounded by date trees, it was the largest building in all of Leodo. It could house hundreds of itinerant entertainers and play host to a days-long feast.

It was the most fabulous of villas that only the wealthiest of people—more specifically, the town's wealthiest merchant—could afford to live in. However, at present, that luxurious estate had been claimed by a certain goddess as her own.

"What are you doing? Food and drinks all around, please."

In the great hall of the villa.

An extravagant fountain—a sculpture of a water elemental pouring water—inside the manor was trickling away in the background as Freya's sweet soprano voice rang out. She was sitting atop a sofa set several steps above the ground, looking down as well over a hundred former slaves hungrily devoured the dishes being brought out one after the other.

Both because of having been forced into slavery due to the impact of the war as well as due to the careless management of the slavers, they had not had a filling meal in a long time. They downed glass after glass of water and wine while grabbing meat and fruits with their bare hands and stuffing their faces.

However, it was not an unsightly scene of people abandoning all manners and reason but a scene of exultation at being alive. They were no longer bound by chains or manacles. Freed from their shackles by a goddess's whims, they were in high spirits, tears flowing as their withered spirits were reinvigorated.

"Mr. Bofman! We don't have enough people!"

"I know! Reach out to people from the other trading companies! Tell them we'll pay for it if we have to—just get them over here!!!"

Meanwhile, the merchant Bofman and his trainees were caught up in a chaotic furor. They had brought the slaves to the estate, bought up all the food they could find at the bazaar, and were preparing countless courses for everyone as if it were a banquet. But the employees of the estate—whom Freya had also inherited from the previous owner of the estate—were extremely understaffed. Anyone could tell by the way they were running dishes around the estate, and employees of the Fazoul Trading Company were being forced to pitch in as well.

"Was it some mortal philosopher who said that wealth is not for feeding your own ego but feeding the hungry? Hmm, if Loki heard me saying that, she'd probably laugh herself to death."

The first thing she had done after acquiring the oasis mansion was to provide a bit of charity to all the slaves she had freed. Not so much out of a philanthropic impulse, but as the bare minimum of resolution to follow through on what she had done. If she had bought up all the slaves and wrecked the market because it was an eyesore only to come out the next day and say, "All right, you may do as you please," then her grace would have been called into question. To her, beauty was not simply a lovely appearance. It was fundamentally based in a character that was befitting a sovereign. And most importantly of all, they were now all her property. So given that, she would accept them all with a smile and have them attend to her as she saw fit.

"Lady Freya, please have some!"

"Oh, thank you."

One of the slaves who Freya had saved was holding out a tray with a colorful assortment of fruits. The brown-skinned beauty paled in comparison to a goddess, of course, but she was nonetheless blessed with looks that would charm many a man. However, it was clear from her eyes that she was enraptured by the goddess. And not just her. All of the beautiful men and women who were set to be sold as the playthings of the wealthy were attending Freya. Not because she had demanded it but of their own volition. Some poured wine, and others fanned her with giant leaves. They were obviously entranced by her, vying for the chance to wait on her hand and foot. At any moment, someone might have led an elephant in to perform for her.

But Freya had by no means truly enthralled them. They were merely filled with a deep sense of loyalty and respect for the alluring goddess who had saved them. It was a scene that occurred purely due to the queenly presence, the absolute charisma that Freya wielded.

An observer could almost hear Freya saying "A harem? A reverse harem? As if either could possibly satisfy me." The lurid fantasy of having dozens of beautiful men and women serve them was one that every mortal had surely dreamed of at least once, and each and every one of the people around Freya was entranced by the silver-haired goddess just as deeply as the members of the familia that had sworn loyalty to her.

It was the pinnacle of luxury.

"Lady Freya, thank you for saving us!"

And there, a young boy and girl approached the goddess. There was no one who would scold them as rude for speaking out of turn. Their pure, earnest thanks were what everyone felt.

"What are your names?" Freya asked.

"M-my name is Y-Yona!" the nervous boy responded.

"I'm Haara!" the younger girl answered cheerfully.

"I see. Those are nice names. But Yona, Haara, you don't need to thank me, because I only freed you all for my own sake."

That was the unvarnished truth. She had not had any kind of merciful or charitable intentions in granting them their freedom. It had all been self-centered, just the whim of a fickle goddess. Yona and Haara tilted their heads, not really comprehending what she said, but they quickly adjusted themselves.

"Ummm, Lady Freya...there was something I wanted to ask!"

"Hee-hee, go ahead. What would you like to ask?"

"Can we join your familia?"

The boy and girl responded with an admirable question. They probably wanted to repay the goddess who had rescued them in their time of need. Faced with those adorable children, Freya responded with a pure smile and no ulterior motives.

"No, not yet. First, you should help out at Bofman's company." Freya admonished the children with a smile.

"Wah?!" Bofman, who was rushing around, stopped in his tracks at suddenly being called out.

She fully intended to leave all the slaves she had bought with the Fazoul Trading Company when she returned to Orario.

"Your souls are still just seeds. They're not even developed enough

to be called immature. I love beautiful flowers and adore sparkling jewels. So first, you must gain some experience in this desert
land."

The qualifications to join *Freya Familia* were entirely based on the
goddess's mood. Freya looked not just at ability but at the sparkle of
a person's soul and chose only those capable of becoming Einherjar. That was why they were the pinnacle. That was why they were
the strongest. *Freya Familia* was a place where those who only had
talent and nothing more would quickly become stepping-stones
for their peers in the intense internal struggle that unfolded every
day. If immature, undeveloped children were thrown into that, they
would undoubtedly be struck down and meet a tragic end. Because
of that, Freya was strict in her choices, allowing only those beings
capable of becoming suitable followers of hers to join.

At the same time, she made the choices she did because she appreciated
the children, because she loved them, and most importantly, because
she had hopes they might show her something new and unknown.

"And once you've grown more, when your souls begin to bloom,
if you catch my eye…when that time comes, I'll gladly welcome you
into my familia," Freya added as she reached out a hand and stroked
the little girl's cheek.

"Y-yes, ma'am!" Haara responded, her voice brimming with joy
and determination.

Judging from the brilliance of those children's souls currently, if
they were to bloom, it would only be after around ten years. However, perhaps with the potential inherent in mortals, they might
betray her expectations and reach their prime in just five years or
maybe even sooner. If that came to pass, Freya would gladly welcome them in, whatever their age. She always kept her word. That
was the kind of goddess Freya was.

"Lady Freya, if it pleases you, I'd like that, too!"

"Please allow your humble servant to sit at the lowest seat of the
table of your followers!"

The children's requests opened the floodgates, and even the adults
began approaching with their supplications. Freya maintained the

same stance as she had with the children, while promising to welcome those who were capable and caught her attention as noncombatant members—those who would not receive her ichor and not gain a status. In short, they would be believers who would support Freya and her familia. She had not particularly been expecting this development, but it ultimately meant she was able to increase her network of supporters outside the city.

Despite the fact that a clear line was being drawn between them and the goddess, the former slaves' devotion to Freya did not waver in the slightest. Every one of them approached the goddess who had saved them and thanked her with an unpracticed formality generally reserved for addressing royalty.

At some point, the feast turned into an audience of people lined up before her.

"Bofman, hire any of these children who wish to work for you. If their loyalty to me is true, then they should rise in stature and become great successes. After I return to Orario, I'll leave this estate to you, so do as you please......Bofman, are you listening?"

"Y-yes, of course, Lady Freya..."

Having finally finished everything, Bofman shakily returned to Freya, exhausted. It was finally sinking in just exactly what it meant to be subjected to the whims of a goddess—just how heavy a load it was to serve as Freya's companion. Absurd and unreasonable requests were the norm. With naught but a single command, he would find himself carrying out tasks that by any measure of common sense should have been impossible.

The various costs incurred would be paid back later from *Freya Familia*'s deep pockets, but even still, he was being forced to bear a significant burden and pushing his limits. He had gained an emaciated look that was a common affliction among the people who tried to curry favor with deities in a calculated fashion.

"L-Lady Freya...my trading company, of course, but I personally have spared nothing in my dedication...so if you might find it in your heart to grant me a reward at such time as your desire has been fulfilled, I would be eternally grateful...gweh...hee-ho-ho...!"

And because of all that, it was inevitable he would continue to hope for some extra return. His eyes were glued to the goddess's bare legs that he could practically smell as he laughed with a creepy, raspy voice. Freya turned around, feeling almost a sense of wonder as four shadows silently appeared.

"What do you think you're doing, swine?"

"Did you wish to be castrated, swine?"

"I'll carve out those eyes of yours, pig."

"Filthy pig."

"*Gweeeeh?!* W-wait! Wh-what are you…?! Stop! My arm! It doesn't bend that waaaaa—*gaaaaaaaaaaaaaaaaaaaaaaaaaaah*!"

The loud, satisfying sound of a kick landing rang out, followed by a dull *thump* as Bofman's swollen body was slammed headfirst into the ground. Immediately, he was placed in a submission hold that threatened to create some new places where his limbs could bend as his whole body creaked.

Four prums were pushing him down to the ground in a pose exactly like that of a pig splayed on all fours.

"Oh, you were here?" Freya asked.

"We combed through the entire residence to be sure no assassins or suspicious elements were here," Alfrik, the eldest of the Gulliver brothers, responded.

From the moment their patron goddess had bought the oasis mansion, they joined Ottar and the others in investigating the grounds from top to bottom, and upon discovering a fool so rude as to look the wrong way at the goddess, they brought down the heavens' wrath upon him.

Leaving the restraint and torture of Bofman to his brothers, Alfrik removed his sand-colored helmet, revealing his clear blue eyes. And then he looked down at the man below him as if he had caught a glimpse of the vilest sewage imaginable.

"Filthy swine with ulterior motives are not fit to be at Lady Freya's side. May we have a little time to *punish* him?"

"As long as he's still useful. Don't finish him off. He is necessary as my eyes and legs here in the desert."

"Understood, milady."

Alfrik saluted and then he and his brothers forcibly carried Bofman away.

"Lady Freya?! Please save meeeeeeeeeeee!" Bofman called out a strangled cry for help as he was hauled off.

The former slaves were startled by the sudden appearance of the Gulliver brothers and started sweating bullets in terror even after they left. It was not hard to imagine the fate that would befall the foolish merchant dragged outside. Their decision, which was the wise response, was to forget what they had just seen and continue to pay their respects to Freya.

"—Oh, so you came."

And then, she appeared right as the line was starting to peter out. Brown skin and disheveled black hair. The girl with such pretty purple eyes. Ali, the slave girl Freya had fallen for at first sight—the person who had the potential to be the goal of this journey, her Odr.

"…Thank you very much for saving me earlier."

There was a nervous tension to Ali's expression as she said her thanks by mimicking the form that the others had used. Freya's eyes narrowed as, for just a second, the girl seemed about to put her hand to her chest before stopping herself and bowing inoffensively instead.

"Ali, how is your body doing?"

"Thanks to you, I'm doing much better…"

She had been freed from bondage and brought along to the estate as a result of that, but her face looked much healthier, probably because of getting enough water and food. But something about the way she spoke was awkward. It almost seemed like she was uneasy or on edge about something. Nonetheless, though, Freya's smile widened, as if even that awkwardness was amusing.

"Then tonight, come to my room," she said, putting a finger beneath the girl's jaw and pulling her in.

"!"

Their faces were so close that the slightest shift might have had their lips touching. The goddess's silver eyes reinforced the command.

Ali's body quivered as the alluring goddess looked into her eyes from so close—but again, she rejected Freya's gaze. Biting her lips, her cheeks flushing, Ali forced herself to look away, fleeing the goddess's charms. A simple girl who had not even been granted a deity's blessing, let alone leveled up. There was no more holding back Freya's curiosity—or her sadism.

"My shopping was a bit extravagant today, but—you were my heart's desire."

"Gh…?!"

"Which is why you won't be getting away," Freya whispered in Ali's ear as she let the girl go.

Ali staggered back, but her face was badly twisted. There had never before been a mortal who looked like that while being allowed to bask in Freya's presence, which only served to increase the goddess's anticipation. As the former slaves' shocked gazes focused on the girl, Freya stood up from her seat.

"Clean yourself up for tonight. And when you come to my chamber, wear something to show off your lovely figure."

Freya instructed Bofman's trainee girls to take Ali to the bathing area. Ali was stunned, and for just a moment before the attendants reached her, she quickly scanned the surroundings. Seeing that, Freya let an "Ahh" slip out as if she had just remembered something and gave the girl a warning.

"I said you wouldn't be getting away before, but to be clear, that was not a threat, just a simple fact. My followers are even now watching over this estate. So don't bother trying anything silly…" Freya said as she left the room, seeming to be enjoying herself.

Her words and smile left the girl utterly astounded. Outside the residence, the sun started to set. The night was only just beginning.

Desert nights are chillingly cold. It was common knowledge in the sandy regions of the world that the intense heat of the noonday sun vanished dramatically come nightfall.

However, that was not the case for Leodo.

It was all thanks to the oasis. The water took more energy to heat up than the earth, and once it was warm, it took longer to release all its heat and cool down. The water absorbed the light of the noon sun and released the heat at night, so at any place with an abundance of water, the difference between day and night lessened. On top of that, the palms and other foliage around the town also had the effect of trapping some of the heat radiating from the ground as the air cooled down, moderating the evening chill. Because of that, the night in Leodo was easier to endure than most anywhere else in the western Kaios.

That was why Freya could comfortably wear a thin negligee in her room as she waited for the girl to arrive.

"Should be any moment now."

Enjoying herself as she sipped the expensive wine that the Fazoul Trading Company had procured, the goddess checked the time.

The location was her bedroom, which had been cleared of people. The chamber on the highest floor of the oasis mansion was dimly lit by magic-stone lamps. The orange light blended with the night air, creating a dreamlike mood. Lounging in a luxurious chair, the goddess recrossed her seductive legs as she suddenly turned to the person beside her.

"Bofman, are you okay?"

"Y-yes, Lady Freya…I'm okay…This filthy swine would never do anything rude in milady's presence…"

The only other person in the room was Bofman. When Alfrik and the brothers released him, he was badly worn down. At a glance, he seemed quite haggard, almost like he was on death's door. He had surely endured a harsh punishment imposed by the brothers.

As evidence of that, he was being quite careful not to look directly at Freya's chest, despite the fact that her night gown was quite boldly cut around her bosom. If it were the earlier him, he would have been gulping audibly, but for now his fear was winning out.

…Well, it was not that he was scared of her body so much as her followers' excruciating punishment, but it left her with mixed feelings to see him trembling like a scared piglet around her like that.

Before long, the door opened.

"…Pardon me."

Ali was brought in by the attendants. Her figure had changed dramatically from that of the pitiful slave earlier. Her disheveled hair had been brushed out nicely, and she was wearing a neat regional dress. Every nook and cranny of her body had been cleaned, and a hearty amount of perfumed oils had been applied. The faint scent of jasmine wafted through the room. Her flawless brown skin was more than a match for the finest silk. Even Bofman, who was scarcely glancing at Freya, was taken aback by her beauty. It would've been difficult to find many slaves as beautiful as she.

"Welcome, Ali. You've become quite lovely. I hardly recognized you," Freya commented.

"Thank you…"

"Or was it that you intentionally dirtied yourself up in order not to stand out?"

"…"

"Hee-hee, don't look like that. It was just the thought that came to mind, is all."

While the attendants bowed and left the room, Ali approached Freya's chair, unable to hide her stiff expression. It was clear she had her guard up against the goddess of beauty, who had grown attached to her. Freya observed the girl closely as she set her wineglass down on a small side table.

"…What did you want of me?" the girl asked, wringing the words out carefully.

However, her attempt to cut to the chase was denied when Freya moved on to something else altogether.

"Ali, do you deplore the current political situation? Or do you perhaps resent what is happening currently?"

"…?"

"The war between Shalzad and Warsa that caused you to be enslaved…what do you think of it?"

© nilitsu

"!"

The change was dramatic.

Ali, who had largely been looking down from the moment she entered the room, immediately raised her head at Freya's comment, and her light purple eyes flared. Freya's eyes narrowed slightly in response.

"I was just curious. Will you not answer my question?"

Faced with the goddess whose smile only seemed to grow deeper, Ali responded by—refusing to answer and closing her eyes.

"You! You're before the Lady Freya! Such insolence is—!" Bofman immediately began to scold her but was halted mid-sentence by Freya's raised hand.

"Apparently Shalzad's fallen capital is still filled with screaming." Freya paid no heed to Ali's silence as she pressed the attack.

"..."

"Most of the royal family has been executed, and only a few still survive."

"..."

"What must the people of Shalzad be thinking right now?"

"...Gh!"

Ali maintained her silence, occasionally trembling as if struggling to hold back a torrent of emotions threatening to break free. The goddess continued to lob questions at her, but the girl persisted in her silence. Unsure of how to react to such an odd scene, Bofman kept glancing back and forth between the two of them, decidedly left out of the loop.

"Bofman, tell me what you know about the prince of Shalzad who was said to have escaped from the enemy."

"Yes? Ah, yes ma'am, of course," Bofman looked surprised by Freya's sudden question as he responded. "The prince's name is Aram Raza Shalzad. He is the first and only son of the king, who was executed when the capital fell. He was rumored to be peerlessly handsome...If I recall correctly, he was sixteen years old."

"Did he have any sisters of a similar age?"

"...? No, not if I remember correctly, at least. The king of Shalzad was apparently not blessed with many children. The prince bore both the royal family's expectations and their obligations..."

Freya's smile did not falter as Bofman finished his explanation. And the girl before her looked like she was trying to endure an onslaught with her eyelids clenched shut. The light of the single magic-stone lamp in the room flickered. Finally, the goddess spoke with an air of confidence.

"Ali, you look like you would be quite handsome dressed in men's clothes. With the proper attire...yes, I'm sure you could pass for a prince..."

At that instant, Ali's mask broke, betraying her efforts at controlling herself. With Freya having said that much, even Bofman could guess what she was implying as shock spread across his face.

"Ali, earlier, you were about to perform the proper way to greet a deity, but you stopped yourself at the last moment, didn't you?"

"...Gh!"

"That was the correct way to pay respect to a deity that the average inhabitant of the desert would likely not have known, let alone a slave, wasn't it?"

While all the former slaves in the estate were giving their thanks, when Ali had approached Freya, she had started to do something different and then stopped short, instead resorting to an inoffensive bow. It had betrayed her as someone who knew the esoteric method of formally addressing a deity. Her awkward movements revealed her unfamiliarity with pretending to be an unknowing commoner, and Freya's eyes had not missed it.

"And regardless of how I try to press you, you respond with only silence. Only someone who knows full well how to interact with deities would be able to do that."

"Wh-what do you mean?" Bofman asked, half in shock.

"Gods can see through all the lies of children. The most effective method of dealing with a god's questioning...is silence," Freya explained, not taking her eyes off Ali.

Mortals could not deceive deities. Or more precisely, the gods could see through all manner of deception. However, even if they knew someone was telling a lie, it was not possible for them to know what exactly the lie was. With their arcanum sealed on the mortal plane, they could not see all the way into mortals' hearts. Because of that, silence was the one and only means of resisting a deity's questioning that mortals had, and it was an effective one.

"In this desert realm, where familias are generally connected with the military, normal people would not have much opportunity to interact with gods. And there surely would not be many who could reflexively respond in the most effective way…Not if they had not already been trained to do so."

In a place where many gods and goddesses gathered, like Orario—where it wasn't too hard to find an adventurer who had been caught lying to a god before or something like that—it was plausible someone might have trained themselves to respond that way. But this was the Kaios Desert, far away from the Labyrinth City. Most of the familias here were treated as part of the military of any given country, from what Bofman said before. That meant that the patron god who led the faction would mostly interact with the nation's elites. In that sort of an environment, someone who purposefully maintained their silence when dealing with a god would have to be a person who interacted with gods on a daily basis or someone who had been trained that way in order to prevent information leaks.

"I-if someone received that kind of training, then it would surely only be someone among a select group of merchants or nobility… or royalty," Bofman said, turning pale, finally realizing everything.

In other words, Freya's questioning of Ali had been a bluff to confirm that she was indeed someone of high-class origin. The actual answers she might have given were irrelevant.

"And more than anything, I could feel it when I first saw you. You possess a dignity that separates you."

A tiger biding its time, waiting for the right moment to strike. From the moment she laid eyes on Ali in the bazaar, Freya realized her true nature.

"Th-then that means Prince Aram is…!"

"Not a son, but a daughter. Raised as a prince by a king who was not blessed with many heirs. A rather conventional sort of trope."

It's not conventional at all! Bofman thought, starting to sweat as he shook his head.

Most likely, while her country was being attacked, an incident had occurred and she had been captured by slave traders. Or perhaps after the capital had fallen, while leading the resistance against Warsa, she had been separated from the rest of her allies and wound up in chains. Bofman's face paled even further.

Now aware he was in the presence of the prince, or rather princess, of a country in a difficult situation, he was surely calculating the merits and demerits of the knowledge that had just fallen into his lap.

"If news spread that Prince Aram was actually a princess…given the current situation, I wonder what would happen?" Freya's lips curled up sadistically for an instant.

The silent girl's eyes snapped open.

"You dare blackmail me?!"

Her tone and mood changed in an instant. Just as Freya had observed before, she displayed the majesty of royalty in spades. Even the self-proclaimed wealthy merchant Bofman quivered at her rebuke, intimidated by the presence her small body seemed to project. However, Freya did not budge one bit from her elegant seat.

"Of course not. I've no intention at all of blackmailing you," she responded casually.

"Wh—?!"

"On top of that, I have no interest in either country or the war that is going on. You, and you alone, are what I am interested in.

"I teased you because I wanted to see your true form," she added with a smile that did not contain any malice. Ali's body stirred beneath the goddess's gaze. It had apparently dawned on her that she was seeing something not of this world.

"…You are truly the Goddess Freya, are you not?"

"Yes. How many times must I say it?"

"Then, Goddess Freya, I would like you to set me free."

Finally, Ali stopped pretending to be a wretched slave and spoke with a royal demeanor while resisting Freya's alluring appearance.

"You have my utmost gratitude for releasing me from slavery. Truly, I mean it. However, as you have realized, despite being a woman, I am playing the role of the prince. I have somewhere I must return to and a people that I must save."

"..."

"I swear I shall repay this debt someday. So, please, allow me to go back to my country."

Ali's purple eyes met Freya's head-on. She surely recognized that a deity might consider her request unreasonable, but her expression was unyielding. She was being targeted by Warsa and could not be sure what fate awaited her tomorrow. And even if she managed to link up with Shalzad's army, what could the prince of a country that had lost its capital offer to repay a goddess?

Bofman was initially overwhelmed by Ali's regal presence, but just as he was about to point out that there would be no value for the goddess in doing that, Freya again checked him with a wave.

"Very well," she responded without any hesitation again.

"What...?"

"You may do as you please. I asked what I wanted to ask, so if you want to go somewhere now, I won't stop you. You may go as you please."

Ali blinked over and over. She had expected to be rejected outright, or at least to have some sort of over-the-top compensation scheme forced on her by a cruel goddess. She was visibly bewildered by Freya's response.

"It's not like I bought you out of a desire for an enslaved puppet in the first place," Freya said. And then her lips curled into a smile. "However, somewhere down the line, you can be sure that I will claim that repayment you mentioned."

Ali was roused from her shock by a bolt of tension that shot right through her the moment she heard those words. Her face looked strained as she nodded, like a criminal making a deal with the devil in the fables of old.

"...You have my thanks, goddess of the world beyond."

Her gratitude was a mere formality. Freya stifled a little giggle.

"That's that, then. Bofman, take her to her room."

"I-is this really okay?"

"Yes, this is fine."

Bofman nervously double-checked with her, but Freya simply urged him on placidly.

Finally, the female attendants summoned by his service bell appeared and led Ali away. As she was leaving, Ali glanced at Freya, but Freya just smiled back at her.

The sun peeked out over the sand dunes stretching out to the horizon. As the darkness started to fade, the Kaios Desert's temperature increased as it escaped the cold embrace of night.

Morning had arrived.

"I overslept...! As if I've got any time to waste!"

Ali leaped out of bed not long after sunrise.

The room she had been led to last night was magnificent, and the soft bed had lured her into a comfortable sleep. She had been constantly on the move, both before she was caught by the slave traders and after they had captured her, pushing her to the limits of exhaustion. Thanks to the inviting bed and a full night's sleep, though, most of that exhaustion was gone, and her head was clear.

She frantically started moving, readying herself for her journey. She wanted to avoid becoming indebted to Freya any more than she already was, but she did accept the travel clothes that the attendants had politely offered her.

At that moment, the only other clothes she had to her name were the slave rags, the dress that Freya had given her for their rendezvous last night, and a light nightgown—and all of which would have drawn unnecessary attention if she walked around outside in them. Given that she intended to leave Leodo and needed to avoid revealing her true identity, Ali did not really have a choice, so she begrudgingly accepted the travel clothes.

I can't figure out what that goddess is thinking. She said I was her heart's desire, but then immediately let me go…No, don't think about it. It's already clear she's the kind of deity that it's best not to get involved with…

Ali had absolute confidence in that analysis as she left the oasis mansion. As she was passing through the gate, the catman standing guard there audibly scoffed in annoyance. Ali was thrown off by his inexplicable hostility, but it was not long before her confusion was resolved.

As she crossed the big wooden bridge connecting the island in the middle of the oasis to the northern side of the city—

"…Why are you here?"

Ali stopped, her face tensed when she saw the goddess leaning against the railing of the bridge, clearly expecting her.

"Because I was waiting for you," Freya responded, intentionally dodging the actual question.

"Wh-what do you mean?! You said last night you were letting me go…!" Ali shouted, paying no heed to the stares of the other people crossing the bridge.

"I said that I wouldn't stop you, but I didn't say anything about not coming with you."

Freya was wearing the same clothes as she was when they first met the other day: a short white dress and red hood, a matching red fabric wrapped around her waist, and a black skirt. The clothes that Bofman had arranged for her were breathable and easy to move in, so they would make for convenient travel clothes. Though Ali had no way of knowing that.

"You?! Come with me?! What are you talking about?!"

"The only thing I'm interested in is you. I told you that last night. So I'm going to watch you. I want to observe you from up close."

Ali abandoned her royal gravitas for a moment as her eyes opened wide in unveiled shock.

What are you talking about?! Are you crazy?! That doesn't make any sense! she screamed in her head. She was utterly confused and well past the point of caring that the goddess could accurately read her state of mind.

"In what way will your soul transform? Will it shine even brighter? That's what I want to see. What I want to confirm."

—*To know whether you are suitable to be my Odr.*

That last part, however, did not reach Ali's ears as her exasperation reached its limit.

"Do you think this is a game?! I must get back to the army as soon as possible for the sake of my country! I don't have time to deal with a goddess's flights of fancy—" *So I have no desire to be shadowed by some weirdo goddess!* was what Ali was about to add, rejecting Freya, but—

"What about traveling expenses?" Freya's one question stopped the girl in her tracks. "It seems you plan to leave this town, but have you made all the necessary arrangements?"

Ali was at a loss for words as the goddess continued.

"I fully understand that you have no desire to be further indebted to me. However, what can you do by yourself? I don't know where you plan to go, but it's not someplace you can easily reach by foot, right? If so, then how will you cross the desert?"

Freya's points were all sound and undeniable. Ali was currently broke, and without the funds to prepare for a desert journey, venturing out into the sands was not just foolish, it was suicidal.

It was not as if Ali had not considered that when she left the manor, though. This was Israfan, after all. There were merchants here who had close ties to the Shalzad royal family. If she was dressed as a man and identified herself as the prince, it would be possible to get help from them, but—

"Which reminds me of something Bofman mentioned. The situation in Shalzad is currently extraordinarily unstable. Many merchants are wagging their tails for Warsa, as they currently hold the advantage... If you started announcing yourself as the missing prince, they might decide the reward for turning you in is better than the risk of hiding you and providing assistance."

Freya rested her cheek on one hand as she, by all appearances, read Ali's mind.

"Are there any merchants who were close to you personally rather than just aligned with your country? Is there someone who would actually set aside profit to side with Shalzad out of loyalty?"

Ali's optimistic plans and the straws she was grasping at were all swept away by the goddess's smile. Without a personal connection with a merchant, none of the trading companies would extend their hands to the prince of a floundering country. And because Ali had had to keep her real gender hidden, she had rarely had any chances to build such connections. Other than those who already knew her secret, she had not been allowed to interact with other people any more than was absolutely necessary.

"Traveling alone in the desert at such a young age...you might just end up in a slave train again, you know?" Freya commented with slight smile.

"*Grrr...!!*" Intercepted at every possible angle, Ali could do nothing more than groan in frustration.

"If you'll allow me to accompany you...then I'd be willing to help you, though."

Freya was still smiling as she offered Ali a way out.

For Ali, who did not have many people she could rely on—any, really—Freya's offer was like a blessing from the heavens. It was possible something worse might happen because of it, but at the very least Freya would not try to help Warsa or hurt Shalzad. If she were going to do that, she would have done it already. Ali suspected that what she had said the night before about not caring about the war was probably the truth.

But getting played around with like this is just...!

Even so, though, Ali still didn't want to let her have her way. It was a combination of caution when dealing with such an incomprehensible person as well as the pride of a prince who knew better than to trifle with deities—but most of all, it was a childish rebelliousness. She just could not stand the smug way the goddess was smiling. Her beauty was such that it threatened to allure Ali, even though she was a girl, too, but Freya's gaze had a certain feel to it, as if she was look-ing down on mortals or perhaps appraising them. That, combined with the goddess's egotistical actions, and Ali just could not help finding Freya distasteful. Despite her own pathetic situation and the direly needed help, she insisted on holding out.

"My compensation."

"…!"

"You swore that you would repay me some day. Today is that day."

That was the clincher. Just as Freya said, Ali was the one who had promised to repay her. It felt an awful lot like minor quibbling, but if she reneged, it would be a stain on the honor of Shalzad—indeed, the request Freya was making was cheap relative to what she owed, so much so that it was debatable whether this request could really be equivalent.

She wanted to tear Freya a new one and scream at her to quit screw-ing around, but she restrained herself as her shoulders slumped.

"I'm the one who made the promise…and I'm the one being helped here…so I'll allow you to accompany me…"

"Very good. Thank you."

In the end, Ali was forced to dance to the goddess's tune. And the reason the catman had scoffed in annoyance was probably because he had realized it would all end up like this. It was not through any fault of Ali's.

At least she was able to repay her debt quickly.

"However! Promise me you won't just get in my way all the time!" Ali refused to budge on that one point.

"But of course. I promise." The goddess simply responded with a provocative little smile.

Resigned to her fate, Ali started walking.

When they crossed the bridge over the oasis, Leodo was lively as noon approached. The bazaar in the northern part of the city was booming, more than equal to the bazaar in the southern half of the city that Ali and Freya had passed through the day before. Compared to that one, the sides of the streets here were filled to the brim with shops and people lined the road. Camels loaded up with goods were having difficulty moving through it.

"Now that I think about it, is Ali a fake name? Should I call you Aram?"

"...My true name is Ali. Out of respect for my dying mother's wish, my father did not steal away my individuality. Though there have been times I wondered if I might end up forgetting my own name..." Ali explained.

We're in the middle of a giant crowd here...Were you seriously about to start calling me by the name of a prince whose disappearance is the subject of so much rumor? She kept that snide quip to herself, though.

Around that time, Ali lightened up on the formal tone toward Freya. It was not how deities were supposed to be addressed, but she nonetheless started using a tone that conveyed her annoyance a bit more readily. However, Freya did not seem to mind it at all. In fact—

"I see—then I'll call you Ali from now on."

She responded with a smile more befitting a girl enjoying herself than a goddess. She seemed happy, as if anticipating how this encounter of theirs would develop. Ali unconsciously was drawn in by that smile and time froze for a few seconds.

"Ali, make sure you entertain me."

"Gh...! Do I look like a clown to you?!"

But that overbearing manner of speech she had was enough for Ali to be able to confirm again that she just could not really get along with this goddess.

"So, where are we going? Surely you don't plan on just walking back to Shalzad like this?"

"...There is a hidden fortress along the border between Israfan and Shalzad. The plan was to meet up there with my retainers in the event that the worst-case scenario came to pass, and we were split up. That is where we are headed."

It was impossible to lie to gods, so given that they were going to be traveling together, there was no point in hiding it. Freya said "Hmmm" as she brushed her hair behind her ear.

"Now for my questions. What funds do you have available?" Ali asked without looking at the goddess as they weaved through the crowd.

It was quite a ways to the border and the hidden fortress when their starting point was Leodo. Food and water would be necessary as well as a means of crossing the desert. Obtaining passage aboard a desert ship would likely be impossible, but at the very least they would want camels. And protection. Thieves and monsters were plentiful in the Kaios Desert. Without some skilled bodyguards, the two would not be able to safely cross the desert. It would be faster to join up with a caravan, but given her secret, Ali was reluctant to spend time around too many other people.

While Ali was thinking through all that, Freya responded without any delay,

"What funds do I have? None. I don't like carrying something as unwieldy as a bunch of gold coins. I just promised contracts with my familia to Bofman for everything."

"What?!"

Ali stopped moving at that and swung back to stare at the goddess with an expression of disbelief on her face.

"Wh-what do you mean?! You said you would take care of the preparations! That's why I even…!" Ali moved in, about to ask whether Freya had been lying to her all along, but she was stopped by Freya's next words.

"This is our first trip together, though. I don't want to bring Bofman's money into it."

It was almost like she was saying this was a date for just the two of them. Ali was taken aback, hit again by a sense of wonder. She had long since lost count of the number of times this goddess had stunned her.

I've felt it ever since I met her…but she is a really, really strange goddess.

Overwhelmingly beautiful, high-handed, and supernatural. One moment her cool smile was causing shivers and bringing slave traders to their knees, the next she could sound like an innocent little girl like just now.

Ali had no way of knowing, but this side of Freya was one that she never displayed in Orario. The side of the goddess that Ali was seeing here was one that Freya had literally never shown anyone except Ali.

"...So then what are we going to do? We still don't have any funds," Ali asked in a quiet voice, having missed her moment to get angry. The goddess's only response was to leave her behind, though, walking ahead.

"On-site procurement," she said as she headed toward a tavern.

Despite being a popular bar, it was well appointed both inside and out. It almost looked like a salon for well-to-do socialites. Freya smoothly headed inside, as if she had been looking for it in particular while walking through the bazaar. Ali frantically followed behind while hiding her face, and by the time she entered, the goddess was talking to a pair of men.

"Hey, mind if I join?"

"Huh?"

The men were seated around a table, playing a board game. The human who turned back with a puzzled look on his face froze like a statue when he saw Freya. And a split second later he was very obviously lovestruck.

"M-milady, is there something I can do for you?"

"I just said it, didn't I? How about a match?"

Glancing at the beastman who had a similar lovestruck expression, Freya ushered him out of his seat and sat down at the table. Ali was having trouble keeping up, wondering what Freya was doing when she finally realized it.

"You're a merchant, aren't you? Not only that, you must be quite well off to be gambling here before noon."

"Y-yes, indeed! My name is Nahzo, one of the big four in this town!"

Everything from the well-tailored clothes and jewels in plain view to the fact that they were drinking the best quality of wine in broad daylight, it was clear they were merchants. And not just any merchants, but quite successful ones at that. The man Freya questioned responded with an obvious desire to flaunt his success.

And what does he even mean, "big four"? Is that guy who got up also a top four?

Ali looked over with an air of annoyance at the waste of time as Freya's eyes narrowed like a cat's.

"If I win against you, will you do me a favor?"

"A-a favor?"

"Yes. I'd like you to give me all the money that you currently have on you," Freya responded with a brazen request.

Ali stared at the goddess, feeling *What are you even saying, lady?* levels of shock and exasperation. And the man sitting across from her had exactly the same sort of look on his face. Glancing over at the other merchant, he responded with a wry smile and a look of consternation.

"E-even if it is a request from a goddess such as you, that's a little…"

"If I lose, I'll give you my body. For one full day, you can do as you please."

At those words, though, the man locked up.

He could run his hands over her body. Those voluptuous breasts. That alluringly narrow waist. The man audibly gulped. In the blink of an eye, his gaze became like that of a hyena at a full feasting table.

"…Are you sure about that? It might be rude to say, but if you're going to wager that much, then I won't really be able to hold back."

"I look forward to it. I mean what I said and would never tell a lie."

"I will have you listen to my favor, so I'll make sure the wager is sufficient to bring you to the table." When Freya put it like that, the man's lips cracked into a desirous smile. Ali was dumbfounded by the negotiations happening before her eyes before finally cutting in frantically:

"W-wait! What do you think your body is?! Betting yourself on something like this…!"

"Oh, are you worried about me?"

"O-of course not! It's just that I can't sit idly by and watch such licentious behavior!" Ali stammered, turning red as she raised her voice.

Freya's shoulders trembled a bit as she restrained a giggle at Ali's response.

"I'm grateful for your concern, but I'm going to have to ask you to just let it go this time," she said. "When the time comes that you want something, it's reasonable that you would put something of equivalent value on the line to get it, right? At the moment, we don't have anything else to offer other than ourselves. So there's nothing to do but wager that. If I can't at least do that, then I would be a fool for saying before that I would cover your travel expenses."

"B-but…"

Freya held out her hand as Ali approached her, still resolutely against this bet. Reaching out her thin fingers behind the girl's neck and pulling her close, the goddess whispered so that only Ali could hear her.

"You're going to be the next king, aren't you?"

"!"

"Then don't forget this. No matter how great the policies implemented by a wise leader, no matter how skilled at war a ruler might be, no matter how tyrannical a despot might be, by laying claim to the title of king, each and every one of them will have to engage in countless gambles."

The voice whispering in Ali's ear threatened to melt her mind as it left her awestruck. She froze for a second before suddenly pulling away from Freya. Pushing her hand to the ear the goddess whispered into, she could feel a loathsome heat burning in her cheeks as she glared back at Freya. But at the same time, she could feel an inexplicable wave spreading through her chest.

And because of that, she did not say anything more to try to stop Freya. The admonition she had just received was like a divine revelation.

"Sorry to keep you waiting. Shall we begin?"

Freya recrossed her legs as she turned to the merchant. Her opponent nodded, looking like he might start licking his lips at any moment as he arranged the pieces on the board. Realizing something, Ali broke free of her stupor and approached Freya again.

"D-do you know the rules? The games here in the desert are different from the rest of the continent. They can be quite complex…!"

"Not in the least. It's my first time seeing this game, so it should be fun."

Ali came close to collapsing when she heard the carefree response. Ali had bounced through a range of different emotions the past few minutes. There was a hint of anger in her voice as she quickly explained the rules.

The game they were about to start playing was called Halvan. It was one of the most popular games in the Kaios Desert region, along the lines of the continent's chess or the Far east's shogi. And as Ali alluded to earlier, the strategy involved in Halvan was more complex than that of chess or shogi. Someone who had just learned the most basic of basic rules about the pieces' movements and formations had virtually no chance of winning. At least that was what Ali thought, and the merchant on the other side of the board who had undoubtedly amused himself playing Halvan countless times before was chuckling to himself, assured of his victory.

After Freya finished attentively listening to the rules, she just said—

"I got it."

And then, toying with one of the pieces in her hand, she declared:

"We don't have time to waste, so let's get this over with quickly."

And then, about fifteen minutes later…

"Th-that's not…?!"

In a corner of the tavern, Ali and the beastman exclaimed as the human man looked down at the board in shock. It went without saying, but it was a complete and utter victory for the goddess. She had finished it with a quick attack, not needing any pauses at all to think through a strategy.

"All right, then, I'll be taking your wallet."

Smiling at the wealthy merchant who was about to slump out of his seat, Freya held out her hand. The man's eyes glanced back and forth between her hand and her silver eyes before weakly holding out his wallet. The sparse crowd in the tavern had all been drawn into the game of Halvan and was shocked that the beautiful goddess won. However, Freya seemed to have already lost interest as she left the tavern. Ali, who had been standing stock-still while watching the game, snapped out of her stupor and chased after Freya.

"Wh-what was that?! You were lying about never having played it before, right?! It was stunning how badly you trounced him…!"

"Even having descended to the mortal realm, deities are still all-knowing. There are lots of amusements here we've never thought of, but once we grasp the key points, we'll win.

"In fact, I'm a little hurt you thought I wouldn't win," she added, as if her victory was as self-evident as the sun rising in the east.

When she put it like that, Ali did not really have any kind of follow-up. There were certainly a lot of foolish gods in the mortal realm, but this just reminded her again how deeply absurd deus-dea really were.

"All right, then, we've collected our war funds—I mean date funds. Time to go shopping."

"It's not a date!"

Ali fired back immediately, but only just barely. She was getting worn down dealing with the goddess.

The two of them proceeded down the lively street, Ali getting half-dragged along by Freya. Because the bazaar in the south of Leodo had the desert ship port, it had more of a trading influence with all sorts of products gathered together. In contrast, the products gathered in the northern bazaar were more aimed at travelers and locals. Packaged rations, travel clothes, and all sorts of day-to-day necessities were on display there.

Almonds were apparently popular at the moment. A beastman with thick fur, perhaps unable to deal with the intense heat, was sitting in the shade of a building as he ate some ice cream. "Oh, so they even have ice rooms in the desert," Freya commented. Then she laughed a little at herself as she glanced over at a stall where the ice cream vendor pulled another treat out of a magic-stone cooler.

"Move along. Don't go buying stuff we don't need. We need to get food and water first—"

"Ali, let's try that kebab. I'm curious what it tastes like."

"—Have just a little self-control!" Ali finally hit her limit and shouted at the free-spirited goddess dragging her around from stall to stall.

Her face was still deep in the shade of the hood she was wearing, but the volume of her shout betrayed the fact that she had forgotten about trying to conceal her identity.

She could not tell whether Freya recognized what she was feeling or not as the goddess simply smiled back at her. Freya was just doing as she pleased in order to experience the sorts of things that could only be experienced there in the desert.

Ali gave strict instructions for her not to move while she went to get water and food, but unsurprisingly the goddess had not listened, and when Ali got back, she was buying some other seemingly point-less things at a different shop. The purchases were various expensive magic-stone items.

"Hey! What are you buying?!"

"You were taking care of the preparations we need for the trip, right? So I decided to gather the indulgences we need so we can enjoy the trip."

"You idiot! Traveling through the desert is difficult enough as it is! And all the more so for an outsider who did not grow up here and has no experience walking the desert!" Ali was staggered, about to fall over as her anger exploded.

"Has anyone ever told you that you're hard-headed, Ali? Worrying about what the future holds is not a bad thing necessarily, but focusing too much on it robs you children of the wealth of your lives. Optimism is the refuge of fools, but a wise man always has a vice or two to amuse themselves. That applies as much to kings as it does to anyone else."

The goddess's admonition was implicitly patronizing, and—though the goddess had no intention of doing so—just further antagonized Ali because it was the same as the gossip that had been spread behind her back in the palace.

For example: "The prince is too serious."

Ali's cheeks reddened as Freya's words struck home, and she responded with her most defiant stance of the day.

"I—I have a duty that I must fulfill no matter what! I don't have any time or mental capacity to spare to be enjoying myself! If you're going to accompany me, shouldn't you be considerate of that?!" she said in a rather childish tone, pressing the goddess to listen to her.

"I don't want to. I have absolutely zero intention of turning this trip into some boring journey like any other," Freya responded without a care in the world.

Her response was the very embodiment of divine freedom, and it left Ali wishing she could tear the goddess's head off. And upon seeing the girl's frustration, the goddess just giggled, enjoying herself. If anyone who knew the goddess could have seen her there, they would have been shocked. She was not just allowing Ali's back talk, she even seemed to be relishing it.

"She's quite enjoying herself today..."

"Today, too, you mean. She's been enjoying herself ever since coming here and finding that girl."

Among the goddess's followers scattered around the pair and watching over Freya from the shadows, the eldest prum brother and the white elf exchanged words. Some of the followers looked dour as they watched the goddess and girl, while others made no effort to hide their distaste, but the boaz warrior alone simply observed the two, his eyes narrowing as he studied the carefree goddess's radiant smile.

"Nggggh! Whatever! Moving on...The next thing we need is protection! Let's find a mercenary familia to hire...!"

"We don't need that. Let's just go find some camels instead. We'll need them to carry the stuff we bought anyway. If possible, I'd like to travel while riding, but do you think it will hurt my bottom?"

"Hey! I said don't just go wherever you want!"

As her followers watched from the shadows, the goddess continued to drag the girl around at her own pace. Freya was in a good

mood as she continued gathering the provisions for the trip, which
led to Ali shouting in frustration time and time again.

There were four entrances to Leodo: the desert ship port constructed
in the south and gates in the north, east, and west where travelers
and caravans traveling on foot and by camel were entering and leaving the city at brisk rate.

Freya and Ali left from the northern gate.

"The fortress is not close enough to reach in just a day or two.
There are several relay points along the way where we can rest. We'll
spend the nights there before setting out again. For today we'll head
for one of the northern oases."

"Do as you please. I'm just along for the ride."

Each straddling a camel loaded up with bags, the two of them set
off across the sea of sand that stretched off into the horizon. And it
really was like a sea of sand. So much so that camels were called the
ships of the desert until literal desert ships took the stage. The dunes
made an amusing sound as the camels' legs stepped into the sand.
In terms of comfort, horses were generally considered more reliable.
Ali was already used to how it felt, but Freya was left furrowing her
brow in quite the dignified manner, which gave Ali a brief moment
of schadenfreude, but—

"Are we going to just keep moving at all times? It seems like it
would be more comfortable to travel at night," Freya asked, seemingly already bored.

"We're not the only ones who feel that way. There are many animals and monsters in the desert that are nocturnal. Factoring in the
possibility of being attacked, it's best for us to move during the day.
And more importantly, I don't have any time to waste. I need to link
back up with the army as soon as possible," Ali explained brusquely.

That was what she said, but in the end she knew that monsters
showed up when they wanted to show up, paying no heed to people's
convenience.

Ali had bought a sword for herself for self-defense at the bazaar and had previously been trained to proficiency, enough for the bare minimum of self-defense, but compared to a mercenary, her combat ability did not amount to much. If she got surrounded, it would be over in an instant.

Ali had gotten into it with the free-spirited goddess already about leaving without finding guards first. She had no idea what the deity was thinking, but in the end all that worry was for naught.

"——Gh?!"

The giant desert lizard was executed instantaneously, not even allowed death throes. The two-meder-long, four-legged carnivorous monster was laid low by a spear tip that flashed like lightning. That was the fifth one, and Ali still could not follow the action with her eyes.

The group of monsters that had appeared before them, attracted by the scent of prey, was eliminated in the blink of an eye by a cat-man with a silver spear.

"...So that's what you meant about not needing guards."

"Yes. My children are here. I had originally intended this trip to be without them, but since they decided to tag along, we might as well put them to work." Freya nodded.

That was when Ali finally understood the goddess's nonchalance. Of all the factions whose fame had spread around the Kaios Desert, *Freya Familia* was known as the strongest. With that sort of protection, Ali had indeed been foolish for trying to hire mercenaries.

"But if they're guarding us, then they could just stay beside us... Where are they even hiding...?"

She glanced at Allen, who had appeared out of nowhere to protect them—or more specifically, to protect Freya. The catman, wearing a simple cloak over his head, just swung his spear once to clean it as if he thought everything going on was pointless. And when it came to Ali, he treated her as if she weren't even there.

"Not very sociable, is he...So is he the only one tagging along while the others stay back in the town?"

"They're all here. They're a bit overprotective."

"Wh-what? Where?! Other than him, I can't see any of them!"

"Right beside us. They're just maintaining a little distance so as not to be an eyesore while protecting us."

Looking all around, there was nothing for the eye to see but the vast desert. Ali could see neither hide nor hair of the guards who were supposedly watching over them. She couldn't tell whether they were hiding or whether she just could not see them. The girl's face tensed a bit as she was reminded once again just what kind of group they were.

Meanwhile, Freya had already climbed down from the camel as she conversed with a carefree tone. "Yep, it really is quite rough on my bottom. Also, I can feel some motion sickness coming on," the goddess commented as she started walking beside her camel while holding the reins. Ali just sighed and got down from her camel, too. Freya was an annoying goddess, but she was reluctant to disregard her and look down on her from atop a camel.

"Not that it matters much now, but how did you end up caught by slave traders anyway?" Freya asked.

Ali had already said before that pointless conversations were just wastes of energy, but perhaps out of boredom, the goddess walking out in front started a new one anyway.

"...It was in order to escape from Warsa's army. While our forces were routed and being scattered, I ran into a gang of slavers and intentionally allowed myself to be caught," Ali finally gave in and responded.

"Intentionally? That's quite brave of you."

"It's just that I didn't have any other way of escaping...I cast aside the royal family's armor and clothes and pretended to be a powerless little girl to avoid detection. In that situation, I needed to prioritize surviving, even if I ended up suffering badly in the short term. With the royal line in the balance...other concerns don't measure up."

Ali paused, hesitating before she finished her thought, but Freya, who was undoubtedly listening closely, said nothing in response

The sun beat down on the goddess, the girl, and their camels as their shadows grew longer. They paused a few times along the way to drink from a leather water bag to wet their throats. No matter how long they walked, the scenery did not change at all. Sand dunes just continued off into the distance. From time to time, they came across bleached skeletons along their path—either animals that had not been able to keep going or perhaps drop items from monsters. Though Ali suspected they were probably the latter.

The desert was wide. Even Ali, who had lived there all her life, was starting to wonder whether there would ever be an end to the sea of sand stretching to the horizon.

"—Tch!"

Along the way, monsters attacked them several times. And every time, Allen's silver spear ended those monsters' lives. His boots would leap off the ground, and while the kicked-up sand was still flying into the air, it would be accompanied by a spray of blood and the beasts' cries.

By the time Ali could sense the monsters' presence, they were annihilated, over and over again. It was a gust of wind accompanied by the slightest cloud of dust. Desert lizards' heads were sent flying, sand scorpions were dismembered, and vulture hunters' wings were clipped and then skewered. She could not even really make out the afterimages of the nimble wild-fighting cat. Even so, though, Ali could not help but be amazed that mortals could become so strong, so overwhelming.

And she could guess why Freya's other followers were not showing themselves. Because Allen was the fastest of them all. Thanks to that, he could protect their patron goddess the most effectively with the minimal chance of danger. That was why the others were leaving the direct combat to him and were probably just keeping an eye on their surroundings. Though Ali could not say whether that was because of the trust they had in one another or because of the reality of the situation they could do nothing other than acknowledge.

"Quit starin' at me, you shitty brat. It's pissing me off."

"Wh-what…?!

Catching a glimpse of *Freya Familia*'s awesomeness—fearsomeness— Ali had been staring at Allen's face as he finished up his latest round of combat.

She was tempted to shout back, *Who's the brat? It's not like I'm any shorter than you!* but she stopped herself right before those words crossed her lips. She had a feeling that that might have broken a taboo. That she might find herself mercilessly torn to pieces if she finished that thought out loud.

"...Why do you go so far for that goddess?"

Instead, what crossed her lips was a simple question born out of irritation at not being able to respond to his verbal abuse, but—

"Why do I have to tell you anything, asshole?"

"...Gh! You were pissy before we left the town, and you've been pissy ever since. You just think it's a pain in the ass to protect your goddess, don't you?!" Ali raised her voice in response to his rude comeback.

Hearing that, Allen just turned his back and responded as if answering her was the most annoying thing of all.

"In order to be who I am, I've offered up my everything—heart and soul—to serve her."

"!"

"If I could have my way, I'd chain her up and lock her away indoors, but if I did that, she would lose what makes her who she is. Just like I would lose what makes me, me. So everything just goes smoother when I'm pissed off at the annoyance. That's all."

Ali experienced a not-insignificant shock at the catman's response.

Her attitude is the worst, and her personality is atrocious...but just how much charisma must that goddess have to get such a powerful follower to go that far for her...

Oddly enough, it was almost a demonstration of the difference between Ali and Freya as sovereigns. On the one hand, Ali had been separated from her allies and caught by slavers; while on the other, the goddess was behaving every part the queen wielding the loyalty of elite retainers. It left Ali lamenting just how much she still needed to grow as a ruler.

There were certainly retainers who would follow Ali—or rather the prince Aram. And they would gladly do whatever they could to support Aram. But put another way, Ali had not done anything herself. It was also taken care of by adept and knowledgeable retainers. All she did was hand down orders. No, not even that, since she could not really say with any certainty whether those orders were even really guiding them. If she had not provided the directions she had, maybe the capital would not have fallen, and they would not have been routed so badly.

A figurehead prince. That was Ali's assessment of herself. Hiding her own gender, unable to reveal her true self. And perhaps provoked by that feeling of inferiority, Ali subconsciously found herself asking—

"…Why are you all so loyal to her?"

"…What?" Allen froze as he was walking back to his guard post and then slowly turned around.

"She's so self-centered. She's certainly divine in her own way, but she's too high-handed. She thinks only of how to best enjoy herself, smiling smugly as she calls it amusement. It's not regal at all. It's almost like she's just an enchantress—"

"You should watch yourself. I don't have permission to rip your throat out, so quit saying things that will make me kill you." Allen spat. There was more of a bite to his tone as his usual annoyance skyrocketed when she insulted his patron goddess.

However, it was still a quiet annoyance. Not worth the effort to care about. It brought to mind the image of a cat licking its fur as a mouse caused a fuss right in front of it. And that fact—that she was not even worth getting worked up for—caused the blood to rush to Ali's head, robbing her of her better senses. Freya, who had been walking ahead, stopped and looked back as Ali shouted:

"You all are just captivated by her beauty anyway! Just pathetic puppets enthralled by her charm!"

All of a sudden, Ali was staring up at the sky.

"—Eh?"

It took one second for her to realize what she was looking at. It took one more second for her to realize that she was lying on her back in the sand. And it took a third second for her to sluggishly lift her head and notice that a spear was being held right in front of her eyes.

"___"

And in the fourth second, she finally realized that she was about to be killed. Allen Fromel had swept her legs out from under her and had drawn his spear, about to stab it home between her eyes. His icy gaze was filled with a merciless readiness to kill.

Standing behind him was a boaz warrior holding the shaft of the spear in place with a single hand. On either side of Ali stood two elves, one dark and one white, their black sword and rhomphaia crossed to hold back the spear's tip. And surrounding the catman were four prums, their swords all drawn and pointed at the cat's neck.

Just as she realized that they were the only reason she was still alive, Ali broke out into a cold sweat.

"Stop it Allen. You're going against the Lady's will."

Allen was still trying to pierce the girl's head as Ottar's deep voice urged restraint. Allen's rage would not be quelled. He had no use for words and was trying to kill Ali with a pure desire to lash out. It was the fury of someone whose master had been belittled and scorned. And as Allen's ferocious gaze stole her breath away, Ali realized it. Ottar and the others had not stopped Allen because they had reservations about him murdering her. Quite the opposite. They were all furious with her, too, but they were stopping him despite that because it was what their goddess willed.

"Allen, lower your spear," Freya spoke gently, having watched it all unfold.

And the catman who had persisted in trying to kill her, even though his weapon had been stopped, and even though there were blades at his neck, finally lowered his spear. However, even that movement was slow, betraying the mixture of rage and loyalty clashing in his heart.

"I'm touched that you got so upset for my sake, but you must not get violent. You're scaring Ali."

"...Are you really okay with that?" Allen responded, stifling the emotion in his voice.

"It's fine. I'm used to it," Freya answered with a smile as if there was really nothing to it.

The goddess walked over and held out her hand. Ali was still in shock from what had transpired and unconsciously accepted Freya's hand and stood up. Ottar and the others lowered their weapons and silently moved away, returning to their stations.

"Let's keep going" was all the goddess said, continuing the trip as if nothing had happened. Her sore bottom seemingly recovered, the goddess smoothly straddled her camel.

Left behind with the second camel, Ali was frozen in place in awe when Allen, the only one who had stayed behind, said:

"If you insult us—no, her—again, I *will* kill you." Allen glared at Ali, causing her to recoil, but then his brow furrowed. "If she ever seriously used her charm, everything would be nothing but a farce," he spat.

Ali looked back at Allen's face in surprise.

"Her going to that town, you, everything. Get a grip. Just how thoughtless can you get, shit-for-brains?"

"What do you mean...?"

But Allen did not answer. He just shot her one last murderous glare and disappeared like a mirage. Scrutinizing her surroundings, she still could not see the *Freya Familia* members anywhere. Ali awkwardly looked forward. Freya was there, riding her camel. Her silver eyes glanced back at the girl.

Unable to move for a few seconds, Ali finally started following the goddess as if drawn in by Freya's back cloaked in a shimmering haze.

They were progressing ever farther north, toward Shalzad's hidden fortress along the border. Thanks to the protection from *Freya Familia*, all they needed to do was ride their camels, allowing them to make good progress on the first day. However, after that incident, Allen did not appear before the two of them again. The dark elf, Hegni, took the role of exterminating the monsters in their path in his stead. The way he cut countless monsters in half with a single flash of his black sword was different from how Allen handled them but no less intense than the cat's technique. Meanwhile, with Allen no longer appearing, Ali was at a loss for words, unable to explain the swirl of feelings filling her chest.

The sun high up in the sky gradually started to sink, painting the western sky a vivid palette of colors as evening finally began to set. A golden crescent moon appeared high in the sky.

"Oh, it's a much nicer oasis than I was expecting."

They had reached one of the small oases connecting north to the border and gotten there earlier than expected. It was surrounded by small sand dunes, palm trees, and other greenery. There were no signs of anyone else. They were the only travelers staying there that night. It was no match for the one in Leodo, but it was understandable Freya might call it cute.

"Let's eat. I'm getting hungry" was Freya's first comment after they tied their camels to trees. Apparently even she could get tired from traveling through the desert.

"…Okay," Ali said as she looked around the surroundings.

There was no trace of the goddess's familia. Perhaps because of Freya's admonition, they apparently had no intention of disrupting the two of them during their journey together.

"You take care of the preparations, please. I'm not very good at cooking."

"Okay…"

"And not just dried meat, please. I want some fruit to eat, too."

"Okay…"

"Actually, the truth is I've never held anything heavier than a pan. So I'm counting on you to feed me."

"Okay…"

"……"

Absentminded, half-hearted replies. The girl could not even

manage a proper conversation as she prepared some food for dinner. Even when Freya intentionally added in little jabs to get a rise out of her, Ali did not get angry or shout or even respond at all. Disappointed in the lack of response, Freya just sighed in boredom. And after they had finished eating—

"Ali, I'm going swimming."

"Okay......Wait, what?"

That was enough to finally get Ali to snap out of her trance. She stopped moving, doubting her ears as Freya's lips curled into a smile.

"I'm going swimming. In this oasis."

"Wh-where'd that come from all of a sudden?!"

"Ever since earlier, you haven't strung together more than a couple words. It's partially Allen's fault, but at this rate I'm going to die from boredom. So if you won't talk with me, then I'm going to go swimming."

There was a sound almost like a catman snorting in annoyance that reached Ali's ears, but she did not have the presence of mind to react to that as she turned on the goddess, who was fishing for something in her bags.

"O-oases are the common bounty of all travelers! They're not something to dirty in order to clean yourself!!"

"Nothing unclean can come off a deusdea, though? But if it bothers you that much, then we can just use the magic-stone items I bought. This tool is for filtering water, so the water will be even cleaner than it was before we used it."

"Th-the nights are cold in the desert! It's already pretty cold as it is! You'll freeze if you bathe yourself in the water!"

"There's a magic-stone item for that, too. I made sure to get it at the bazaar before we left."

The goddess met each and every one of the complaints that Ali threw out with magic-stone items. The goddess who lived in the one and only Labyrinth City in the world pulled the magic-stone items made in that city from her bags one after the other, as if raising a toast to Orario.

—I thought the bags were a little heavy, but this is what she bought?!

Ali was in danger of forgetting the situation she was in and exploding in frustration.

The item that looked at first glance like a largeish lantern was actually a kind of stove. It had both lighting and heating functions combined in one item, and the model Freya bought was both compact and high-spec, trading that convenience for a relatively short life span. Incidentally, it was also unbelievably expensive.

Grrr, buying such a frivolous item, even though the ironclad rule of traveling in the desert is that water is the most important thing, with food a close second!

"If I put it next to the water's edge...see, it gets warm!"

She placed several torches at intervals along the edge of the oasis and then turned them on. After a short while, the air, which was uncomfortable without insulating clothes, suddenly warmed up significantly. At that temperature, it would definitely be possible to go swimming. And on top of that, perhaps because Freya had messed with some setting, the torches started randomly shifting between blue, purple, and yellow lights.

"Once is enough, but I just had to have a desert oasis all to myself... I so wanted to try turning it into a night pool."

You had this freaking planned from the start!

Thanks to the shine of the magic-stone lamps, the tranquil night scene of the oasis turned into a resplendent spring that reeked of man-made modifications. It was certainly a new and different scene. One that she could acknowledge was befitting the "night pool" that the goddess spoke of.

But she has to be the only one in the world who would think to do a night pool in the desert.

"—Wait, you're really going to take your clothes off?!" Ali shouted, turning red as the goddess unhesitatingly began to strip.

"We're both girls, so there's nothing to hide, right? Besides, we're the only ones here."

"B-but what if someone tried to peep...!"

"Don't worry. Right now, this is the safest oasis in the world."

Ali was stunned by the goddess's boast, but she readily accepted it.

Freya Familia was standing guard. Forget thieves or monsters, they would never allow anyone to lay even a single eye on their goddess bathing. The small oasis had already transformed into an impenetrable fortress, a one-hundred-meder-diameter zone that no one would ever be allowed to enter.

"...gh!"

Undoing the rings holding her lower skirt up, the goddess let the black skirt fall to the ground and removed her white dress. Ali immediately looked away as the alluring goddess undressed herself. Her voluptuous breasts broke free, and a lock of her silver hair rested atop them. It was clear from a glance just how soft the round butt that revealed itself was. And it went without saying, of course, that the goddess's skin was vibrant and sensuous.

It was an otherworldly nude form. Ali was on the verge of being entranced by it despite herself, almost gulping audibly at the sight.

It's almost like I really am some naive, inexperienced prince!

"Woo, it's cold, but...it feels good!"

Meanwhile, Freya had jumped straight into the pool without hesitation. The splash of water lit by the light of the lamps twinkled like jewels in the air. As the goddess played and the water sparkled in a rainbow of colors, she really did look like she was in a world of gems, an owner of a beauty that was truly not of this world.

"...Sheesh, no consideration at all for others..." Ali sighed as she sat on the edge of the water and watched the goddess splashing around in the water.

Sitting cross-legged with her cheek propped up by her hand, she looked at Freya and the oasis. She did not realize it herself, but she was sitting in the seat that many a man or god in the world would kill to have. Freya was beautiful. Utterly and incomparably beautiful. The way she looked swimming around, the way she lifted a handful of water over her head, the laughing voice that crossed her lips. The oasis had already become the goddess's personal slice of paradise. Countless people would probably be filled with bliss just by seeing it. The way the desert's night breeze rustled the trees, it seemed to be overcome with emotion at the scene. And the way the moon hung in the night sky shining down almost seemed as if it was blessing the goddess.

"...So she can smile like that, too?"

At the slave market, she had behaved like a detached, tyrannical queen. And during the journey here, she had taken quite a bit of pleasure in constantly teasing Ali, the quintessential goddess's demeanor. And now, her smile was like that of an innocent girl. She was just simply enjoying herself in the oasis of a foreign country—living in the moment. Ali was nearly certain it was a smile she did not show in the Labyrinth City. A side of the goddess that could only be seen here, in this time and place. A side of the goddess that perhaps no one other than Ali had ever seen.

Ali was seeing more and more of Freya, sides that she had not even imagined, and it was flustering her. She felt that Freya was truly divine. She was both a queen and a girl, two sides of the same coin. She was like a capricious wind, and Ali could not pin her down.

"Hey, Ali? What are you sitting there worrying about?"

"...! Wh-what are you talking about?"

Ali had gotten lost in thought as the scene before her stole her attention, but Freya's question dragged her back to reality as she feigned composure.

"I can see the radiance of souls. And right now, yours is faintly clouded."

"Gh..."

"It has been since before your quarrel with Allen. It was even when I first met you. Something has been troubling you," Freya said without looking at her, still playing in the water.

Ali stirred as her deepest thoughts were laid bare. She suspected that the goddess knew what was in her heart better than she did herself. Freya glanced over as Ali pursed her lips, not attempting to respond.

"Ali, do you know why I left Orario?" Freya unexpectedly changed the topic.

"Hmm?" Ali glanced up, seeing that the goddess had lain down, floating on the water.

"I came to this desert in search of a companion…to find my fated partner."

"—So it really is just about sex, then!" Ali shouted back in a loud voice, the serenity of the moment broken by Freya's silly reason.

"Don't ruin the mood right when I was starting to have a little faith in you!" she shouted, but Freya paid it no heed as she started swimming slowly on her back.

"I wanted to see if there was a child—a soul—in this world that could suit me. And I found you. Noble and beautiful, dazzling like amethyst."

The goddess's breasts floated like peaches on the surface of the water, as if emphasizing their volume. Her entire body was a lethal weapon that could be wielded against any man or woman. Ali had long since abandoned any illusions of going through life as a woman, but she still could not help glaring a bit at such a prominent demonstration of something she could not have herself.

"Ali, you with your beautiful soul might be able to become my Odr."

"I'm a woman just like you are!"

"That doesn't matter in the face of love."

"Quit just saying whatever you want. Jerk…"

"That's why I want to clear away whatever it is that's clouding your radiant soul."

"!"

"I want you to overcome that listlessness and shine even brighter."

Those words, spoken as Freya floated on the surface of the water and looked up at the desert night sky, caused Ali's eyes to widen. The goddess lying there, rocking in a cradle of water as the moonlight shone down, seemed to be saying, *If you want to talk to me, then go ahead. I'll listen and even grant you an oracle.*

Ali was silent for a little while before finally speaking up.

"…I'm consumed by doubt about myself as the prince," she gradually started to explain. "Am I really adequate to bear the weight of my country's future? Can I truly become a proper king? Can I fulfill my duty and leave an heir to continue the line?"

"That's a pretty common concern. All those who call themselves royalty will face it at one point or another."

"I know. But, I can't help but wonder. If I had been more suited to ruling when Warsa attacked, would the capital have not fallen? Would all my innocent countrymen currently suffering be better off?"

"…"

"Warsa is strong. No matter what we did, there was no stopping that invasion. I understand that logically. But I still…"

Those were the words of the girl Ali, not the prince Aram. That was the anguish that had always gripped her. The true nature of the unease she felt. Her trip with Freya had been too distant from danger, too peaceful, so she could almost forget it, but the blood of her people, her country, was still flowing, even at that very moment. The valiant generals were still resisting, and the people were still being trampled. And with her father dead, she could not change that course. On top of all that, it had taken all she could muster to allow her allies to flee while acting as bait and then escaping by letting herself be captured by slave traders.

"With my country being ravaged right now, closer to the edge of the abyss than ever before, I find myself thinking again how all I can do is just impatiently stand by and watch." Ali looked down as she finally aired all of the concerns that had been bothering her.

She could not help thinking how small and pathetic she was for whining like that. As she fell silent, it felt like the oasis itself was laughing scornfully at her. She was sure she could see the goddess's followers' sneers, and that hallucination shaved away at her confidence even further. Having admitted her own incompetence, Ali felt more ashamed than at any other point in her short life.

"Everyone will tell you that a king is a being who stands alone," the goddess spoke. "And everyone admires kings for their isolation."

"…?"

"It's obvious, really. Because to be a king means that you cannot pass your responsibility on to anyone else."

It was as if she was saying that a king who tried to share responsibility, to share decisions, was not fit to be king. Ali looked over and

Freya was stretching a hand up to the sky as she floated on the water. As if she were tenderly caressing the outline of the moon shining all alone by itself in the sky.

"So worrying like this, suffering like this, is perfectly healthy.

"There's nothing wrong about what you are feeling. It's the same wall that countless other kings have been faced with."

The goddess's voice echoed, as if comforting Ali, who had felt so ashamed of herself.

"So let me tell you something obvious, Ali."

Freya stood up, planting her feet on the ground and facing away from Ali as everything from her waist up was visible out of the water. And, as if in time with her movement, the magic-stone lamps ran out of power and switched off. The moment the sparkling lights cut out, the oasis was consumed by darkness. The only thing outlining the goddess was the pale light of the moon. Time stopped for Ali as she looked at Freya's back.

"Just be yourself. Stop worrying about what others think of you. Don't mistake all the burdens you are bearing for your own weakness. And before cursing your own powerlessness, stand and face the reality before you."

The goddess's sweet voice. The tranquility of the desert. The cool moonlight and the lapping waves on the surface of the water. The oasis had transformed into its own little world, a small domain of profound mystery. And that dreamlike scene stole Ali's sight, her consciousness, and even her soul.

"Live nobly and resolutely.—Like a hero."

The goddess looked toward Ali. Drops of water ran across her skin and the silver hair covering her back swayed. Ali's widened eyes met the goddess's gaze.

"Even if you fail and your country is destroyed...even if everyone comes to resent you...we gods will praise you."

Without realizing it, Ali had stood up. Freya's voice, her eyes, her smile—they all had drawn her in, pulling her to her feet.

"We will celebrate those decisive kings who bear that lonely pain that none can understand without turning their back on it."

Neither the prince Aram Raza Shalzad nor the girl Ali would ever forget that scene. The moonlit moment when they touched upon the most beautiful thing in the world, the goddess Freya's divine will.

"You resisted my beauty of your own volition in order to sacrifice yourself. The radiance of your soul in that moment captivated me. So take pride—"

"…"

"—because you really do have the makings of a king."

Perhaps Freya had been trying to teach Ali that all along during the trip. Even if it was only calculated to increase the brilliance of her soul, Freya had probably been trying to guide her. Ali thought back to their earlier interactions. Freya had always been teasing her, but there was a meaning hidden in everything she said. She had a deity's point of view, but her gaze was almost motherly.

The naked goddess's unvarnished words caused Ali's chest to tighten.

"Ali? I want to embrace you. A you who shines even brighter than you do now."

"I…am a prince. I cannot reciprocate your affection," Ali struggled to respond, saying nothing more than that.

"A wonderful answer. I wouldn't have it any other way."

The goddess's voice and expression were gentle. The breeze blew between the two of them. It was a cool night breeze, filled with grains of sand. The wind of the desert. It was utterly familiar to Ali, but to Freya it was a new and fresh experience. As if provoked by the wind stirring up waves in the water, Ali drew her shoulders back.

And then kicked off the ground.

"!"

Freya was surprised as Ali leaped into the oasis, still wearing her clothes. She swam underwater with all her might, as if washing away all the restraints holding her back, as if wiping away all the idle doubts filling her heart. Taking off her shoes and top, Ali felt her body became more and more free. Finally, she sunk all the way to the bottom of the pool and kicked off the ground, breaking free from the surface with a splash.

Catching her breath and shaking her head, Ali realized the goddess was right in front of her and not very far away. For once, Freya looked visibly surprised.

"Umm…I'm sorry!" she shouted as she pulled her hair back, her soaked undergarments clinging to her brown skin. "I lost my temper like a child! As your follower said, I insulted you!"

There were still too many complex feelings swirling in Ali's heart for her to be able to express her gratitude to the goddess who had illuminated her heart, but even so, she could at least apologize, so she honestly conveyed the feeling that had been gnawing away at her since earlier.

"…Hee-hee, ah-ha-ha-ha! What, that?! That was still bothering you?"

"I-it's important to me to take responsibility for my mistakes!"

"Don't worry about it. I said before, I'm used to it."

The goddess's laughter rang out from the center of the oasis. Ali realized she had been unconsciously biting her lip as she finally managed to relax.

"Your clouded soul has gotten a tiny bit clearer. At this rate, it will shine even brighter."

Still just saying whatever she pleased, Freya turned around and walked to the shore. Ali watched her as she placed a hand on her chest. Her clouded soul had gotten a little clearer. That also meant there was still some hesitation left.

The misgivings plaguing her had not entirely been resolved. Hardships were sure to continue. And there would undoubtedly be many more times where she would not be able to forgive herself. But, for today, she would try to live as the goddess had said—nobly and resolutely, heroically.

That was what she thought as she looked up at the solitary crescent moon shining high in the night sky.

"What's going on with the search for Prince Aram?!"

A deep, manly voice boomed out in the tent city constructed in the conquered capital of Shalzad, Solshana. The man's name was

Gorza, the general commanding the Warsa army that had invaded Shalzad. At just short of two meders tall and with his commanding presence and burly figure, he looked every part a great general. He had deep brown skin and the air of a fabled desert warrior.

"W-we still have not been able to determine his whereabouts... However, it is known that he was among the enemy forces we clashed with and routed in the south of Shalzad..."

"Fool! We have to find him! Shalzad is a country that reveres their royal family! If we don't hunt down every last member, this war will never end!"

The soldier fell back in the face of Gorza's thunderous shout.

Despite the fact that they had lost their king and their capital had fallen, Shalzad forces were still continuing to fight back all around the country. Their resistance was entirely due to the generals holding on to the single thread of hope embodied with Prince Aram, who would become the next king. As long as the enemy still rallied behind the prince, the resistance would continue.

For Warsa, who had planned a lightning strike, the war dragging on was terrible news. Both in the obvious sense that it exhausted the country and because their country risked being targeted by its neighbors given how many troops it had committed to carrying out the invasion. Part of the reason no country had emerged as the dominant force in this part of the western Kaios was because the cluster of countries here would never allow a neighbor to rise to the top and were always watching for the opportunity to strike.

"At Serein, in the north of Shalzad, an elite division is attempting to push back our forces. If we don't do something soon, they might break through...!"

The country of Warsa was in a particularly poor position in the desert, so it had to resort to pillaging and violence to get by. Shalzad, with its enormous belt of oases, had always been a juicy target for them and a territory they could not afford to let slip away. Just stealing a piece of land and not finishing the job would be unacceptable.

We have to force Shalzad to accept defeat. If we can't even do that much, then why did we join hands with that scourge—

"Heeeeeeeeeeeeeey! Resheph enters stage right! How's the war going, General Gorza? ☆"

Just as Gorza was groaning to himself, a single god with long black hair tied back appeared in the tent.

"Wh-why are you here, Lord Resheph?!"

"What do you mean? I'm the patron god of the familia, right? It's part of the job description to at least show my face!"

The god was accompanied by a male elf, one of his followers.

He was a relatively short god, even when not compared to such a giant of a man as Gorza. He wore a hat that was pointed at the front, like an arrowhead. And though he was a deity, his insincerity was plain to see. No sane person would ever consider following him.

"You should have gotten word to pin down the enemy forces putting up a resistance in the northwest! So why are you here?!"

Warsa's royal family had been unable to contain their displeasure with the familia that was formerly in charge of their military for never being able to invade Shalzad, so they had summoned a different familia from outside the desert. *Resheph Familia* had been the ones to answer their call. A god and followers who were not even born in the desert, they had been charged with the most recent attack on Shalzad. And the results were self-evident. They had broken through the enemy's defensive line that Gorza's army had not been able to break for years and even toppled the capital. There was probably a days-long feast in celebration going on in Warsa right at that very moment. However—

Our country may have no talent beyond raiding, but compared to them?! Burning the villages, pillaging, rape! Resheph's followers lay waste to everything in their path! It was like the work of devils! To think I'd see the day where I'd feel pity for the accursed Shalzad...!

An atrocity. That word alone was enough to describe *Resheph Familia*.

Gorza, who had been chosen as the overall commander of the forces, could be called the buffer between the existing army and *Resheph Familia*. He was the one who drew the short straw to try to keep them from getting too out of control.

"I'm aware I'm a mere mortal, but as the representative of my patron god who stayed behind in Warsa to protect the capital, I hope you can please accept my instruct—"

"Isn't it obvious? I'm here 'cause I murdered the shit out of the enemy already. ☆"

Gorza and all the other soldiers around froze as Resheph cackled.

"The ones you were saying were strong—at Serein, was it? We slaughtered the soldiers there. Just straight up genocided the lot of 'em! So where's my reward? Ha-ha-ha!"

Gorza was at a loss for words. And as if to confirm what the god was saying, a soldier frantically dashed into the tent to report that the enemy forces near Serein had been wiped out. It took everything Gorza had not to keep his giant body from staggering back in shock.

The main forces of *Resheph Familia* were all elites who had leveled up at least once. There were not too many people in the desert realms who could measure up in terms of pure strength, and theirs was a familia full of them. Gorza should have known that. He did know that. But even so, that report was just too—

"Since we've got nothing else to do, can we join in with the search for Prince Aram? We can help out torturing whoever is hiding him. ☆"

"…! Wait! You should deal with the remnant forces—"

"There's basically none left. The resistance is on death's door already, so you can take care of that yourself. If you can't even do that much, then there's no choice but to judge you to be as incompetent as your patron god. ☆"

Gorza's cheek twitched as the god laughed mischievously.

"The prince was near the southern front when you lost track of him, right? So he probably fled to Israfan. Maybe he even disguised himself as a slave to blend in?"

He was lacking in dignity and grace, but there was still no mistaking the fact that Resheph was a deity. He was more than capable of gauging the state of a game board, even with only the slightest bit of information.

"Let's put a little fire to the feet of Israfan. If he's a good little prince, he'll rush forward all teary-eyed to announce himself!"

"Don't, Lord Resheph! We can't afford to drag a third country into this!"

"Come on, man, the king is getting on your case to end the war already, isn't he? So just leave it to us. My kids will murder everyone who gets in the way. Every last one of them!"

There was a chilling grin on Resheph's face as he left the camp with his follower.

"Pestilent beast!" Once the god had left the encampment, Gorza's shout was loud enough to cause the soldiers to shrink back again.

Currently many of the soldiers of Warsa were being drawn to the strength of Resheph's followers, entranced by that power and swearing to convert over to his familia. The army had always been wild to begin with, but it was becoming less and less controllable by the day and could barely even be called an army anymore.

And with regard to the proposed assault on Israfan, even if Gorza handed down a strict order not to carry it out, there would be many people who went ahead with it anyway because of Resheph's instigations. Gorza was little more than commander in name only.

The vile god was just spreading the flames of war for entertainment. For Warsa and for Shalzad, Resheph was assuredly a country-destroying pestilence. Gorza's boulder-like fists trembled as he was convinced again that that god would bring chaos to the desert world.

They finally spotted the fortress on the border three days after they set out from Leodo. The scenery of sand dunes had long since disappeared. The area around the border was a rocky hamada. It was a craggy valley region with boulders scattered all around.

"There it is! That's where the hidden fortress is!" Ali shouted from astride her camel. She was pointing to a bunch of rocks that soared into the air like a mountain. Perhaps because she had been there before, a confident smile filled with joy at the end of their journey crossed her face as she looked at the location that appeared at a glance like a little more than a pile of rocks.

"..."

Meanwhile, Freya furrowed her brow. Her vision was excellent, more than capable of distinguishing individual souls' glimmers from the top floor of Babel in Orario, and her silver eyes had noticed something strange.

"Alfrik."

"Yes, I see it."

Immediately responding to her call, the prum warrior materialized out of the shadows. As Ali looked in shock, the eldest Gulliver brother lifted the faceguard of his sand-colored helm, revealing his blue eyes that narrowed as he looked into the distance. Prums had the best vision of all demi-humans, and he confirmed the goddess's suspicions.

"It's faint, but there are traces of magic particles. And there is a smell of blood in the wind."

"...Huh?"

Initially a look of confusion crossed Ali's face as she listened to Alfrik. But realizing what he was implying, she turned pale and urged her camel into a run. Freya and Alfrik followed behind her.

Dismounting at the foot of the towering bedrock, she ran up the gentle slope that resembled a trench. The moment she crossed through the entry cave and set foot in the fortress, she was greeted by the smell of burned flesh and the sight of countless corpses scattered around the floor in a pool of blood.

"No...but that's—?!" Ali screamed.

The inside of the fortress was horrifying. There were signs of resistance, but every last one of Shalzad's soldiers had been mercilessly slaughtered. Cut by swords, run through by spears, scorched by magic. The armored corpses told a mortifying story with their wounds on full display. Tables, chairs, weapons lining the wall—everything had been overturned and trampled.

"Aaaah, aaargh?! Douglas! This can't be true! Not like this...!"

Ali ran to one of the fallen officers, reaching a hand out to his body, but it was already cold. His eyes would never open again. Ali cried as she embraced the corpse that had lost an arm and been impaled through the chest.

"The enemy attacked with magic indiscriminately and then charged in, taking advantage of the confusion among the fortress's forces…They are experienced in conducting surprise attacks. It seems clear the perpetrators were the aforementioned Warsa troops," Alfrik said, calmly analyzing the cruel scene of the fortress while Ali collapsed in tears.

"How many people carried this out?" Freya asked.

The remaining three prum brothers, who had immediately examined the surroundings of the fortress, appeared.

"Likely around fifty. They were also lying in wait at the hidden passage in the rear where they loosed a fusillade of arrows at those who tried to flee," reported Dvalinn.

"The majority of them were riffraff, but there was likely at least one who was skilled," added Berling.

"Some of the magic remnants are a bit stronger. Perhaps someone who has leveled up," Grer said, before adding, "Also, inside the fortress…there are characters written in blood."

As Ali looked up, tears still streaming down her face, Freya asked Grer to lead her to the room. The place he took her was likely the command center. The Shalzad flag, a crescent moon and wreath of jasmine, hung on the wall, torn tragically apart, and in its place, a message was written in the blood of one of the soldiers.

"Come forward, Prince Aram. If you don't, Israfan will be consumed by a sea of flames…"

Ali read the words written in blood, covering her mouth as she struggled not to vomit at the repulsive deed. Perhaps it was because of a merchant's report or perhaps it was just the keen insight of a god, but either way Warsa had apparently realized that Aram had headed for Israfan. And—

"Leodo will be the first warning…"

Freya's eyes arrived at the final passage of blood. She had not been shaken at all by anything else, but that line caused her to suppress her emotions. Her frozen eyes narrowed as she turned on her heels.

"We're going."

"Wh...wh-where?"

"Leodo, obviously," Freya responded without any hesitation.

Ali had not recovered yet from the shock of the all the soldiers who had been killed as she tried to keep up.

"B-but the enemy left here long ago. We must have crossed paths somewhere along the way. Even if we chase them, we won't make it in time...!"

"That's irrelevant," she said, disregarding the words Ali struggled to get out. She took Ali's hand as she headed for the fortress's exit. "It's unfortunate, but we're leaving the camels here. Tell Ottar to carry me and Allen to carry Ali."

"That stupid cat will probably complain about not wanting anyone other than Lady Freya to touch him."

"Tell him I will never again ride a chariot that won't do as it's told."

""""Understood.""""

Four sets of footsteps rang out as the Gulliver brothers acknowledged their orders. Freya and Ali would be departing from the hidden fortress without delay.

The boaz carrying a goddess under his arm, the cat person with a look of an annoyance on his face and a girl over his right shoulder, and the other first-tier adventurers accompanying them were all moving at extreme speed. They sprinted across a distance that had taken camels three days in just a few hours. Leodo came into view before the sun had even started to rise. Even though she had been complaining quite loudly about being handled like luggage, Ali could not hide her shock at how quickly they arrived.

But even so, it was already too late.

"Th-the town...?!"

Leodo was ablaze. The red flames and smoke beneath the desert's night sky looked like a funeral pyre. The lamentations of women and children filled the air, and the shouts begging for mercy were probably the merchants'.

When they reached the northern gate, Ali scrambled toward the center of the town. Freya and her familia followed behind her. On the way, they discovered that the bazaar had been wrecked before being set ablaze. The colorful goods that had been so pleasing to Freya's eyes before were scattered all over, interspersed with the corpses lying everywhere.

There were no survivors anywhere to be seen, but screams could be heard coming from the center of the town. Ali could not keep herself from trembling as she saw the carnage. The results of her actions were laid out before her.

The people of an entirely uninvolved country were attacked, all because of me. Because I came here!

She despaired but did not allow herself to fall apart there. The goddess striding through the town as she looked around would not allow it.

"Even the oasis..." Ali whispered.

The giant emerald blue oasis still fresh in her mind was now crimson with blood. Freya and her procession crossed the bridge to the island at the heart of the oasis. There were many residents of the town who had been cornered there after fleeing from the burning bazaars. And the inhumane soldiers of Warsa were also there, having chased down the residents to amuse themselves. Ali was frozen in shock at the hideous scene as a figure ran toward them.

"L-Lady Freyaaaaaaa!" It was the merchant Bofman, his clothes scorched here and there. "You've returned?! P-please! Please save us!"

"Situation report first." "Make it fast." "What of Lady Freya's property?"

The Gulliver brothers stood in front of the goddess, blocking the way. Bofman recoiled from the memory of their punishment and explained himself, driven by a fear even greater than they evoked.

"W-Warsa's forces suddenly attacked and broke through the city's defense! They started burning the town without announcing any demands or accepting any negotiations! They just pillaged every-thing, demanding to know where Prince Aram was and killing those who could not answer them…!" Bofman responded with a torrent of words, his shoulders heaving as he knelt on the ground. He timidly looked up at the goddess, who had not glanced at him even once, struggling to finish his report. "Lady Freya's property, too…Warsa broke into the manor…the former slaves are already…"

Freya did not hear the rest as he finished by explaining he had been running away with the rest of the employees of the Fazoul Trading Company. She proceeded down the path to the oasis man-sion. Strewn across the path were two bodies. The young boy and girl whom she had freed from the slave's collar, who had asked to become her followers.

"…"

They were clinging to each other, lying in a pool of blood. Their eyes were wide, and tears and blood had streamed down their cheeks. Freya silently lowered a hand over their faces and closed their eyes, without any concern about getting her hand dirty.

They had clearly tried to let the others get away, since there were many others collapsed farther down the path. All of them former slaves that Freya had freed. And every last one of them had been killed. There was no emotion on the goddess's face.

"Stop…Stop iiiiiiiiiiiit!" Ali's scream resounded.

Tears were streaming down her face as she took in the scene. Her shout was filled with a rage that seared her body as she broke through the grief.

"Who's there?!"

The attackers noticed Ali's scream as well as Ottar and the others, who were armed and ready for battle. The people who had torched the town gathered. They were soldiers wearing official uniforms.

"Warsa…!" Ali growled, her voice filled with loathing.

"Purple eyes…could it be Prince Aram?! Ha-ha-ha-ha, that's Lord Resheph for you! His eyes really are all-seeing!" A masculine human wearing a cape laughed.

He had higher quality armor than the average soldiers, and he was wielding a mage's staff. He was probably the skilled magic user who had led the troops that assaulted the fortress that the Gulliver brothers had mentioned.

"I am the warrior Marzner, who has been blessed by the god Resheph! Surrender, Prince Aram! If you don't, I, who have leveled up, shall burn everything before me! Behold my Level Two—"

While Marzner haughtily bragged of his strength, Ali pierced him with a wrath-filled gaze, and Allen and the other adventurers watched with a dry look that did not even rise to the level of disgust, a single deity stepped forward. The goddess's silver hair swayed.

"Lady Freya!"

"…? You're…"

Allen and the others tried to warn her it might be dangerous as Marzner looked at her dubiously. Ali's eyes widened. Freya stopped right between both groups. She drew the eyes of every last one of the Warsa soldiers to her with her beauty. As more and more of them became entranced, their eyes started to crawl over her body, their vulgar thoughts obvious to all. The commander Marzner licked his lips.

"What business do you have here, Goddess of Beauty?"

"You were the ones who did this, were you not?"

"Indeed. All of it was done in accordance with our Lord Resheph's divine will!" Marzner maintained his haughty pose, gesturing overdramatically as he spoke. "Are you perhaps…displeased? Perchance, is a righteous indignation burning you like we burned this town?" He asked in a jeering tone, not realizing his death was quietly approaching as he stirred *Freya Familia*'s murderous ire.

However, Freya rejected his implication without any indication of caring.

"There's nothing strange about victims in a war between children. If I got angry about it or grieved over every victim, there'd be no end to it."

"Wh…?!" Ali was rocked by the goddess's response.

"That's just how it goes. Nothing to be done about it."

And her shock was all the stronger because, though it had only been a short journey, she could tell from the time they had been together that Freya meant every last bit of what she was saying. Meanwhile, Marzner was laughing loudly.

"Ha-ha-ha-ha-ha-ha! That's a true goddess for you! No need to beat around the bush! So could you step aside, please? Our target is Prince Aram over there—"

However, that was where she cut off the man's annoying voice.

"But, when it comes to what you stole, that's a different matter."

The goddess's voice was like a crescent blade, silencing everyone around her. The soldiers and Ali felt a chill as Freya continued.

"Yona, Haara," she started listing off names.

"…?"

"Anwar, Latifah, Murat, Hicham, Hazid, Sere, Khanna, Ohza, Nacer, Nadia, Leila, Ruqaiya, Zahir, Karathona—"

The Warsa troops, Marzner, and even Ali were shocked by how eloquently she listed off so many people's names. And, just as Marzner was about to shout something, perhaps irritated by the goddess's seemingly never-ending list, Freya's tone shifted, reaching the end of her litany. For the first time, Ali heard an intense power in her soprano voice.

"Those are the names of my children that you killed."

A spark shot through Ali's body.

"I've no interest in the victims of war. But those who lay a hand on my children—on my property—those people I shall never forgive."

Freya had remembered them. The names of those slaves she had freed. The faces of those whom she had saved on a whim, who had praised her name. She remembered every last child whom she had claimed as her own!

"Wh-what…"

"No one likes having something of theirs taken, right? Whether it's a physical item, memories…or even lives."

Perhaps finally noticing that something strange was going on with Freya, Marzner became overwhelmed. He pulled back in the face of her supernatural force and presence.

"So I'm going to have to demand an equivalent recompense."

Freya's eyes opened wide. Her silver gaze sparkled bewitchingly. An eerie divine gravitas emanated from her body.

"——gh!"

Allen and the others were the first to react. The strongest adventurers who were unmoved no matter the situation or the enemy became visibly nervous.

"Close your eyes!" Allen shouted, paying no heed to appearances.

"Huh?" Ali did not move.

The cat person growled in annoyance as he leaped to her and forcibly covered her eyes and ears. Despite her vision and hearing being cut off, though, Ali could still sense Freya's divine majesty. It pierced through everything, as if it had her very soul in its grip.

"Prostrate thyself."

The heart of every mortal there leaped. Every living being there trembled. Ali felt her body jerk in response. The billowing flames trembled, the desert breeze died down, and the moon froze in the sky. It was the word of god.

However, with that one command, Marzner and the other Warsa soldiers dropped to the ground, prostrating themselves before the goddess with a well-trained reaction.

"Ha-ha-ha——!"

Freed from Allen's protection, Ali's eyes widened as she saw the bizarre scene of Marzner and the other soldiers obediently kneeling there in the sand. There was something off about all of them. Their cheeks were flushed, and drool was dripping from the corners of their mouths as they peered up at the goddess calmly standing before them.

There was no longer any vulgar or lecherous thoughts lurking in their eyes. There was nothing left other than a desire to please the being before them. They were utterly enthralled. It was as if their souls had been removed.

"Do you want my love?"

"Y-yes, milady! More than anything in this world! Please, milady!"

"I see. But that's a problem. I already decided I wouldn't forgive you. If I don't exact some kind of punishment, I won't be satisfied. How could I love children such as you?"

"B-but...?!"

Marzner and the others were being trifled with by the goddess's every word, battered by sadness and despair. There was already a smile on Freya's face as her silver eyes sparkled, and the witch's words continued.

"But I've got an idea that might work. If you kill yourselves and wait for me in heaven, then maybe—"

The next instant, the soldiers' face warped into manic grins as they drew their weapons.

"Understood! I'll be waiting, beloved goddess!"

The tragedy was over in just an instant. The soldiers all slit their own throats with their swords or else thrust the blades into their chests. Marzner spun what sounded like a ritual prayer as he pressed his staff to his throat and cast his spell. There was a flash of light and a thunderous boom. His smiling head flew high into the air, falling to the ground before it reached the heavens.

"......What...happened...?" Ali whispered as she trembled at the sight.

There was a synchronized splash of blood and then they all tumbled to the ground, forming a mountain of corpses. Their eyes were still rapturous as their souls passed beyond the desert's sky and raced off to the heavens. In obedience with Freya's divine will, they had all killed themselves. As Ali struggled to remain standing, Allen's low voice rang out behind her.

"She charmed them."

"What...?"

"*That* is her charm." His face twisted as he hid the awe he felt toward his patron goddess.

"What you said before, about how we were all enthralled by her beauty."

"That isn't true at all."

"As if."

"She hasn't used her charm even once since she first came to this town."

The Gulliver brothers chimed in in response.

Time froze for Ali as she realized what they were saying. *Freya hasn't used her power to charm anyone in the entire time we've been together? So everyone who set eyes on her until now was simply captivated by her beauty?*

The phenomenon that had just shaken Ali's soul to its core, that was Freya's true charm—

"If she were to use her charm…it would put an end to everything."

"Even we in her familia would become nothing more than puppets."

Hegni's and Hedin's eyes narrowed as they looked at the goddess before them.

Even the followers who bore Freya's ichor on their backs were dizzied by the force of it. And Ali, who had resisted the goddess's beauty, would have crumpled over had Allen not protected her. Incidentally, Bofman had been kicked in the back of the head by Grer, and his head was half-buried in the ground while the rest of his body twitched. The bundle of carnal desire managed to avoid being charmed thanks to the pain and the shock.

"We can crush ten thousand armies. But she…she can seize absolute control over those same ten thousand armies," Ottar finished.

The reality of what he was saying left Ali utterly speechless. If Freya felt like it, she could literally end everything—steal a country, usurp a throne, even rule the entire mortal realm. Her power was overwhelming, capable even of affecting beings on the same level as her. And other than deities and monsters, she could captivate every being in the mortal realm in an instant. It was absolute domination. Not a beauty whose face could launch a thousand ships but a witch who would rule the world. Her domain extended to as far as her gaze and voice could carry.

But despite that, the reason Freya did not try to rule everything was so that she could amuse herself. And more than anything else, it was out of respect for the mortal realm. Freya understood that there was nothing more empty, more meaningless than her ability. For what value was there in effortlessly acquiring everything? If she charmed everything and moved the whole world according to her whims, it would be as if the world were dead. That was why she did not use her charm in matters involving the mortal realm. The one and only exception was when her divine wrath was incurred.

"So then she…"

Meaning Freya's charm was invincible. And from everything they were saying, Ali realized that even what Freya had carried out just now was not actually serious, which elicited an unstoppable shudder.

—If she ever seriously used her charm, everything would be nothing but a farce.

She finally understood the true meaning of what Allen had said during their journey. And why he had gotten so enraged by what she had said. They had sworn their loyalty to Freya of their own volition. It had nothing to do with being charmed by her. They were not puppets in thrall to her but followers who had willingly offered up everything for her.

"…"

Regaining her composure, Ali looked at the goddess before her who stood right in front of a fountain of blood and yet had not been marred by a single drop of it. The soldiers were stained with blood, every one of them still grinning, still clinging to their faith in her as they collapsed. It almost evoked the image of a crimson lotus. The goddess of beauty stood in the middle of it all, smiling as their souls began their journeys to the heavens.

"When I go back to the heavens, if I can still remember this day, I'll grant you my love. Only if I remember it, though."

Her smile was that of a queen who mercilessly toys with the souls of others.

© nilitsu

4

The desert wind brings mirage-like dreams. Particularly on nights when people are already tossing and turning.

Ali had borne two names from birth: her true name, Ali, and her royal name, Aram Raza Shalzad.

Her father, King Shalzad, was troubled by the problem of needing a successor. He had not been blessed with a child by his wife, his harem, or any of his various mistresses. It troubled him such that he could even hear voices whispering behind his back about his lack of an heir, despite the fact that no one was around.

Shalzad was a country that adored its king, and in order to solidify his support, her father had obsessed over producing an heir. Because of that, his long-awaited first child, Ali, was given the life of a prince, despite being born a girl. And because of the teachings of the country's founder, queens were not acknowledged in Shalzad, so Ali's position was to serve as the last resort until a male heir was born or until Ali herself could bear a son.

Ali never felt like she was being limited by the burden placed on her, though. Quite the opposite. She felt a strong sense of duty; a belief that she must serve as king for her country. The fear of being found out was something she lived with daily, but until she could bear a rightful successor, she was determined to fulfill her duty as a member of the royal family.

"Ali. I'm sorry you were not born a man. I could not even grant you happiness as a woman—"

Her mother died, leaving those words behind, when Ali was still young and unable to understand the true meaning of her mother's tears. Standing before her mother's body, she swore, *Ali is not necessary. The one who is needed is Aram—and also, the true prince of the next generation.*

In the first place, she was nothing more than a placeholder. Her name would be little more than trivia in the long history of her country. It was true she had mocked herself for merely being a placeholder, but she could accept it because she was able to love her beautiful homeland blessed by oases and the smiles of the people who lived there more than she cursed her own fate.

She believed that her retainers generally had a good opinion of her. Both those who knew her secret and those who did not followed her—or rather him. Aram enjoyed a mostly favorable reception: he tried to do well, though he had a tendency to spin his wheels pointlessly because of his deeply rooted sense of justice. And the generals who actually went out into battle threw themselves into the fray with the knowledge that he would shed tears for their sacrifice.

She recognized she was raised well. But to her way of thinking, that did not necessarily mean she was acknowledged as a full-fledged ruler in her own right. Reality would not wait for Aram's growth. "Someday" could not last forever. In time, a tragedy would visit their land.

When it finally arrived, the capital fell, and innocent citizens were sacrificed. Those crazed villains had rampaged through the city. And Ali had been unable to act. Unable to do anything but be dragged from the capital by her retainers in order to escape.

"Someday." That naïveté had only invited destruction. She should have pushed further, harder. From the very moment she decided to live as Aram. Even if she was nothing more than a placeholder until the next king was born.

Ali had to make a decision. She needed the resolve to become the cornerstone for her country.

The day after Warsa's army had set fire to Leodo.

Ali had barely slept, and bags were still visible under her eyes. The merchant Bofman was desperately trying to keep up with her as she looked around the torched ruins.

The lively merchant town was not even a shadow of its former self. The north, west, and central bazaars had been burned. The soldiers left scorched earth in their wake. Apparently they had also set fire to the port in the south to prevent the prince from escaping. The desert ships, save a small handful that managed to escape, and even the warehouses storing goods had all been reduced to cinders. It was an open question whether the bloodstained oasis would ever return to normal no matter how much time and effort was spent on rebuilding it. Ironically, the slave market had been passed over because it did not have any items in it.

All around the city, there were those whose bodies were covered in ash, hugging each other and crying at their safe reunions. But there were just as many kneeling beside corpses, weeping.

If anyone there knew Ali's identity, if they knew why Warsa had attacked their town, they would surely have glared at her with eyes filled with hatred. They would have stoned her.

Ali took in all of the tragic scenes and steeled her will.

She had gone out into the town at daybreak, and night fell by the time she finished looking at everything. As darkness set in and the temperature dropped, Ali returned to the oasis mansion at the center of the city. It had barely managed to escape the fate of the wider town and was where the goddess was staying after she lost her children.

"Goddess Freya."

The manor's mistress was in her bedroom on the top floor. She was sitting in a velvet pillowed chair, sipping at a glass of wine, and looking out the window across the scorched town.

At her side was the boaz warrior, at the ready like a loyal retainer. Ali assumed a formal tone and manner, befitting an audience with a goddess, just like the last time they had met there.

"If it pleases you, I'd like to ask your aid in order to extract vengeance on the villainous scum of Warsa."

There was no stopping Warsa at present. Not with the forces Shalzad and the rest of the western Kaios could bring to bear. The reckless assault on Israfan—the burning of Leodo had sent shock waves through the region and tensions were rising, but Warsa itself showed no signs of being concerned. It was an expression of their confidence in their own strength—in the strength of *Resheph Familia*—that they were not afraid no matter how many countries joined forces against them.

"I spoke with Bofman and gathered information. Shalzad's elite forces in Serein were apparently wiped out just the other day. Warsa's military, *Resheph Familia*, undoubtedly has several kavir. In this part of the western Kaios, that's an overwhelming amount of military power."

The harsh desert world—though it paled in comparison to Orario—was capable of producing many Level-2 warriors. And above all, those who managed to level up a second time, known as kavir, were a precious resource. So much so that even in the large, powerful countries along the Nire River, they were promised the status of general with no strings attached. And *Resheph Familia* boasted several of those kavir. Or perhaps warriors even stronger than that. In the age of deities when quality was superior to quantity, the enemy's forces were overpowering.

"I'm aware just how shameless my request is at this point. However, right now I have no other deity to whom I can turn."

"…"

"My country is ravaged, my people victimized, and the flames of war are now spreading to an entirely neutral country. I brought them into this. I cannot turn a blind eye to such villainy. So for the sake of that…I will debase myself as much as I have to. I will pay whatever price I must."

The only way she had to repel Warsa's attacks was by borrowing the power of the goddess before her eyes.

"I will…offer myself up to you. I shall become the Odr you desire." Ali presented herself, stifling the tremble that threatened to creep into her voice. "I was never anything more than a placeholder until the next king could be born. If a rightful successor is born, then I can accept whatever may happen to this body of mine. I will devote my all to you. So please!"

Ali had steeled her resolve to become a sacrifice in order to save her homeland, and because she had nothing to her name now, all she could do was offer herself in return. So that was exactly what she did in her appeal to the goddess.

"I beseech you, take your followers and—"

Destroy my enemy. But the goddess did not allow her to finish her request.

"I don't want to," she rejected it bluntly.

"Wh—...?!"

"Why do I have to save your country? Why must I be bothered to have mercy upon the children of the desert?" she said as she sat with crossed legs.

Ali had no doubt the negotiations would not be simple, but she had not expected Freya to so adamantly refuse. She should still be upset about her property—the former slaves—being killed. Ali was about to press her about whether she had forgiven Warsa already, but Freya answered it before she could even ask, as if she already knew everything in her mind.

"I already punished those who laid hands on my property. They will despair over the promise that can never be fulfilled before eventually being purified. I'm satisfied with that."

"...!"

"I have no obligation or duty to butt into some pointless war. At least not as far as I'm concerned," she finished.

Ali was standing there, about to step forward, to ask for any kind of help, but Freya stopped it with a glance.

"Besides, have you no shame? Clinging to the fact that I'm looking for my Odr?"

"Gh...?!"

"You didn't seriously think I would agree to such a boring exchange, did you?" Freya's eyes narrowed as she openly expressed her disappointment for the first time. "Really, Ali? I'm disappointed."

Scorned for trying to cling to an easy answer, disappointing the goddess before being cast away. For some reason, those feelings were especially painful. Ali felt like an invisible blade was slicing into her body. And the fact that she was so hurt by the goddess's words flustered her all the more.

Then what should I do...?!

Without Freya's support, she had no way to stop Warsa's barbarity. Ali was about to look down at the floor in disappointment in herself, when—

"I can't be satisfied with you like that. Your soul will never shine this way." The goddess's lips curled up into a grin. "Don't offer me something. *Come and take* what you want."

There was a crack as something was set down on the round table at the center of the room. Ali spun in shock at the loud noise and saw that Ottar had moved at some point and prepared something.

"A placeholder until the next king is born? Irrelevant. You were still earnestly, foolishly, sincerely trying to find the correct path to be a righteous king, were you not? So then follow that path all the way to the end."

There was a board game on the table.

"Walk the path of kings."

It was Halvan.

"You can't mean—" Ali shuddered.

"Let's have a match, Ali. I'll wager that which you desire," Freya said, her silver eyes narrowing provocatively as she looked through Ali. "I said it before, Ali. No matter the king, there would come a time when they had to make a gamble. There would come a time when they would have to rise to the challenge."

"Gh...?!"

"If you win, I'll lend you my followers. You can use them as you please. Whether that's to protect your country or to destroy your hated enemy is entirely up to you."

Ali was at a loss for words as the goddess's soprano voice slid into her ears. Freya stood up, approaching Ali before she realized it and cupping her hands over the girl's cheeks.

"In exchange, if you lose—I will take your everything."

She pulled the girl's face in close to hers. The goddess's expression was alluring like a witch of destruction. It was the look of a haughty, inhuman queen. There was no trace of the divine goddess's face that had stolen Ali's heart that night in the oasis. Two sides of the same coin. That was the true nature of the free and cruel goddess.

Ali caught her breath.

"It's true that I want you. So the moment you lose to me in this game, I will be taking you with me and leaving this desert."

"Wh—?!"

"I'll return to Orario and take my time dissolving you in pleasure as you moan until you have become my personal little doll."

Ali's speechless face was reflected in the goddess's eyes as she smiled at the girl. Those eyes were filled with a sadistic, rapturous, dark desire.

—*She'll do it. She really would do it.*

She would embrace her own desires without reserve, embrace Ali's body and spirit, and devour every last bit of her. The goddess would ravage the soul that had fascinated her. And she would not doubt for a moment that it was a pure expression of her love—a blessing.

"So, have a seat, Ali."

She released the girl and moved to the center of the room and sat down, but Ali didn't budge.

It's impossible. I can't win.

Before they had left Leodo, she had seen Freya's skill at the game. Or rather she had been shown just what kind of beings that deities were. All-knowing. She could examine the board while in perfect knowledge of the truth, never make a mistake, and mercilessly cut down her opponent. Every move she made would be flawless, and she would never be baffled by the state of the board, literally playing a godlike game.

There was no way for Ali to match that. A cold sweat broke across her brow, and her hands trembled. She was being consumed by despair in the face of a match with a goddess who could not be escaped.

Freya watched all of that silently before finally opening her mouth.

"Ali."

For just that one moment, her voice changed back. She smiled, as if placing a wreath of flowers in the girl's hands.

*   *   *

"Are you really being resolute and noble right now?"

"___"

Hearing that question, a memory flashed through her mind.
Live nobly and resolutely.—Like a hero.
The scene from the oasis that night that Ali would never forget. The message from the goddess that had been engraved in her soul. The most beautiful divine will in the world.
...I see. That's what she meant...
Hearing Freya's words, Ali realized her misunderstanding. If challenging this goddess to a board game was too much for her, then she was never going to be able to fight Warsa anyway.

Ali was walking a razor's edge between recklessness and despair, and in order to achieve her wish, she had to stake herself, demonstrate her resolve, and nobly break out of her predicament.

Ali had misunderstood her situation. Her assumptions were all wrong. She did not need to show a tragic resolve in the face of Warsa. If she were truly suited to be king, then it was the goddess before her whom she needed to fight, to whom she needed to demonstrate her resolve.

"Ghhh!"
Ali resolved herself.
I mustn't shame myself any further before her.
She quickly sat down across from Freya. The goddess's eyes narrowed, and her smile deepened as Ali's light purple eyes stared her down. Ali had made her decision. Not the resolve to become a cornerstone for her country, but the resolve to live nobly—to heroically stake her life on the royal path that had led her to that point.

She stepped to the table and challenged the goddess to a gamble.

Halvan.
It was the most-played board game in the Kaios Desert. In all,

there were eight starting types of pieces: the king, called malik; the queen, called malikah; the general, called faiz; the chariot, called merkabah; the sprite, called rauch; the pawn, called junud; the thief, called las; the slave, called obadiah. It was played on a ten-by-ten board, and much like chess and shogi, the goal was to capture the opposing malik. There were two rules in particular that distinguished Halvan: the initial formation and the sacrifice.

At the beginning of the game, the players were allowed to place their pieces freely within a predetermined region: their formation. And by giving up a single turn, a player was able to remove one of their own pieces and exchange it for certain other pieces they could later spend a move to drop anywhere on the board: the sacrifice. The drop pieces they gained from the sacrifice depended on what piece was sacrificed. For example, by exchanging a junud, a player could gain a single las and a single obadiah.

Because of those two rules, Halvan strategy had developed marked peculiarities that separated it from those of other similar board games. In exchange for getting to move first, the player was forced to expose their formation before the second player had set their own pieces. If the formation the first player chose was one that the second had studied well, they would be at a significant disadvantage. It was said that between players of equivalent skill, the match was decided before a single move had even been made.

"Will you go first or second?" Freya asked as she sat back in her chair, smiling ever so slightly.

"...Second," Ali responded after slight hesitation.

Nowadays, with every possible opening having been studied, it was clear that moving second was advantageous in Halvan. At least among mortals.

I played quite a bit of Halvan in the court and am familiar with all the standard openings. I'm sure that alone won't be enough to beat her, but...the depth of my knowledge should at least be of some value on the path to victory!

It was not something she would boast about, but Ali was the best Halvan player in the court of Shalzad.

As a member of the royal family, she was blessed in her heritage, and while she did have some hardheaded tendencies, she made it a point to internalize all of the knowledge and teachings she had received in the court. The weight Ali bore while passing as a male prince was not something the average person could understand, and she had put in an equivalent effort in order to play her role. And Halvan, which was popular among the aristocracy, was just one more part of that effort.

"All right, then, let me set up my pieces."

Picking up the black pieces, Freya began to systematically place them atop the board. Her formation was…the pieces were lined up symmetrically from left to right at the front of her area. Essentially just the default formation. It was the most basic of basics. Ali caught herself feeling momentarily disappointed as she watched the formation take shape, but she immediately switched to carefully analyzing the structure. And when it was her turn to lay out her pieces, she carefully and deliberately set up her own formation.

The formation she had chosen was a flying V with the pieces gathered to the right side of her area. It was an offensive formation that took advantage of the rauch's mobility to open holes in the enemy's formation, and it was Ali's best formation. She decided to put her faith in her rauch.

"An attack without any concern for defense…Hee-hee, that resolve of yours is exquisite. In that case, I'll also yield the turn to you."

"Wh-what?!"

"Move as you please."

Admiring Ali's determination, Freya confidently skipped her turn, even though Ali had been able to place her pieces in response to the goddess's formation. It was obviously an enormous advantage for Ali.

Is she looking down on me? Giving herself a handicap? No—it doesn't matter! First things first, I have to win this match! If she is looking down on me, then it's her funeral!

Just like a tiger lying in wait, Ali readied her strike.

Ali's gaze contained a regal pressure, but Freya weathered it as if it were a comfortable breeze.

And, with Ottar watching on from the side, the game began.

Ali's first move was to advance the junud in order to open the way. Between using the default formation and allowing Ali to move first, Freya's defense would be slow. Ali could choose to either continue pushing with her junud or attack through the opening with her rauch depending on how her opponent responded.

Next was Freya's turn. Ali was on guard for what the goddess's move would be—

"—What?!"

Freya took the malikah in her formation and moved it to the side, taking the malik standing beside it.

"Regicide?!"

It was one of the possible sacrifices in Halvan. However, for reasons both tactical and cultural, it wasn't a move that anyone ever made. It could even be called taboo.

It was a natural sort of development. In the desert world filled with kingdoms of various shapes and sizes, killing the piece that represented the king was taken as an offense against the royal family. If anyone used that move in the royal court, it would undoubtedly be judged as lèse-majesté. But even setting that aspect aside, there were none who would choose that move for purely tactical reasons.

In the event of regicide, the piece that took the malik became the king in its stead. In exchange, the player received another copy of every piece other than the malik and malikah to be used as drop pieces. And then, in exchange for being granted such an abundance of pieces, the player would be forced to yield three turns instead of the usual one turn for a sacrifice. Three straight turns without being able to move.

That was the risk that accompanied regicide. And yet, the goddess before Ali had not only done it but done it as if it were natural.

"I don't like having anyone standing over me, giving me orders," Freya said with the smile of the one and only Vanadis.

"Gh…!" Ali strangled the agitation she felt.

Combined with the first move that Freya had yielded, she had already ceded a total of four moves. She had given Ali four turns with which to attack. From the perspective of any board game, that was a fatal move. There was no way she could overcome that. No matter how godlike her moves might be, there should be no way out.

That was what Ali thought, but she did not gleefully cling to those three moves she was given, nor did she struggle with how to manage them. She was shocked by Freya's choice, but she put her hand to her mouth and thought hard about how best to use her moves.

While Ottar solemnly prepared the goddess's newly acquired pieces for her, Ali took her own piece in hand. For the first move, she used her junud to take Freya's slave, easily advancing into the enemy's camp, which allowed her to promote her foot soldier to a faris—a knight. And then for her second move, she took one more piece with the faris. And with her final free move, she pushed into the goddess's formation from the other direction with her rauch, using the faris as a wedge while she set up on both flanks.

With that, it was finally Freya's turn again. Ali had taken free rein of the board and could attack from either the left or the right depending on how Freya responded.

The position already looked hopeless for Freya. But despite that, the goddess smiled.

"All right, then, let's get this started."

She picked up one of the pieces she had gained by killing the king. The goddess placed the faiz on the board with confidence, as if she were sending out her most trusted warrior.

The desert nights are quiet and cold.

Even around oases that moderated the change, the night was still much cooler when compared to the blistering sun. Leodo was no exception. The tranquil moonlight chilled everything.

However, Ali could not tell whether her body was boiling or freezing over. An intense torrent of emotions, a mixture of passion and chills ran through her.

"Ghhhh…?!"

Beneath her eyes was a Halvan board filled with black and white pieces. The position that should have been overwhelmingly advantageous to her had long ago been turned on its head.

Her position had been favorable from the start, and there had not been any obvious turning points, but before she realized it, the balance of power had become even. And then, the goddess's advance began like a flaring inferno.

Ali had not even been able to stammer in awe at how or why. Freya merely proceeded to turn the tables with each move she made, as if it were obvious, as if it were divine providence. Ali had not made any incorrect moves at all. On the contrary even, she had made several excellent, even brilliant moves. And yet, every line of attack she readied was crushed, and all her defenses were broken.

She never knew. Ali had never imagined that a Halvan like that could exist. Every time she thought she had studied all there was to study in the state of the board, it was transformed into an entirely new and never-before-seen beast by a single move from Freya. And what she first thought was a giant beast, or perhaps some kind of dragon, changed into a torrent of countless slashes.

She broke through the center with her faiz, then used her free merkabah in a hit-and-run before crippling my defenses with a rauch, letting her tightly knit junud pieces tear into my formation—!

The pieces smashing through her defenses transformed into swords and spears, arrows and axes, carving away at her body as they broke through her formation. She could clearly see it, could see the unmatched brutality of the Einherjar obeying their Vanadis.

If I lure the faiz so my merkabah…no, that won't work! Her rauch will break through my flank! And I can't deal with her merkabah because of the way her junud are positioned!

She had already been pushed into a one-sided defense. The game Freya was playing out in her head was far beyond anything Ali could imagine. Countless times, the board in the girl's mind collapsed in submission like a castle made of sand.

She was still threatening the goddess a little. There was no denying she was still maintaining some kind of a grip on the board. But she could not help thinking that even those struggles were all within Freya's calculations. That she was being toyed with and the outcome was already set in stone. That her hopes of saving her country were already gone and she was already as good as the goddess's puppet.

The helplessness she felt spawned a terror that was unbearable.

By any reasonable look at the board, this isn't over. You can still fight. You must...

The scolding voice in her head that kept telling her it was not over yet was like a candle in the breeze.

"..., ..., ...gh!"

Ali realized that her lungs were screaming for air. She was gasping like a fish out of water, but she did not have any composure left to care about how comical the wheezing sound she was making sounded.

There was no one in the room to read the record of the game. The only other person in the room, the boaz warrior, was standing over the board taking a neutral stance, simply watching the flow of the match.

The only other sound was that of the pieces moving across the board, their movement transforming into a lonely tone that gradually cornered Ali. It was as if she were tracing the outlines of her life with her moves, and it felt like that life were being chipped away with every advance that Freya's pieces made. Ali had already lost count of how many times she had paused to ponder the state of the game, but the goddess never admonished her for it. Ali could imagine the goddess amusing herself with how despair clung to this desperate girl's face. She could not stop the sweat pouring down her brow as she acknowledged that she was standing on the edge of a cliff.

They were already in the final stages of the game. If she did not do something, Freya would be able to checkmate her within three moves. She was close enough now to guarantee there would be no escape.

Was there any way out? Any move that would allow her to survive? Or was it an inescapable death? Ali could not see anything anymore. She did not know what move to make. She did not know how to advance.

It's no good—I lose—It's over—I already—

Her hand became limp. Her body was on the verge of toppling forward like a marionette whose strings had been cut. She was overwhelmed by a sense of resignation as she stared at the board—and for the first time, she looked up.

Sitting across from her was the goddess she was fighting. The smile on her face as she watched Ali was the same as it had been all along. There was no joy or scorn in her eyes. She was just waiting to see what path Ali would create for herself.

"—gh."

That smile. That gaze.

It made Ali's hand tremble. Before she realized it, she was clenching her fingers. Her hand had become a fist. A spark flashed to life in her frozen heart, filling the rest of her body with heat.

No, I can't! I won't!

She could not give up. She could not cower. She would not allow herself to run away in the face of the goddess.

I can't. Not in front of her—I can't show her such a pathetic figure!

It was just stubbornness, but that was her truest feeling. She did not want to lose to Freya, to the goddess who had wreaked such havoc on her heart. She did not want to be cast aside by the goddess who had guided her in that moonlit oasis. Freya alone, she did not want to ever disappoint.

"—That's why!"

And with that wholehearted voice, Ali took her own malikah. There was no strategy. No goal. She just moved the piece along the board, following the flash of light, the guidance from the solitary moon she was sure she had seen.

She had the feeling that the reflection of herself in Freya's eyes shone dazzlingly.

"——...gh."

It was just a single move provoked by her heart. The blazing passion and determination that had gripped her was fleeting.

—*It's over.*

It was a blunder made in desperation. Just a vain struggle. When the boiling heat that ignited her whole body passed, Ali could see it. She hung her head silently. She did not even try to pray. She could do nothing but wait for the goddess to carry out her punishment.

Her head hung like a criminal's awaiting the executioner's blade, merely waiting for the proclamation—

"........."

But Freya stopped moving. Her silver eyes opened wide as she stared at the board.

"...?"

Freya had made every single move up to that point without taking any time to plan, so when she paused, Ali looked up in confusion. Ottar also looked on, puzzled, as Freya looked down at the board for a second.

"Heh...Heh-heh-heh...Ah-ha-ha-ha-ha-ha-ha!"

And then she laughed. A pealing laughter, like an uncontrollable wind. The goddess's voice sounded more joyous than Ali had ever heard her before, which caused her to recoil in surprise. And, ignoring the girl's confusion, the goddess reached out to her piece, her shoulders still quivering in uncontained mirth.

"E-four malikah, C-three merkabah, D-two rauch—"

And before Ali could say anything, she also started moving the girl's pieces. The black and white pieces moved without hesitation as she revealed a board dozens of moves into the future. Ali could not hide her shock at what was happening when—all of a sudden, her eyes shot open.

"Your chariot corners me, and—it's your win."

Checkmate. Not for Ali, but for Freya. All because of the single move with the malikah that Ali had just made. Even Ottar looked awestruck at the result.

"Th-that's...it can't be!"

Ali was astonished. It was a board dozens of moves into the future.

She had by no means seen that far in advance, and she would never have been able to make it there herself. If Freya had not performed the moves herself, she would never have noticed the path to victory and would surely have lost only a few turns later.

The move Ali had made contained an unknown potential that only a deity could have noticed.

"I beat you…?! No! But—! This is just…I could never have…"

That one move had come from following her instincts. It could be written off as nothing more than a burst of emotion. There was no way she would have been able to actually follow through and corner Freya.

"A king is not one who must accomplish everything themselves."

However, even if she could not have carried it out, she had demonstrated it. The possibility of a move that could tear the unrivaled queen down from her throne. The potential of mortals to overcome the impossible.

"A king is someone who exemplifies hope to others and proves the glory that lies beyond the light."

Ali sluggishly looked back at Freya, who had suddenly started speaking.

As if acknowledging that right at the end Ali's soul had demonstrated the glimmer of a king, and she had found the path to victory, Freya tipped over her malikah—the embodiment of herself. She resigned.

Ali caught her breath, unable to process what was going on.

"It's your victory, Ali," Freya said, rising from her seat.

"Gh…! W-wait a minute! I—!" Ali stood as well as she started to argue, but Freya stopped it with a glance

"Just accept it. I'm in a wonderful mood right now."

Ali could not tell what those narrowed silver eyes were looking at. But Freya could not hide her good cheer as she addressed her retainer.

"Ottar, obey Ali. Until the battle she desires is finished, you are to treat her as your mistress."

"Understood."

"Convey the same to Allen and the others as well."

The goddess was already moving things along as she ignored Ali standing there in shock. The boaz retainer nodded in acknowledgment of his true mistress's command and shifted to stand behind Ali, waiting in silence. Ali turned awkwardly to look behind her, her eyes trembling as she saw the boulder-like warrior standing there, looking down at her.

"I'll be changing rooms. This is your castle now. So carry yourself like a king."

"...!"

"From now on, everything that happens is entirely up to you. Will you stop their invasion? Or destroy a country you find offensive? You can do anything you want now. You wield a power that can achieve anything."

Ali gasped at Freya's words as the goddess moved toward the door. It did not feel real. But her pulse raced. There was nervousness and exaltation and an emotion she had never felt before.

And, as she placed her hand on the door, the goddess gave her one piece of advice out of generosity before leaving the room.

"If you're ever unsure what to do, then rely on Hedin. Other than that, do as you please."

Ali's victory was immediately reported to the first-tier adventurers of *Freya Familia*. Their initial reaction was disbelief, but they unquestioningly obeyed their patron goddess's divine will.

They accepted that they would play the part of Ali's arms and legs, though there was one, a certain catman, who made no effort to hide his displeasure at the situation.

"This is a farce."

That night in a meeting behind closed doors.

Several tables were pushed together with multiple maps spread out across them. The magic-stone lamp on the wall gave off a faint glow as those gathered in the room—Ottar and the other first-tier adventurers—looked to Ali while Allen made his displeasure known.

"It is her divine will. Obey, Allen."

"You got any other lines in your repertoire besides that, dumbass? She is who she is, and she went and let this brat who can't do anything other than beg for help screw around with us."

"Gh…"

"I didn't come all the way out here just so I could be some brat's plaything to boost her ego."

Saying she had defeated Freya in a match certainly sounded impressive, but she would never have noticed the opportunity if Freya herself had not pointed it out, and even that was only after the devastating handicap the goddess had imposed on herself. So what gave her the right to order them around? Ali could not really disagree with the clear implication behind Allen's blunt statement.

The silver-haired goddess was not there. She had told Ali to do as she pleased and then disappeared off somewhere.

"We're not getting anywhere like this. If you don't like it then just take back your oath to Lady Freya and get lost, you stray. We won't miss a cat or two leaving," the elf Hedin responded calmly. There was no anger or disgust in his voice. Just a professional desire to move things along.

The dark elf and prum brothers did not even glance at Allen.

"Tch…" The cat's annoyance was clear, but he did not leave the room.

They're supposed to be comrades, aren't they…? It's so tense.

Ali, who by all rights should have been an outsider to the group, was ready to collapse from the stress of dealing with them. She was struck again with awe at the fact that Freya somehow managed to command a group of such strong-willed people. At the same time, though, she could feel a weight in the pit of her stomach as she realized she was going to have to command them all herself now. Hedin glanced over as Ali subconsciously rubbed her stomach.

"Let's begin the discussion. You are short on time, are you not, milady-for-the-time-being?"

"Ah…yes!"

It was the dead of night.

This war room had been thrown together immediately after she had finished her game of Halvan with Freya. Her mind was already frayed from the intense match with a goddess, so she would have liked to have a long break, but she managed to get moving again thanks to the strength of her determination. While all of this was going on, her country and Israfan were still under threat from Warsa. She needed to come up with a plan to deal with them immediately.

"Bofman, was it? What are the particulars of Warsa's army?"

"Y-yes, sir?! Me, sir?!"

"Hurry it up, swine." "What are you waiting for, swine?" "Do you want to scream some more, pig?" "There's more where that came from, pig."

"Eeep?! I can report! I'll tell you everything I know! Without delay!"

Bofman had also been dragged into the room. He was on the verge of wetting himself as he recoiled from the Gulliver brothers' glares. Ali still did not really understand what connection he had with Freya, but she was starting to feel bad for him, suspecting he might have drawn the worst lot of them all.

"W-Warsa's forces are apparently currently occupying Shalzad in their bid to gain total control of the country. Reports indicate they have scattered several small groups all over in order to search for Prince Aram, but…"

The profits of merchants were affected significantly by the economy and politics of countries. And that was more true than ever during times of war. Bofman had surely been using his trading company to gather all the information he could about the ongoing war in order to determine any possible business opportunities, long before he had gotten dragged into this situation by Freya. Bofman glanced at Ali, trembling a bit as if what he wanted to say was difficult to address, before mustering the will to continue.

"I can't put an exact number on it, but…based on the information

I've gathered, the enemy forces likely number around eighty thousand."

"E-eighty thousand?!"

"It's not just Warsa soldiers, either. Countless mercenaries have been joining the war on their side as well…"

Ali felt her throat quiver when she heard that number. The numbers she had heard from back when the capital was taken were nowhere near as high as what Bofman was reporting. Shalzad and Warsa were both preeminent powers in the western Kaios's central region, but even so, raising eighty thousand troops should have been an impossible feat for either of them. As Bofman indicated, that number was unthinkable without thousands of mercenaries also entering the war.

But even if he's right about that, that number is still unreasonable. Not unless that mercenary group Warsa has been courting the past few years, Resheph Familia, *has been brining other mercenaries in as well…!*

Ali felt a chill. The war between Shalzad and Warsa was no longer merely a problem between their two countries. She could sense that she was being drawn into a different, stronger current. A contagion that would shake the entire Kaios region was starting to spread.

"Eighty thousand, huh?"

"Better than the Dungeon at least."

"But that's still a pain in the ass."

"A giant pain in the ass."

—However, despite the earth-shattering projection, *Freya Familia* was entirely unmoved. In fact they did not seem even the slightest bit concerned. Ali and Bofman found that difference in reaction disturbing.

"People with no talents to their name besides banding together can hardly be called capable. Indeed, I would write them off as incompetent. That's just how it is."

Hedin paid the two residents of the desert no heed as he looked down at the table. Amid all the maps spread out across the tables, he was focused on the areas surrounding Leodo and the area where the borders of Israfan, Shalzad, and Warsa all met. Examining the terrain in that area, his eyes suddenly narrowed, as if he had hit upon a plan.

"Milady-for-the-time-being is royalty, so even if I gave you an order, I could not enforce it. However, I'm going to provide directions. If you wish to end this quickly, then I suggest you follow them."

"..."

"If there are no objections, then I'll explain the plan."

As Hedin looked up, he appeared every bit the strategist supporting the king as he seized the initiative. His intelligence was seemingly common knowledge, as Ottar and the other adventurers did not interject.

"First of all, as a brief overview of the plan—"

Freya had told Ali to rely on this elf, Hedin.

I see, even his appearance has an air of intelligence to it. With the glasses he's wearing, he really does look the part of a brilliant tactician.

Ali was sure he would have a secret plan to break out of the predicament they were in, even though they were so overwhelmingly outnumbered, so she was tensely waiting with bated breath for his next words,

"—The eight of us will annihilate the enemy army. That is all."

"That's way too vague!!!" Ali howled at the ceiling.

There was no secret plan or strategy or anything. Just brute force. No consideration for ideas like winning tactical or strategic victories. Indeed, the overview was so lacking in detail as to be utterly useless.

"What are you talking about?! There's no way you can do that! Beating eighty thousand people with just eight?!"

But Hedin easily waved away her complaints.

"This is the most *efficient* method."

"What?!"

"And this way, there will be no innocent victims, which you wanted to avoid. I'm proposing a simple and clear plan that will meet your demands."

FAMILIA CHRONICLE: EPISODE FREYA 125

Hedin did not back down at all, as if he were simply stating the reality of the matter. Meanwhile, Ottar and the others took it all in stride without any comment.

He's serious. He meant every word. He—all of them—seriously think that they can wipe out an army of eighty thousand with just eight people!

"Did you think I would have a plan to scrounge together some soldiers and somehow overcome their advantage in numbers through some ingenious strategy?"

"O-obviously! That's how this sort of thing goes, right...?!"

"My apologies for not rising to your expectations, but even for us that method would be incredibly painstaking. It's just too unrealistic."

—Then what is realistic?!

Ali's jaw clenched as Hedin patiently explained to her that eight people defeating eighty thousand was the most reasonable choice when the alternative was trying to gather allies in order to meet the eighty thousand in battle—as if it were the most obvious thing in the world.

She broke into a cold sweat, wondering whether maybe she was the weird one for thinking it was ludicrous, but then she saw Bofman across the room with his mouth hanging open.

"...I-it's not just the numbers, the overall level of skill in the enemy's army is also high. They surely have countless kavirs!" Ali barely maintained the presence of mind to object.

The enemy troops were followers of a deity, warriors who had been granted Falna. Warsa was a militaristic country and they had several other subordinate gods in addition to the patron god of their military. And it was clear that *Resheph Familia* had several members who had leveled up as well.

"What of it? Are you suggesting that people equivalent to second-tier adventurers would be capable of stopping us?"

However, throughout it all, the elf's stance was unchanged. This was the era of gods. Quality over quantity was the ironclad rule of the times. *Why would a rabble be able to properly cross blades with an*

© nilitsu

elegantly polished and refined individual? Hedin's implicit response made Ali realize she was taking them too lightly. She was underestimating just how brokenly powerful the strongest faction—*Freya Familia*—really was.

"Whether through their own efforts or the work of a deity, the enemy has realized that Prince Aram is hidden in Israfan. They should be targeting other communities along the border besides just Leodo," Hedin continued as Ali stood there in shock.

The elf pointed to the communities in Israfan that were near the Shalzad border. He glanced over toward Bofman, who immediately stammered, "Y-yes, sir, there are reports that they have assaulted other towns and villages."

"While all that was going on, the forward elements they sent to Leodo stopped reporting all of a sudden. They will undoubtedly send in a new force. If they have already noticed the disturbance, then…they will likely arrive tomorrow evening," Hedin announced confidently.

He was basing his analysis on the equipment and the level of training of the Warsa troops they had encountered, combined with the information provided by Bofman regarding the enemy army's location and distance.

"First of all, we will crush that force to make them suspect that there is an unknown force in Leodo."

Ali had finally recovered from her shock and focused intently on what Hedin was saying. *An unknown force of the strongest adventurers in the world*…But she had no more energy left for rejoinders.

"If the second force they sent here does not return, they will become a bit more cautious, which will buy us some time. During that time, we will take care of our preparations."

"Preparations…?"

"To force the enemy to assemble their entire army in the location of the decisive battle."

"What?!" But Ali was flabbergasted yet again by the new bomb that Hedin dropped.

"I said before that it would be most efficient for the eight of us to take care of the enemy. So our challenge now is drawing all of the enemy forces onto the battlefield so that we leave no remnants that will need to be cleaned up later. If we can do that, then we'll be able to end everything in one fell swoop."

"Wh-what are you talking about…?!"

"It's the same when Rakia decided to attack Orario, but even for us, annihilating tens of thousands of enemies spread out across multiple fronts requires significant time and effort."

It was as if he was saying *"I'd rather get this annoyance over with all at once."*

There's no way we can do that. If we had a similar-sized force, then Warsa might meet us on the battlefield. But even with how over-whelming our combat strength is, it is still only eight people. They won't just rally for an all-out assault just because we ask them to. How are you going to convince a force of eighty thousand to all join the battle?!

Perhaps the voice screaming in Ali's mind was conveyed by her gaze, since Hedin looked back at her.

"If you desire peace for your country, then the method you should take is not to repel the enemy, but to annihilate them."

"!"

"I mean that quite literally. Not the colloquial usage where you dramatically reduce their forces and leave them significantly dam-aged. If you half-heartedly leave remnants behind, it will simply transform the conflict into a quagmire. If the enemy's army escapes without a decisive confrontation, they will undoubtedly continue to be a source of trouble for you in the future."

"Th-that's…!"

"We could begin an assault with surprise attacks now, but if we did that, there would be no way to prevent some from slipping through the cracks. That's why I want to gather them all in one place."

There was a clear logic and coherence to what Hedin was saying, but only to those who could accept his premise. It was not some-thing an average person could comprehend.

"We are going to go back to Orario after this. We will only fight this one time. So in order to fulfill your wish, it is necessary to comprehensively crush them so that they will never be able to attempt something like this again."

In truth, they had no interest in the fate of Shalzad. This was simply Hedin's considered advice to his current mistress, temporary though she might be. Understanding that, Ali felt her throat tremble.

"Because of that, I'm going to need you to do your part as well, Milady-for-the-time-being."

"...!"

"It is necessary for you to become the lure to draw out both the enemy and your allies...Can you do that?"

Behind his glasses, Hedin's coral eyes met Ali's gaze. It was not just him, either. Ottar, Allen, and the others, they were all looking at her. Eight pairs of eyes focused on her, appraising her. Ali clenched her hands.

"I'll do it! Whatever it takes!"

She responded firmly, accepting his challenge head-on.

"My capital has fallen, I failed to protect my people, and even my retainers are gone! I've done nothing but disgrace myself throughout all of this! If after all that, I couldn't even put myself on the line, then the royal family's name is worthless!"

"..."

"Use me, Hedin! If that's what it takes to make your unbelievable nonsense reality, then so be it!"

Her face took on the regal presence of Aram as she finally spoke her mind. It was already obvious she was going to have to do this herself, as she had been urged on so much by the goddess.

Ottar and the others quietly watched her. As both a king and a lone girl, there was still one thing that Ali had not told them.

"Please save my country, gallant warriors!"

And she said it with the spirit of a king.

Hedin's lips curled ever so slightly into a muted smile—at least that was how it looked to Ali.

"Very well. Then, let's commence the operation."

But on second glance Hedin's expression was unchanged from before as he solemnly continued, so Ali suspected it might have just been her imagination. However, as if responding to her royal decree, he began to shoot off instructions.

"Hegni and the brothers, it's your turn. And you four split up."

The dark elf and prums looked up as they were addressed. The elf tactician announced the beginning of the initial skirmish.

"Drive out any Warsa forces that come within a five-kirlo radius of this town."

That night, a wisp of cloud was covering the crescent moon.

The desert night was even darker than usual without the moonlight, and that darkness evoked a primal fear. The outline of the desert turned into clusters of darkness that seemed to almost grow into mountains, and the shining eyes of the monsters milling around flashed menacingly like disembodied souls.

Instead of the moon, countless stars in the sky looked down over the ruins. Stone pillars and broken walls rose out of a sea of sand, granting a window into the culture of the time they were built. The ceiling was half-collapsed, barely able to block out the cool night breeze. It was just right for monsters or humans to use as a place to rest their heads.

That same ancient ruin was currently ringing with screams.

"Ugh! Uwaaaaaaaaaaaa?!"

Shrouded in darkness, the cries from inside those ruins echoed across the desert night sky. Sprays of blood took to the air like countless flower petals. Crimson blood spurting from a severed neck painted the walls red. The sound of dozens of footsteps raised a great clamor. And each time a wail went up, the number of footsteps decreased by one.

Warsa's troops fell into disarray. They had invaded Israfan territory and were on their way toward Leodo to find out what had happened to Marzner and his advance unit that had failed to report back. They had set up camp in those ruins to avoid detection and were just taking a break when they were suddenly attacked without warning.

"R-report in! What the hell is goi—? *Gargh!*"

The man who was apparently in charge was mercilessly relieved of his head, and as a result, there was no longer any stopping the soldiers' panic. The shadow of a single attacker danced across the wall, coalescing into a silhouette as it cut down several more soldiers, bringing yet more death. The shadow sent the magic-stone lamps flying with a kick, transforming the interior of the ruins into pure darkness as the massacre continued.

"—AAARGH!"

Fittingly, the last thing the soldiers saw before they died was a dark fairy bearing death.

"Ahhhh, nights are good. It feels good striking from the shadows."

Taking advantage of the darkness to cut down yet another soldier. Simply repeating that over and over. To Hegni, it was a very easy task, freeing his speech from the usual nervousness he struggled with.

"No need to worry about other people looking at me. No need to be anxious about what I look like to anyone else."

Because the darkness hides it all.

His unburdened speech was accompanied by an intense flash of steel and enormous blooms of blood. The Warsa soldiers met their death one after the other without ever knowing what was happening.

"Honestly, I don't really like killing people, but you all did much worse things to the powerless masses, didn't you? That means there has to be atonement for your sins, so it's best if you just die here."

The only response he got was panicked screams. However, undeterred, the dark elf swordsman composed a melody with his blade as he confessed.

"If you don't, you'll eventually reach a point where just being alive fills you with shame. Just like me."

His green eyes bore a mixture of emotions as they narrowed earnestly.

©-nilitsu

"I'm jealous of you being able to die like this. I'd like to be able to be killed by me, too, but I haven't settled things with Hedin yet, and most important of all, Lady Freya has stolen my heart. Until I've given my all for her sake, I can't die."

The fairy began speaking faster, but even as he spun a passage befitting a bard lamenting the world, the melody of his black sword never paused. His pitch-black cloak snapped sharply as another five soldiers fell to the ground coughing up blood.

"So die for me. Our goddess is looking forward to the path that girl is treading. So for the sake of that pleasure, die. I also would like to see what becomes of her. My bad, sorry, my deepest apologies. But I've heard that the heavens aren't such a bad place, so you probably don't need to be scared. I'm sure you'll return down here someday. Probably."

To the Warsa soldiers, his voice was like a lullaby murmured by a terrifying god of death. The dark elf whipping up a vortex of blood was undoubtedly a demon of the desert.

"...Ahhhh, it's like I've returned to my old self. I really hate war. I hate killing people."

Right around when the screams died out.

Hegni was standing alone amid the dark red sand that marked where so much blood had been spilled. Dozens of corpses were facing the opening in the ceiling of the ruins, their hands outstretched toward the sky.

The dark elf had not been touched by even a drop of blood as he looked out across the scene of devastation emotionlessly before disappearing into the night to hunt another unit.

"AHHHHHHHH!"

The Warsa squad was screaming as they ran away. The four prum brothers had blended into the darkness, making noise with their weapons as they watched the soldiers run.

"Just like Hedin said, we let *two* enemy squads through," said the eldest brother as he swung his spear.

His expression was not visible through the helmet he wore as his three brothers picked up where he left off.

"This is so boring."

"That snooty elf's acting like a tactician."

"A miserable elf who thinks he can increase his brainpower by pushing up his glasses just so. He should die in a fire."

"Oy, give it a break—you're making me feel bad for Hedin…At least he's better than Allen."

While his younger brothers tore into the elf, the more worldly Alfrik covered for the elf magic swordsman a tiny bit.

The Gulliver brothers were driving exactly two squads that were fleeing in a panic after the prums attacked. Watching the Warsa soldiers running to the south ahead of them, Alfrik switched gears.

"We're splitting up here. Dvalinn, Berling, you two guide them toward Leodo. Make sure when you're done that the tormented animals mindlessly snap at the bait."

"A monster parade with soldiers, huh?"

"It's harder to hold back than it is to finish them off. They're too damn weak."

The hammer-wielding and ax-wielding prums dashed off like the wind. Grer with his greatsword was left with the eldest brother.

"Alfrik, we don't have to do this annoying stuff anymore now, right?" Grer asked.

"Yeah, there's no need to let anyone else through the defensive lines now. We'll split up and maintain the perimeter."

They were five kirlos away from Leodo.

In the vast desert sea with nothing to block the way, the prums, whose already-keen vision had been enhanced by their multiple level-ups, were able to spot any suspicious figures no matter how far away they might be.

"If anyone is fool enough to test their luck, wipe them all out."

Allen was in peak foul mood.

"Warsa's soldiers are attacking again!"

"But there's this absurdly strong catman and boaz who are crushing them like insects!"

"Who is that noble able to command such powerful warriors?!"

The reason was because he was being forced to play a part in a farce in front of the masses.

Right around when people were getting up in the morning, as if it had been perfectly timed, Warsa soldiers surged into Leodo. The residents screamed as visions of their town being burned again flashed through their minds, but then, as if it had all been arranged in advance, Allen and Ottar gallantly appeared, along with Ali.

"My powerful kavirs—no, my batars! Protect the people from those Warsa fiends, my heroes!"

As the people of Leodo were reliving their nightmares, a mysterious group appeared to rescue them.

The residents and merchants were moved by the powerful warriors and filled with a profound gratitude and respect for the king who led them—was the scenario that Hedin had constructed.

In the first place, basically no one knew that Allen and the other adventurers had been in the town secretly guarding Freya. And no one would recognize that Aram in his shining armor was Ali, the former slave girl. Even the slave merchants were deceived by the sight of Aram riding astride a camel while handing down orders with a regal authority.

The three of them behaved as if they had happened upon the scene by chance, looking for all the world like heroes from an epic who rose to defeat the villains.

"Amazing! They beat Warsa's soldiers so easily!"

"Who are they...?"

"Ahhh, please save this town!"

Seeing the overwhelming display of power that Allen and Ottar put on in the scorched bazaar, the residents of the town cheered them on in a booming roar of support.

Perhaps as a reaction to the despair of having their town burned before, they were responding exactly as Hedin intended, deeply inspired by the sight—incidentally, the first few voices that almost sounded like they were setting the scene were plants from the Fazoul Trading Company—

Making me be part of this stupid farce. Fuck off and die.

Allen's annoyance was rising by the second, and because of that, it was impossible for him to make a dramatic show of crushing the Warsa troops.

"Quit it, Allen! Don't be so brutal!"

Eat shit. I'll murder you.

The voice of the girl behind him who was pretending to be his master only served to send his annoyance through the roof.

"...Nrgh!"

"Igyaaaaaaaaaaaaaaaaaaaaaaaaaaaaaaaa?!"

Looking closer, Ottar also appeared vaguely displeased as he haughtily sent the enemy soldiers flying high into the air. The soldiers who had been driven hard by Dvalinn and Berling were already worn out even before the "battle" had begun.

"This is why I hate goddamn farces."

Allen grumbled as he showily mowed through the Warsa soldiers, who could do little more than whimper in fear.

"So tired..."

Ali made her way back to the oasis mansion while trying to avoid some of the warm greetings from the residents of the town. The residents had readily accepted the explanation that the valorous desert warriors had rented out the manor from Freya.

Ali removed her gaudy armor and started to walk down a corridor.

"It's going to be a problem if you are already complaining after only this much," Hedin remarked as he fell in step behind her.

"It's not physical exhaustion; it's mental exhaustion...Allen very obviously wants to murder me. He might actually try to kill me when I go to sleep tonight..."

"If he does, I will pray that you can rest in peace."

She glanced at the elf resentfully, but if he cared, he didn't show it.

"Thanks to the events of this morning, you are a hero to this town. Most people will lend an ear to the savior who appeared in their time of need. That will make our plan significantly easier to achieve."

"It was all just a charade, though…Deceiving people who don't know any better…"

"No residents were harmed in the staging of the performance, so it is fine. As with ruling a country, pretty words are not always enough."

As far as Ali was concerned, rather than being a hero, it was effectively her fault the town had been burned at all, but Hedin would not allow her to wallow in guilt. According to him, "'Warsa and their barbaric behavior are clearly in the wrong. It is not my fault they behave as beasts.' Please snap back like that." That was how she was supposed to respond.

Ali could only sigh as the elf demanded efficiency while not allowing any room for individual emotion.

"Alfrik and the others guarding the perimeter around Leodo have wiped out all of the Warsa forces in the vicinity. They should finally start to be wary of an undiscovered threat here."

"…How are they able to search for enemy soldiers and attack them so quickly without any means of contact?"

"Nights in the desert are clear. As long as we take up the right positions, it is trivial for us to catch any enemies approaching."

He said that as if it was natural that they could see enemies approaching from over a kirlo away. Ali managed to contain the twitch in her cheek that had become something of a habit lately. It was just dumb to argue when dealing with a battle strength that could eliminate all comers as easily as breathing.

"More importantly, milady-for-the-time-being, have you finished your preparations for the speech? Tomorrow it will be your turn to put on a whole performance."

Hedin opened the door leading into the command center, immediately receiving a report from Bofman's protégé, who hurriedly dashed over to him and stood there as he read through it. Because she was tired, Ali did not hesitate to sit in the chair that he yielded to her.

"I've finished my preparations, and I'll pull it off. If it will save Shalzad…save the western Kaios, I'll do it." She clenched her right fist as tension seeped into her voice.

Hedin stood at her side in the role of aide-de-camp, as she demonstrated her resolve. He glanced over, and then—staring directly at her head, he sighed.

"?!"

And then stretched out his hand and ran it through her hair near the base of her neck.

"*Uwaaah?!* Wh-what are you doing?!"

"You should take better care of your hair. Do you really think a shabby-looking king can inspire thousands to follow them?"

She jumped out of the chair, blushing. Ali had forgotten all pretenses of the role of Aram as her heart threatened to leap out of her chest. Hedin looked at her in exasperation.

"Let's get your hair brushed out. I can do it better than the attendants here, so I'll come to your room tonight. Make sure to leave it unlocked, please."

"Wh-wh-wh-wh-wh…?!"

A man visiting a lady's room at night. Ali's face turned beet red as she imagined for a second that he meant something else, but Hedin, who looked back down at the report in his hands, his face as unchanging as the vast desert, quite clearly did not have any intentions of the sort.

To him—no, to all of them, all women other than Freya are probably no different from any other stone on the side of the road.

Before she could breathe a sigh of relief, what little maiden's pride she had was shattered, and Ali was left with a complicated feeling. Or rather she was pissed off.

"Proper grooming is a fundamental requirement for those who would stand at the top. There are many other areas where you need to put in the effort, but that is not one you can afford to neglect."

As expected of an elf, Hedin's appearance was outstanding. Even compared to Hegni and the rest of Freya's followers, he was a clear cut above the rest. In particular, his long, beautiful blond hair would be the envy of most women. In fact, even though he had just scolded Ali, she still could not shake the jealousy she felt. Aside from that, though, there was something about what he said that caught her attention.

"Hedin, if you don't mind me asking, before you joined *Freya Familia*, were you an attendant to a king somewhere? No…were you yourself…?"

The way he carried himself, coupled with his advisory rebukes, gave off a scent that was familiar to Ali. She had a feeling that he was of noble heritage, just like she was.

"What meaning would there be in you knowing my past? I can't find any value in it," Hedin responded without looking up from the report.

And it felt more like he really could not think of any reason in revealing his past rather than a desire not to have it dredged up.

He really is just an intellectual, hyperefficient elf.

That thought guided her next question.

"Then, why are you putting in this much effort as a retainer? Even if it was an order from your goddess, you're the only one who goes that far, unlike Allen and the others…like using such formal language to address me…"

He called her milady-for-the-time-being, but out of all the members of *Freya Familia* she had met, he was the one who had been the gentlest in his treatment of her by far. His polite words were just one example. It had only been a few days, but Ali could sense what felt like a small amount of actual respect from him.

And that question, at least, Hedin deemed worthy of answering.

"Those who have never suffered with how to carry out their duty have no right to call themselves kings."

"Eh…?"

"You faced the reality of your situation and did not flee from the grief or hatred. Not only that, you even rose to challenge the most beautiful and terrifying goddess. There is no one who understands the true meaning of that better than we do," the fair elf said as he glanced up from the paperwork and looked Ali in the eyes. "You have demonstrated the bare minimum pride required of royalty. Thus, I have decided to treat you as such, regardless of what others think or say.

"I suspect Hegni also has a better opinion of you now, too," he added.

Ali was dumbfounded. She by all rights should have been happy with Hedin's appraisal, since she had been so worried about her own suitability to the crown, but she was also struck by an odd feeling. The fact that Freya's followers had acknowledged her, even a little bit, was confusing to her. Especially given that she was relying on them completely and had done nothing herself.

Has anything about me really changed enough to earn their acknowledgment?

"I'm going to notify the others. There are too many useless incompetents here."

As Hedin got ready to leave, he left Ali with one last admonition.

"Milady-for-the-time-being, I won't ask much of you…But please, don't let us down."

Since you were chosen by milady.

That was all he said before he left. Facing his back as he walked away, Ali mustered her resolve and determination to respond, "I won't."

The Kaios Desert was even hotter than normal that day. The air was heavy in Leodo as the sun beat down from high in the sky.

Though reconstruction was progressing, unease still gripped the town. There was a fear that Israfan would be next after Shalzad, that every country in the region would be ground underfoot by Warsa. And while the townspeople were worrying about the future, Ali was in Leodo's southern district along with Hedin and the rest.

"More came than expected…"

They were in a plaza. Normally used as part of the bazaar, today it was filled with a crowd of people. Ali's palms started to sweat a little as she peeked out from behind a building. It looked like everyone in the town had gathered there.

Ali—or more precisely, Hedin—had assembled them by saying she had an important message to share. And since it came from the hero who had saved the town, the residents were happy to accommodate the request.

The crowd was buzzing as people wondered what would be said. Some must have been hoping that the town's hero would pledge to continue protecting them.

"Hee, hee-hee...now is the time to raise the sacred signal...the holy pledge of the king who will lead the people of the sand..."

"Don't talk, Hegni...*Prince Aram*, this is your battlefield. I wish you good fortune in battle."

As Ali choked back her nerves, Hegni and Hedin spoke up. Their words made her realize the import of the moment.

—*Right, this is my battlefield. I can't defeat the enemy on the field like they can, so this is where I make my stand.*

Ali nodded to them as she stepped out. Her splendorous white armor—a light armor with a cape carried by the breeze when she moved—brought to mind jasmine blossoms as she stepped out onto the podium that had been prepared for her.

"...People of Leodo. You have my thanks for taking some of your precious time to lend me an ear. I called you here today because there is a favor I must ask of you."

Thanks to the magic-stone amplifier at the top of the podium, her voice carried all the way to the outskirts of the city. It truly was like a pledge being broadcast out to all of the people of the desert.

"There are some who believe me a nameless wanderer, so first allow me to clear that misunderstanding. I am the prince of the Shalzad family, Aram Raza Shalzad."

A murmur spread through the crowd. Many of the residents were shocked by the prince's name alone, but there were others who could not hide their disbelief. The merchants. Ali met their gazes as they looked up at the podium, probing whether she was telling the truth as she continued.

"I'm sure some of you may have heard rumors about me. The incompetent prince who disappeared without a trace as his capital fell and his country was ravaged by the Warsa army—However, that is far from the truth. In my country's hour of need, when the royal family's destiny was on the line, I split off from the army for a time in order to gather legendary warriors who would lend us their strength. And upon doing so, when I heard that this town was being threatened by the beasts of Warsa, I rushed here with all haste."

She was just repeating a perfunctory intro that Hedin had prepared. But this was where the real battle would start. This was where she would have to prove she was truly a king.

"—Merchants, and people of great Israfan! I won't command you to cast your lot with me! However, I pray that you can carry my words! Spread them on the wind, beyond the sand dunes to my beloved Shalzad!"

As emotion filled her voice, Ali thought back to the other day.

"A speech?"

In the command center, the same evening she had defeated the goddess at Halvan.

She was looking at Hedin in disbelief, not believing her ears, as he nodded.

"We do not have many pieces we can use. It is difficult to share information and plans, not to mention carrying out espionage and sensitive operations. Even if we want to eliminate the enemy's entire forces, we do not currently know their precise location—That's why we need to call out from our end in order to convince the enemy to move for us."

As the other adventurers listened, Hedin spoke while studying the maps spread out on the table before him.

"Call out? Have them move for us…? What are we trying to send out?"

"A signal for the entire Shalzad army. The message that we have a plan to settle everything in a single decisive battle."

Ali's eyes widened in shock.

"In order to allow Prince Aram's voice to reach them, we'll have to use the merchants. Merchants' rumors move faster than the wind, and this is a merchants' town in a country of merchants. They should be able to disseminate our message throughout Shalzad even with Warsa occupying it."

"…!"

"The speech is the crucial point. It can't be some anonymous rumor that can't be verified. The time and place of the decisive battle have to be proclaimed loud and clear for all to see and hear. We need Prince Aram's resolute action to be known by all around the desert world."

From the perspective of the Warsa army, Leodo should seem like an inscrutable land of ghosts where all of the units they dispatched disappear without a trace. And then all of a sudden, a declaration of war would emanate from that void. One directed not just at Warsa and Shalzad, but at the entirety of the Kaios Desert.

"You will declare the time and place of the decisive all-out battle. And you will have to be inspiring enough to gather the momentum and support needed to force both Shalzad and Warsa to deploy their entire armies."

"W-wait a minute! Even if my voice reached Shalzad's generals and they moved as I asked, there's no way to know whether Warsa will obediently come along! The difference in military strength is evident! They'll be on guard, but they won't just blindly commit everything they have...!"

In response to her argument, Hedin pointed at a certain location on the map.

"The location you'll have Shalzad's army deploy is an area to the northeast of Leodo, the Gazoob Wasteland. The rocky desert area near where the borders of Shalzad, Israfan, and Warsa meet. As long as the soldiers gather there, they'll be poised to advance into Shalzad or even into Warsa itself."

"!!"

"That's not something the main forces of Warsa occupying Shalzad's capital can afford to ignore. If their country was toppled then everything they have done would be for naught."

Ali was awestruck as she realized what Hedin was suggesting. He intended to threaten Warsa itself. If their army did not respond to the call for a decisive final battle, then the Shalzad forces would simply take their army and destroy Warsa.

There was no mistaking that Warsa had devoted a significant

amount of their military force to the conquest of Shalzad. Their defenses back home were surely thin.

"Worst case, we can also call on Israfan to deploy troops as well, since they have also suffered from Warsa's barbaric assault. They have more than enough just cause," Hedin said, coolly mentioning a monumental contingency.

Ali unconsciously stared long and hard at Hedin.

Despite the fact that we don't have any retainers or soldiers, this elf is seriously trying to move the full armies of two different countries with a single plan. And he can probably do it.

Ali felt a shiver of terror.

"As a rule, you should always leave your opponent with two options to choose from."

"Eh?"

"And ensure that either of the two options is convenient for your needs. That way, you don't force the opponent's hand, but allow them the illusion of choice. In the royal court, as in war, that method is crucial for dealing with people, milady-for-the-time-being."

"!"

"You would be well-served by learning more unfair tactics."

Hedin matched Ali's gaze as he advised her, as if bestowing the extension of Freya's divine will. Seeing his coral eyes, Ali had a realization. He was both probing her and expecting her to develop even more as a king.

"However, all of that will hinge on the speech. Whether you can stir the desert world into motion is entirely up to you."

"Solshana fell, and my father, the king, was executed! All at the hands of Warsa! I have never cursed my powerlessness more than I did that day!"

Her gestures changed as she drew in the crowd's gaze and looked out over the throng. They had used all of Bofman's connections to summon countless merchants from other towns. And Leodo was a merchant town to begin with. This place's web of connections encompassed the whole of the Kaios region.

Incidentally, the high-class armor Ali was wearing had also been provided by the Fazoul Trading Company. Ali wondered in the back of her mind when the Fazoul Trading Company, and particularly Bofman, was going to collapse from overwork.

"However, now we have a powerful ally! The legendary warriors who will aid Shalzad, the eight great heroes who will crush the armies of Warsa! Their strength is as you have seen!"

When the crowd looked over at Ottar and the others, their excitement ratcheted up another level. Borrowing the dignity and presence that *Freya Familia* wielded, Ali fanned the crowd's excitement higher. Even the merchants started to stir. After all, they could not remain indifferent to Warsa's barbarity.

The crowd was being drawn in by Ali's plea that they need only spread her words. Many were still enraged by the fact that their town had been put to the torch. All that was left was for Ali to prove that she was indeed Prince Aram. Then everything else would fall into place.

"I'll ask you again! People of Israfan, please carry my message word for word to my beloved homeland! To my people's brave generals!"

The words she said here on this day—all of the merchants would spread that message to Shalzad's army. But the loyal retainers would have to consider whether the prince in Israfan was a pretender or a trap set by Warsa. Reports of purple eyes inherited by members of the royal family would not do. That was not proof enough by itself. Because of that, she needed to include something in the message itself that showed without a doubt that she was the prince.

"I swear by *Ali*, the name of our family's great founder, that the decisive battle shall take place five days hence in the Gazoob Wasteland! Gather all our forces! We shall retake the capital!"

Ali's proof—her real name.

The true identity of the prince was not something a fake could possibly know.

The excitement of the people and the merchants bubbled over at her display of a sovereign's authority and her declaration that righteousness would triumph over villainy.

Ali thrust her fist toward the sky and shouted with a resolve to accomplish everything she had said.

"I declare here and now! As the surviving son of the house of Shalzad, I shall become the new king and strike down the villains of Warsa!"

The crowd swelled with cheers, and the burning sands of the desert trembled with hope. The merchants' determination rode the wind and spread its wings as it took to the Kaios sky.

And seeing that, the members of *Freya Familia* also acknowledged the girl who would be king.

"Ah, the princess…! She still lives!"

The speech in Leodo spread across the desert that very day, carried by the merchants. And loyal retainers of Shalzad who heard it fell to their knees and cried tears of joy.

"The princess—no, the prince! If he swore it on the name of our great founder *Ali*, then there is no mistaking that it is Prince Aram!"

All around Shalzad.

Battle cries roared out among the pockets of resistance that were still struggling against the invaders.

There was, of course, no one named Ali among the founders of Shalzad. That secret signal proved Ali's identity and invigorated those few retainers who knew Aram's secret.

"Inform the other forces! The prince in Israfan is the true prince! Gather our forces in Gazoob for the decisive battle!"

In the encampments where morale was sinking because of how poorly the resistance was faring, the old general Jafar, Ali's right-hand man and her most trusted retainer, bellowed his orders.

The Shalzad army, which had been worn down and was losing hope, roused themselves in the blink of an eye as they began marching east as one.

*   *   *

"Reporting! The remaining pockets of resistance on all fronts have begun advancing east! The Shalzad forces are splitting into small groups as they advance…we can't pin them all down!"

The Warsa encampment in Solshana.

Gorza slammed his fists down on the map spread across the table when he heard the soldier's report.

"Damn it! They got us!"

The now famous speech in Leodo had also reached their ears. He would never have dreamed of using the merchants to re-form the scattered army. It went without saying, of course, that Shalzad's army had a much better grasp of the terrain there, so it would be impossible for Warsa to stop them from using various back doors in order to regroup and form backup. And if Shalzad embarked on a full-scale counteroffensive, then Israfan would surely support them. *Resheph Familia*'s barbarism was coming home to roost.

Five days hence. The Gazoob Wasteland.

It was obviously an invitation. Gorza could clearly hear a certain elf's implicit threat: If you don't feel inclined to settle things here then we'll simply attack Warsa itself.

"Prince Aram…! To think he was planning this when he vanished! What a bold move! I'd heard he was skilled, but to think he had such potential!"

Or perhaps he had an excellent wise adviser at his side. However, even so, there are none more sensitive to the birth of a new king than the country's populace, and Gorza could feel the foreign prince's resolution in his bones as the furor gripping the people of Shalzad reached his army camped out in Solshana.

"HOT DAMN! This reeks to high heaven! This here's one helluva of a scam!"

In a different camp from Gorza and the main forces, the god Resheph was roaring with laughter.

"This so-called choice is nasty! 'Meet us where we want, or we'll raze your country.' Whoever thought this one up is pretty great!"

Dignity and grace aside, as expected of a deity, Resheph correctly recognized what lay behind Hedin's plan. And despite understanding it, he could still do nothing but respond to it. Even knowing that the enemy was hiding something, he had no way of knowing what their secret plan was. Until the lid was opened, even a god could not know for certain what lay in store.

"We could have the army disband into bandit bands and scatter around the desert realm…Well, that'd be fine, too, but I can't deny it would feel like a bit of a step down. And honestly just a bit boring."

Resheph had no interest in winning the war. As Ali and Gorza feared, he was making plays according to another plan that had nothing to do with what either country had in mind. It was a pastime that could be called a hobby for a certain subset of deities; his was the plan of an evil god trying to sow chaos in the mortal realm.

"Well, fine. I'll call your bluff. ☆ That sounds more fun anyway, and I've got an ace up my sleeve, too—right, Seal?"

"Yes, Lord Resheph. Unfortunately, though, it won't get its chance to shine," responded the elf at Resheph's side, his familia's captain, Seal.

He had a dark smile unbefitting a member of the fairy race. He was tall, lean, and sported long black hair. He was topless other than a cloak draped over both shoulders, with ominous-looking tattoos covering his skin. He looked like a cultist born of darkness.

"I'll slaughter the Shalzad and Aram by myself and then I'll skin him to make a flag of his hide for you."

"That's what I love about you, always spewing such sleazebag shit with such a handsome looking face! Ha-ha-ha!" Resheph cackled at his closest aide and captain.

Resheph was inhuman and his followers were all devilish in their own right.

Their plan was callous and wretched to the extreme, one that would bring chaos to the mortal realm, but—

Put bluntly, that plan would not come to light due to this battle.

"I don't know what that 'eight great heroes' shit is about, but there's no way any power in this neck of the woods could match us!"

For the simple reason that an unparalleled strength that Resheph could not foresee was currently in the Kaios Desert.

"Hedin, can you gather everyone for me?" Ali asked.

The night before the battle.

The location was, as always, Leodo. With the adventurers' legs, they could arrive at the scene of the battle within hours, and because Aram had appeared there in order to deliver his speech, Warsa might try to strike back, so Ali wanted to wait and protect it until the last moment.

"I've gathered those who can be gathered, but to what end? You aren't planning on giving us rousing encouragement before the battle tomorrow, are you?"

Hegni, Ottar, and Alfrik had gathered in the hall.

The younger Gulliver brothers were on watch at the perimeter outside Leodo, and Allen was apparently not inclined to respond to her request.

Still, Ali shook her head at Hedin's question after he had gathered them. She realized that *Freya Familia*, the strongest of all, did not have any need for encouragement or really any of her sentiments. It was just that she suspected this night would be her last chance to really have a word with them.

"First of all, I'd like to say my thanks for lending me your strength. I'm sure Hedin would tell me that as king I should not so readily lower my head, but…in truth, this is the only thing I can offer you at the moment. So—thank you." She met each of their eyes in turn as she spoke her mind without pretense or artifice.

The goddess's followers were unsurprisingly not moved in the least. However—

"Nothing's over yet, so don't be getting ahead of yourself. But…I'll be sure to tell my brothers." Alfrik's tone was calm, but at the end, his voice sounded a bit more affable.

"...Y-you were significantly less foolish a ruler than I expected, so...I mean because...ugggggggh——Now is the time for me to break free from the robes of darkness and scorch thy foes with an all-consuming hellfire! Hee-hee-hee-hee!" Hegni, who apparently had trouble speaking, seemed to be trying to say something, but it ended up collapsing into a moan and then things only become more unintelligible from there.

"Shine. That is the potential the goddess saw in you as well as your duty." Ottar said only that, his expression entirely unchanged.

"There is nothing more I need to tell you. However, if I were to add one final intrusion, then...I suspect that the troublesome cat is on the third-floor balcony."

Thanking Hedin, Ali headed toward the troublesome, feral cat.

"Allen."

The catman with black and gray—almost silver—fur was on the balcony as Hedin had said, looking out at the desert night. He did not show any sign of acknowledging Ali's greeting, so she quietly approached him.

"Stay away from me. Figure it out already that I've got no damn intention of pretending to be friends with you."

"Okay. Then I'll say what I wanted to say from here." She stopped five steps away from him on the spacious balcony. "I said my thanks to the others already, but...I want to apologize to you. I insulted you during the journey."

On the first day after they had left Leodo, Ali had thoughtlessly lashed out in a childish fit of anger. She had almost been killed on the spot for it, but she had been wanting to apologize to Allen ever since.

"I'm sorry Allen. I was narrow-minded. I slandered the devotion you all have toward your goddess."

"Quit acting like some dignified leader, stupid brat. It's making me sick."

Curt and to the point. He really only ever had abuse to hurl. However, Ali already knew that was the kind of person he was, so she did not lose her temper. Instead, she just smiled softly.

"...Something funny?" Sensing her smile, Allen's head turned to look at her.

"No..." Ali said as she looked up, still smiling. "Hey, Allen, are you glad to be able to devote your everything to a single master...to your beloved goddess?"

"What?"

"The thought just crossed my mind. During these few days, Hedin and the rest of you, your devotion was directed at the goddess behind me instead of at me. And more than I was jealous of her...for some reason I was jealous of you."

The starry sky spread out before her. And the solitary crescent moon hanging high above. Ali found that the words tumbled from her lips without any thought as she took in that beautiful night sky.

"Goddess Freya is...mysterious. There's no telling what she's thinking. But her words, her eyes, something about her somehow draws my heart in anyway."

"..."

"She truly is more beautiful than anything. But the thing about her that is most alluring isn't her looks...It's her capricious, brilliantly noble personality."

Ali suspected she knew now why Allen had gotten so incensed with her before. Those who had devoted themselves to Freya were those who had had their hearts cleansed by her, who had been saved by her. But Ali could not kneel before the goddess because she needed to sacrifice her own desires, to become king for the sake of her country. The moon shone so high in the sky, but it still could not reach the heavens. It could not wait at the foot of the deities who were able to look down on everything, even the moon.

"I have a country. I have my duty as king. But if I could abandon myself entirely like you have, devote myself wholeheartedly to something..."

How long had she had that thought? Since the Halvan game? Since that night in the oasis? Or was it ever since they had first met?

Ali did not really know what she wanted to say, so she stopped there, realizing that those pure feelings were not something she should be putting into words.

"...Sorry, I ran my mouth about something I shouldn't have. Just pretend that didn't happen." Ali grinned to cover it and started to leave.

"Just cast it aside if you want. It's only a country."

But Allen's words stopped her in her tracks.

"What?"

"If you're jealous of our allegiance, then that's because we're just being faithful to our desires. Because we've no need for anything other than her and desire nothing else."

Allen turned to face her, meeting her head-on. Ali was shocked as he hit her with a voice that for once had a tone of something other than censure.

"Don't try to blame your own weak will on something else. That country is just a parasite leeching off you."

"!"

His sharp gaze piercing her was unlike any other he had turned toward her. Ali was visibly shaken by his argument as Allen rocked her with another explosion.

"For her love, I cast aside my own family...my little sister."

"—"

"To society, I'm the lowest of the low...but what of it? You think I'm gonna give up because of what other people think? If that's enough to stop you, then it isn't fit to be called love. At least not as far as she's concerned."

So follow through to the end. That's what it means to really want something.

Ali was unable to respond, floored by the impact of Allen's conclusion. And Allen did not say anything else. He passed right beside her and left the balcony.

Left alone, Ali awkwardly peered back up at the sky.

"..."

The moon could not reach the heavens. But could it be forgiven for forgetting to look down on the earth, for forgetting to shine—so that it could look up to the heavens itself?

The doubt that crossed Ali's mind left her with a heavy heart and unshakable questions.

As he walked down a long corridor filled with columns, a voice called out to Allen, who was carrying his spear on his shoulder after he left Ali with his parting words.

"Liar."

Freya was leaning against a pillar with a smile on her face. That goddess's smile that even Allen acknowledged he could not best.

"You still care about Ahnya."

"…"

Allen stopped.

"Surely you jest," he said and then started walking again, actually leaving this time.

The goddess's eyes twinkled as she watched him walk away. Freya had been watching over the girl on the balcony all along.

The room was dark, dimly lit by the moonlight shining in from the window. The white curtain rustled faintly.

Ali was suffering alone in her room. It was hardly the time for it, since the battle that would determine the fate of her country was going to happen the next day, but she was troubled.

Cast aside my country…? Me…?

Cast aside Aram and become one of the goddess's followers. It was a thought that had never crossed Ali's mind. To the girl who had never known anything other than life as royalty, it was an option that she should decisively reject, and yet it was an alluring possibility.

No, that's not right.

Ali herself was—

"Ali."

"!?"

Ali's shoulders twitched as she heard the door open and a voice call out to her.

"A-at least knock!" she shouted at Freya, who entered without any hesitation.

"I did, but you didn't answer," the goddess responded as she approached Ali. "It seemed like you were a little preoccupied. Is something on your mind?"

Freya sat down next to Ali on the bed like it was the most natural thing in the world.

"Nothing of any importance..." Ali responded as coolly as she could manage, not wanting the goddess to realize what she had been thinking about.

Freya giggled a little as she studied Ali from the side.

"Allen's actually a bit of a softy in his own way."

"...? What are you talking about?"

"His tone's a bit harsh, but he's always acting with me in mind. Because he knew that I wanted you, he tested your feelings."

"!?"

She was shocked to realize that Freya had overheard her conversation with Allen, and at the same time, she thought, *She sees through me. She can tell exactly what I feel deep in my heart.*

Ali looked away from the goddess to hide the fact that her cheeks were burning.

"I mean, you are someone I'm attracted to, so it's understandable that you would be caught up on me."

What sort of logic is that?! You're too self-centered in every possible way!

But that explanation did not draw the sharp-tongued rebuke from Ali that it was designed to evoke. Instead, the girl was just silent, her hands full dealing with the feelings in her heart that she had not yet gotten a handle on. It took Ali a few seconds to respond.

"...Even if what you said were true...it's not a yearning sort of love."

"Ohh? Then what is it?"

Ali averted her eyes as she carefully chose the words to describe the swirl of emotions she felt deep inside.

"When I see you...I'm sure I see some of my mother, too."

In her memories, Ali's mother had long black hair. She was a fragile, beautiful woman. The image that was burned into her eyes was of her mother's last smile as she lay on her bed and caressed Ali's cheek. Ali was bawling her eyes out while her mother also cried as she apologized to her child.

Her reserved mother and the free-spirited and high-handed Freya did not really have anything in common. But in Ali's mind, their faces seemed to overlap. No, perhaps it was better to say that Ali's heart was making them overlap. Perhaps she was seeking the warmth of a phantom of her mother who died when she was young.

It was embarrassing enough for Ali to admit that she missed her mother at her age, but Freya did not tease her about it. The goddess merely shrugged.

"Well, I am a goddess, so it's not really wrong to think of me as a mother figure. To me, all of you residing down here in the mortal realm are children, after all."

"Th-that's not what I meant!"

Freya giggled as if there was something funny about Ali's denial. Her eyes narrowed, finding it charming that that was where Ali decided to interject.

"But I like that side of you. That sincerity that will honestly share what you are feeling in your heart, and the serious way you face the fact that you still don't know yourself and continue to worry about what to do."

Ali's heart throbbed as she met the goddess's gaze and listened to what she was saying. Freya softly caressed Ali's cheek, brushing her hair back.

"You've done well, Ali. You've worked hard to get here today. I'll swear it on my name. You have handled yourself more regally than anyone else in this desert realm to get here."

"Gh...!"

"There are no more impurities in your soul. That amethyst radiance has bloomed."

She treated each strand of hair with a tender affection, like she would a child—or a lover. The bed creaked. Ali was flustered as she noticed the warmth of the goddess's hand next to hers on the bed. She could not deny that she was deeply attracted to Freya.

As a goddess? As a mother figure? Or as—

Ali shook her head at the thoughts racing through her mind. The heat in her cheeks refused to fade. She was struck by a boyish annoyance that had no focus.

I see…I wanted someone to praise me…

Not as Aram, but as Ali.

She could not tell whether those maddening feelings were an extension of her childlike desires or whether they were the cravings of a love-starved person, but either way, she longed for Freya's love. She could not deny that.

Ali smiled. It had been bothering her, but once she admitted it, her heart was lighter. She was satisfied with that. She should have been satisfied with just that, but—

"—So I'll give you a little treat, Ali."

Creak. The bed groaned again, even louder than last time.

"?!"

Ali was pushed down onto the bed. It was a gentle push, but it had no difficulty bringing her down. The goddess looking down at her brushed her hair behind her ear and then slowly lay atop her.

"Wh-wh-what are you doing?!"

"I told you, didn't I? I'm giving you a treat."

The furniture in the room had been matched to Freya's tastes, since it had originally been intended for her use. And the bed the two of them were lying on was no exception. It was extremely big and had an extravagant canopy. It was more than large enough to comfortably fit both of them.

The goddess's face moved closer to Ali, her hand caressing the girl's cheek. A shock of pleasure raced down her spine.

"...No, it might just be that I can't restrain myself anymore," Freya said with a smile that was simultaneously innocent and alluring.

A crimson color like nothing she had felt before filled Ali's head.

"W-wait! Why is this happening?!"

"Because I'm Freya, the Goddess of Love and Beauty."

"But we're both women!"

"I don't mind either way."

"Wh...? W-wait a minute...D-don't."

"Hee-hee, so cute."

Before Ali realized it, her nightclothes had been removed. Their hands were tightly clasped like lovers. An unbelievably mind-bending scent tickled her nose. Her purple eyes dimmed as tears welled up, meeting the dewy silver eyes above her.

"Shall we share a sweet dream tonight?"

That night, the girl dreamed of being consumed by a giant dragon.

"*Aaaaaaaaaaaaaaaaaaaaaaaaaaaaaaaaaaaaaaaaaaaaaaaaaaaaaaaaaaa aaaaaaaaaah!*"

"Where...where...?"

Late that night in the hallway of the estate. A suspicious shadow emitted an uncanny voice.

"Where is Lady Freya...?"

It was Bofman.

He was breathing raggedly, and his eyes were entirely bloodshot.

Bofman seemed almost on the verge of death.

In addition to the goddess's unreasonable requests, he had also been tasked with Hedin's frequently absurd demands.

Between gathering boatloads of information on Warsa so that Ali could take back her beloved Shalzad, straining his connections to their limits in order to reel in as many merchants as possible, and many other things, he had been forced to work long and hard, neglecting sleep and not allowed any rest. Despite being a mere merchant, he had made every effort in every endeavor and endured the harsh treatment of *Freya Familia*, whose stance was effectively "of course you have to work day and night, swine." There was no question that he rendered distinguished service from the shadows.

And now, the night before the final battle, finally freed from that nightmarish labor, he was wandering through the manor like a zombie.

"This debt won't be repaid until I've experienced the goddess's sweet nectar…!"

—It was inevitable he would want something in exchange. The connection with her familia that Freya had promised to grant his company would not be enough! This debt could not be cleared until he was soothed by the peerless and incomparable goddess's body!

Driven to the edge, Bofman lost all restraint, surrendering himself to his desires.

"Gee-hee…hee-ho-ho-ho…! I'll have her let me join in while their lovely little tryst blossoms…!!"

Perhaps his senses had been enhanced after having been pushed to the brink of death, but Bofman could sense clearly that the goddess and the girl were already quite entangled, and he fully intended to join in and gee-hee-hee-ho-ho-ho.

Finally reaching the highest floor of the estate, he was about to sneak through the door to his goal—

""""You filthy pig!"""""

"?!"

Shadows appeared out of the darkness and dragged him away.

"Where do you think you're going, swine?"

"Are you looking down on us, pig?"

"You're awfully brave, swine."

"And unbelievably stupid, pig."

"Eeeeeeeeeeeeeeeeeep?!"

His pupils widened as the devilish Gulliver brothers pummeled him into the floor. And it was not just them.

"Don't scream."

"I'll murder you."

"Rot in hell."

"Bugyaaaaaaaaaaa?!"

The all-stars of *Freya Familia* were all there. Hedin with his cool gaze was serious as always, but even Hegni's tone dripped with murder. And Allen had already landed a kick right in Bofman's gut.

"—A beast like you has no right to enter the goddess's chambers."

And the last to appear was the enormous, boulder-like warrior.

"Come. We'll house-train you."

The strongest warrior, Ottar, delivered Bofman's sentence with a stern voice.

"N-noooooooooooooooooo! Save meeeeeeeeeeeeeeeeeee!"

His fattened body was dragged down the hall into the darkness. That night, he dreamed of being killed by the Einherjar countless times, only to be forcibly revived for more suffering each time.

"Aaaaaaaaaaaaaaaaaaaaaaaaaaaaaaaaaaaaaaaaaaaaaaaaaaaaaaaaaa aaaaaaaaagh!"

There was a faint scent of jasmine.

She was still dreaming after the goddess had granted her a special gift.

Her eyes opened. Crossing the line between dream and reality, she noticed the room was dim. A desert with a brightening blue sky unfolded outside the window. A coolness shrouded her body, telling her it was early morning.

"Are you awake?"

A soft voice rang in her ears, and turning to the side, she saw a beautiful goddess. Ali's sleepy eyes jolted open, and she looked extremely annoyed.

"I'm awake…I just woke up. And next to you, of all people."

"I see. I'm still sleepy." Freya yawned cutely, pressing her hand to her mouth to cover it.

Thinking back to what had happened last night, Ali felt like her face might catch on fire. Her body was still sluggish. The only thing she could do was glare weakly at the goddess.

"You just wouldn't let me sleep at all last night, Ali."

"You were the one ravaging me!"

Ali shouted "Don't try to put the blame on me!" as she averted her eyes and turned bright red.

The goddess was her usual free-spirited self today, too. Her voluptuous breasts were pressed into the bed as she lay on her stomach, her head lying on the pillow as she behaved like a listless cat. The sheets were in disarray, leaving her naked upper body entirely on display. Ali could feel her cheeks burning as Freya's eyes narrowed like a cat's, and her shoulders shuddered slightly as she suppressed her giggle.

"We're both women, so wh-why did…!"

"You're really so fastidious. I told you before that a wise man always has a vice or two to amuse themselves, didn't I? Have you really never played around before?"

"Of course not! I could never risk my secret coming out!"

Ali raised her body up, naked as the day she was born. She suspected she was still blushing as she rubbed her dark skin and pouted at the goddess.

"I at least learned the basics…so I would be prepared for my companion once I'm king.

"So don't make fun of me," Ali said, doing her best to keep a hold on what dignity she had left as Freya lifted herself up.

And then, sliding her legs behind her, she faced Ali and gave her a hug. Her full bosom pressed against the girl's flatter chest. Ali unconsciously groaned in frustration as she couldn't help but be conscious of the goddess's well-endowed body.

"Then make sure you remember this night so you can make the woman you marry happy."

"…Whatever unfortunate girl takes my hand will undoubtedly know Aram's true identity beforehand. If she didn't, she would never be chosen as the official wife of a king hiding his gender," Ali responded with her face nestled against the top of the goddess's soft bosom before reluctantly peeling herself away. "Ensuring the royal family's lineage doesn't end is my duty. I have to find a fitting man to grant me a child to ensure the next true prince can…"

Her words trailed off as a sharp pain rippled in her chest.

She had been raised to do that and had long ago resigned herself to it. But it was terribly painful all of a sudden. Now, after she had experienced this goddess's love.

"If it were me, I would fulfill your every need, whether as a man or a woman…" Freya put her hands on the girl's cheeks and pressed her lips on her forehead. "…Whatever the future may bring is up to your decisions today. The battle will be settled by Ottar and them, but you are the one who will decide your own destiny."

The goddess caressed Ali's cheeks tenderly. Her gaze and her hands were simultaneously like a lover's and a mother's.

I don't want this to end. I don't want to have to leave. Not after I've felt this warmth.

Suppressing those feelings in her heart, Ali stood up. She poured some water from the pitcher at the corner of the room and dumped it over her head. Her body shivered from the cold as her senses sharpened, allowing her foolish thoughts to shrink back to the depths of her heart. Taking the washcloth soaking in the water, she carefully cleaned every nook and cranny of her body, washing away the traces of the night before, before putting her clothes on.

The goddess watched over her from the bed.

"Do your best, Ali."

When the girl had finished all her preparations, the goddess smiled kindly.

"And go forth, Aram."

A fearless smile appeared on the face of the king who radiated determination.

Ali nodded once in response. She did not look back at the goddess. Her eyes were focused on what lay before her as she left the room, a king.

5

The Kaios Desert was arid and sunny that day.

As searing rays of sunlight poured down, thousands of soldiers marched through swirling heat hazes.

The Gazoob Wasteland was a rocky desert region where the borders of Shalzad, Warsa, and Israfan all met. Though it was rocky, that did not mean it was not also a desert. Most importantly, there was a place in the Gazoob Wasteland with even terrain and unobstructed views that made it a perfect battlefield. And the armies of Shalzad and Warsa were both marching toward that location.

"Prince Aram's loyal retainer, Jafar, has arrived!"

"Jafar, sir! So you came, too!"

The soldiers led by the old general joined the forces from Shalzad that had answered the call.

Finally gathering up for the first time after the capital had fallen, the Shalzad army's morale was high. The signal that Prince Aram had risked himself to send out had revived their spirits, and about twenty thousand troops were currently making their way to the battlefield.

"So! Where is Prince Aram?! Where is the next sun to illuminate the hearts of all Shalzad?!"

"...About that, well...he has yet to be seen..."

"What?!"

However, the all-important Ali herself was nowhere to be found in the Gazoob region. And not just her. The Warsa army was yet to be seen, either, despite the reports indicating they had already departed from the capital. At the very least they were not anywhere visible from the Shalzad army's current position.

Jafar and the triumphant Shalzad forces froze at the soldier's report as the dry desert wind blew through their camp.

"Advance! The Shalzad army must have gathered and deployed along the Gazoob Wasteland! At most there will be twenty thousand of them! Against our force of eighty thousand, that's little more than a breeze!"

Around that time, the Warsa army was approaching the Sindh Expanse. It was a pure sand desert that enclosed the Gazoob Wasteland. Their supreme commander, Gorza, had split the host of eighty thousand into five different divisions before they clashed with the enemy.

"Surround their army both to insure they don't advance into Warsa, and to make sure they can't flee into Israfan! Warriors of Warsa, this is where we crush the last of Shalzad's resistance!"

"WOOOOOOOOOOOOOOOOOOOOOOOOOOOOOOO!"

The main division raised a thundering battle cry and the second, third, fourth, and reserve divisions spread across the dunes roared in response. The soldiers of Shalzad had only just reformed their army, so their chain of command would not be consolidated yet. That was where Warsa would strike.

Gorza's plan was logical and reasonable, clear evidence of his competence as a commander. However—precisely because of that, *he* could predict it.

"Sir! Enemy at twelve o'clock!"

"What?! How many!"

On both the right and left flanks, there was a commotion spreading among the units at the edges of the formation as soldiers raised the alarm. The officers in charge of those units looked around, wondering if their strategy had been figured out when each of them saw it.

"Th-the thing is…you can't even call it a force, sir…"

As their subordinates reported, it was not an army nor a smaller unit launching a surprise attack. It was just one person. Or rather four people.

One report of a white elf, one of a dark elf, one of a catman, and one of a set of four prums appearing in front of the second, third, fourth, and reserve divisions.

—Who could have predicted this? The gathering of Shalzad's army was, in fact, just bait. The true final battle would not be in the wasteland but in the Sindh Expanse.

Eight followers would take on an army of eighty thousand.

As the Warsa troops looked on, dumbfounded, Hedin, who had devised all of this, pushed his glasses up,

"The preparations are all complete. Now to exterminate them. Leave none alive," he declared

The adventurers readied themselves for battle, and immediately after that, the rout began.

"Gaaaaaaaaaaaaaaaaaaaaaaaaaaaaaaaaaaaaaaaaaaaaaaaaaaaa rgh?!"

The war began with a scream.

An enormous cloud of sand wafted—no, exploded into the air. Seeing the cascade of sand, the commander in charge of the left flank raised his voice.

"Wh-what's happening?!"

"The second division is being attacked!"

"A sneak attack by Shalzad?! How many are there?!"

At those words, the soldier's voice trembled as he responded,

"I-it's *one person!*"

"…What?"

Not one division or even one squad. One person. The commander could not believe his ears as a terrified report rang out.

"We're being bombarded by a single elf!"

"Struggle for eternity, indestructible soldiers of lightning."

Just a single stanza was chanted. The white elf was unleashing a torrent of magic with a super-short cast specialized for quick attacks.

"Caurus Hildr."

A rain of white lightning fell on the battlefield. Despite being a super-short cast spell, an enormous number of lightning orbs devastated the Warsa forces. Each ball was the size of a human's head. It was a thunderstorm of certain death.

The deluge of lightning was unavoidable, and the soldiers could do nothing but be blown away by it, their armor shattering as the electricity scorched their bodies.

"Don't scream and don't move. It messes with my aiming and lowers the efficiency. How irritating."

Hedin continued his fusillade of magic as he muttered to himself. He was rapidly casting his magic calmly, coolly, and mercilessly.

"This is why I despise dealing with trifling people. You fools are always messing with my careful calculations."

Deployed across the clear desert plain, the ten-thousand-strong second division was in utter disarray. All because of a single elf foolishly barring the way, unleashing a storm of magic capable of erasing hundreds of troops at once. The lightning balls seemed like a rain of arrows as it split the division straight down the middle like a hot knife through butter. The crazed symphony of thunder even blasted away the sand, causing the Warsa force's formation to collapse almost immediately.

To a falcon overlooking the scene from the air, it was clearly visible. The magic attack left a giant gash in the ground where Warsa's second division was deployed, like a dragon leaving a swath of destruction in its wake.

"Though most are cowards who cry out and try to flee, there are also warriors who wield a reckless valor and charge. Fear and excitement. Drown in the winds of battle, all of you slaves to the paradox of battle."

Hedin mercilessly bathed in magic those mercenaries who turned and fled, and just as readily fired off a thunderclap to incinerate those tragically gallant warriors who charged forward to allow their comrades to escape.

Lowering his right arm, which held his rhomphaia, he held out his left arm and cast his magic. The rhomphaia boasted a long blade and a hilt designed to resemble a holy tree. Its name was Dizaria. Hedin's first-tier weapon was both an excellent polearm while also serving as a staff to boost magic power.

"You will all be routed just the same, so at least maintain some discipline, you failures."

Cries and screams went up all around. Hedin did not allow them any opening to approach him. His single-handed unending barrage crushed every charge the enemy mustered and incinerated any in the rear who attempted to retaliate with their own magic.

From the moment they had been caught off guard while spread out across an expanse of sand dunes where they could be seen clearly, they had had all their options taken away from them. It was impossible to have a unit stealthily sneak up on him from behind or pull off any other surprise attack. Those elven eyes, that race famed as fairy marksmen, caught every squad that attempted any covert movements and slammed them with another ball of thunder.

"What is ha—...What kind of monster is heeeeeeeeeeeeeeeeeeeeee?!"

The general in charge of the division cried out in unbridled panic.

Several messengers bearing more confusion reported in. Bombarded by that torrent of reports, he was the only person on that side of the battlefield who knew exactly what was happening. Every single person with a rank of squad leader or higher was being erased from the battle. The enemy possessed a terrifying, demonic eye—and by fully utilizing that keen insight that could interpret the miniscule ebbs and flows of the battlefield, their foe was annihilating the entire chain of command with sickening precision.

There was nothing more pitiful than an animal that had lost its head. The orders being sent to each unit became meaningless and the surviving soldiers had become little more than helpless targets. The aftershocks of their rising fear only exacerbated the meaningless deaths.

Precise marksmanship. Incomparable accuracy. And a command crueler than anyone's. The white elf was a ruthless king who looked down on a force of thousands as he slaughtered them with lightning strikes.

"Ah—"

A second later, the moment the wall of soldiers being shredded by his magic started to thin out, a magic blast mercilessly filled the general's field of view with impenetrable white. Consumed by the flash of light, he readily departed the battlefield that was swirling with screams and despair.

Having been obliterated by a lightning lance, that general was actually exceedingly lucky. Thanks to that, he was able to pass on without experiencing the suffering of losing a limb or the intense pain of having his skin scorched by a bolt of lightning.

"Shooting off magic everywhere as if I didn't know any better... This may be the pinnacle of boorishness, but I suppose it can't be helped." Hedin was just calmly talking to himself as the soldiers' cries filled the air. "Who in their right mind would face a force of ten thousand head-on, after all? Extermination via magic is the most efficient method. This way at least minimizes the annoyance."

He spoke as if he was explaining the most obvious of facts as he nocked yet another magic arrow to loose, continuing to lay waste to the barbarians.

He did not allow anyone to flee the field. By the time a unit took a step that might have led them to safety, he had already shot off another bolt of lightning that landed right where they were moving toward. Hedin was very precisely and carefully making use of his mind even then, enveloping the battlefield in a lightning barrier to trap the Warsa army.

The moment they realized that no one would be allowed to retreat from the sand dunes that had come alive with lightning, the soldiers finally started to call out, pleading for their lives with no concern for how unsightly or pathetic it appeared. And because of those offensive cries, for the very first time, Hedin's face, which had stayed calm throughout the entire massacre, finally changed.

"Why in the world...Why in the world did you seriously think your cries would reach anyone who would listen? You seem to have gravely misunderstood your situation. Who would allow even one of you to live?"

As bolts of lightning crackled in the air, a single core member of *Resheph Familia*—a Level-2 man—saw the elf's lips moving and turned pale.

"A faction of people close to you cast aside their humanity and defiled the Lady's property. You dishonored the goddess's love in that oasis town. You covetously desecrated a sacred domain that must never be touched!"

After Leodo had been razed, Hedin had buried the corpses of the former slaves, Freya's property, with full honors. He understood. He knew full well that their dignity had been trampled upon. He knew that every last one of those slaves who were being sold for their looks and abilities had passed from the mortal realm in the depths of despair.

This was the obvious result. Axiomatic. If Warsa were inclined to laugh and brush off such things as merely the vagaries of war, then it was only natural that they would go on a spree of pillaging and rape. But given their position, there was no reason for a high-minded elf like Hedin to turn a blind eye to their behavior. Once he had sworn to become an executioner, there was nothing left for those soldiers beyond every last one of them being wiped off the face of the planet.

"You dare claim you are without sin? That you weren't responsible? Do you take me for a fool? You reek of the same stench. You have already embraced that same sadism and carry that same beastly stench!"

A blazing rage was ignited by his goddess's defiled love. And faced with that conflagration of wrath and spirit, the Warsa forces near Hedin even forgot their thoughts of escaping as the blood drained from their faces, and they despaired, quivering in abject terror.

Hedin's coral eyes narrowed sharply, and the next moment the corners of his eyes flared up as he clenched his glasses, tearing them from his face and shattering them in his clenched fist.

"There is no reason that I of all people would overlook such a flawed world!!"

The fairy's fury. The intellectual mask that Hedin wore fell away as he revealed his true self, unleashing the storm of murderous rage that he had not allowed to erupt before.

"And on top of all that, you hunted down and pushed that girl to such lengths—if I don't impose the true meaning of havoc upon you myself, then how will I face my mistress or that young king!"

His loyalty to his goddess and the indignation he felt for that girl whose country had been ravaged. All of those emotions exploded as the fairy transformed into an apostle of destruction.

Hedin roared his duty.

"Your sentence is death! Barbarians of the desert!"

"…That's the kind of thing Hedin would say," Hegni murmured to himself.

"*No—noooooooooooooooooooooooooooo!*"

Countless corpses were scattered all around him. The people screaming in fear were, of course, the soldiers of Warsa. He was the right wing of the assembled army. Facing off against the third division, which consisted of another ten thousand men, Hegni, a magic swordsman just like his old foe Hedin, had chosen not a long-range magic battle but a hand-to-hand, head-on brawl.

"But unlike him, my magic doesn't have a very good range and isn't nearly as convenient…"

As the soldiers cowered before him, he stood there, immersed in his own world. The dark elf swordsman lowered his eyes, hiding his mouth behind a high collar as he muttered quietly.

"…This is just more my style…"

And then, he raised his sinister black sword in one hand and caressed the surface of it with his other hand. It was a first-tier weapon, Victim Abyss. Hegni's most trusted weapon, his comrade in battle, it was a jet-black blade with a jagged lightning-bolt shape to it and was capable of unleashing an incomparably sharp slash. It was a superior-grade cursed blade made for him by a certain hexer that boasted an ability to extend its slash in exchange for consuming more of his stamina.

The black blade that was seemingly forged from condensed darkness caused the brown desert to absorb pools of crimson blood, staining it red.

"…Hee-hee, hee-hee-hee-hee, your chance encounter with my pitch-black blade has sealed your fates…The fiery sands flutter and crimson flies…My blade calls for sacrifices. Meaning…y-y-you will die."

He had preemptively slashed his way into the center of the enemy's formation. He was secretly scared of all the eyes staring at him as he tried to explain himself. What he had intended to say was something along the lines of "I'm the one assigned to deal with your group, so I'm going to exterminate you. I've already broken through and completed the initial skirmish, so please prepare yourselves," but what actually came out of his mouth was quite different.

And faced with that, the soldiers of Warsa responded pitifully.

"Wh-who is this guy?!"

"I wondered who the hell was slashing at us, but this guy is crazy!"

"Why's he grinning like that while babbling like a lunatic?!"

"He's an elf, but that grin is like a damn ogre's!"

"He looks like he might start licking his sword any second now!"

"Seriously, what the hell is he even saying?!"

His incomprehensible rambling did a fantastic job of aggravating his already poor communication ability, and the ghastly grin was a consequence of his face tensing up from the nervousness, but the storm of comments from the Warsa soldiers stung Hegni, who by any measure was the absolute strongest there.

Argh, I can't take it. I want to die.

So the pitiful dark elf hid face behind his deep collar and slashed away as his cheeks burned in shame.

"Guaaaaaaaaaaaaaaaaaaaaaaaaaaaaaagh?!"

He flew into an intense sword dance. His black sword became a flash of light, slicing through several soldiers at once like it was nothing. Their shield walls, ready spears, swinging swords, and everything else in the blade's path were all cut down. Each swing of his sword composed a rondo of cries and suffering. His black cloak danced through the air behind him as if he were a conductor leading a gruesome orchestra.

There was no darkness to hide his shame or his silliness. It was not night like when he had fought before. The desert sun shone bright, exposing Hegni's wild sword dance to the world. To the enemy forces, it was an incarnation of terror, and to Hegni it was the equivalent of a hellish one-man performance atop a stage for all to see.

Argh, they're watching me. They're all looking at meeeee. Arrrrgh, I can't, I can't, I can't, I can't. Why did I ever become a first-tier adventurer? I don't need the attention, just let me sink into the darkness to fight! Or even just become the darkness itself. Why didn't I become an assassin? I can't do it, this is too hard, I just want to hide in the forest, aaaaarrrrrgh. I just wanna lay my head in Lady Freya's lap—no, the other way around, I want her to lay her head on my lap.

He was facing ten thousand enemies. It was a concentration of gazes unlike any he had experienced before. Unlike monsters in the Dungeon, they were people with intelligence, which just made it all the worse for Hegni, causing the incoherent thoughts in his head to mix and merge. While he was performing a cruel dance of blades, his stress was threatening to break past his limits.

I can't do it…I guess I have to use it.

Because of that, Hegni fled to his magic.

"*Draw thine sword, King of the fiendish blades.*"

He plunged his black sword into the sand before him, and a black magic circle appeared around it, then expanded as he closed his eyes and began chanting fluently.

"*Sacrifice reason and offer up blood. Slaughter all until the feast is finished.*"

The soldiers did not even have time to defend themselves as they watched in shock. The dark elf's short cast ended, and he spoke the name of his spell.

"*Dáinsleif.*"

The black magic circle at his feet shone and then shattered. The fragments of lights were absorbed into his body. A veil of light seemed to envelop him completely, but it disappeared in an instant as he slowly opened his eyes. And then he suddenly spoke:

"—You villains who have acted as you pleased in this desert, offer up your blood. Only through that may there be forgiveness for the grave treason you have committed."

It was a firm, resolute voice and menacing attitude entirely at odds with how he had been acting before, which just confused the soldiers even more because of the sudden change in demeanor. His eyes did not betray any hidden insecurities. Instead they were raised sharply, like a true swordsman's.

Hegni's magic, *Dáinsleif*. It had the unusual effect of modifying his personality. It was counted as a rare magic, one that allowed Hegni to embody the mental image he had of himself. It was the key to the ritual that allowed the weak-willed, nervous elf to become a true warrior. It bore a resemblance to a certain prum hero's fighting spirit buff magic, but *Dáinsleif* did not have an effect that increased his status. It merely manipulated his personality, making it a seemingly plain ability among a rather flashy class of magics.

"Speak your final words should you have any. There shan't be mercy."

However, his magic was so specialized in manipulating his psyche that it surpassed autosuggestion and was a genuine modification of his self. Its effect literally turned his personality and vocabulary into that of another person, effectively making his ideal self a reality.

It was a magic that summoned the strongest possible version of himself that had grown out of an obsessive self-hatred. The moment he cast that spell, Hegni transformed into a merciless, cruel, murderous, and domineering warrior king, like a cursed sword that once drawn could not be sheathed until it had satisfied itself by shedding the blood of countless people.

"—Shuffle off this mortal coil, rabble. Unseemly tributes who have been forsaken by the goddess's love, you are best dead."

In an instant, Hegni disappeared. The desert sand exploded up into the air from his unexpected step as he dashed forward, cutting down an entire platoon before the enemies even realized he had moved.

"Ahh—Ahhhhhhhhhhhhhhhhhhhhhhhhhhhhhh!"

That was how the true banquet of despair began. Having activated *Dáinsleif*, Hegni had rid himself of every last shred of mercy. The limiters inhibiting his full strength had been removed by magic. He transformed into a man-eating fiend that even his old foe Hedin would say, "That rogue is the strongest among all elves when it comes to hand-to-hand combat."

Moving like a black sliver through the soldiers' ranks, he struck each and every one down, leaving none alive as he created a storm of slashes. The soldiers of the third division who saw him were more terrified than the soldiers on any other battlefield, because what they saw was the personification of a demon blade. A manifestation of death itself that paused only to dedicate more blood and viscera. The soldiers understood it instinctively as they cried and their teeth chattered, until a split second later, they became the next offerings to his sword.

Hegni's title, Dáinsleif, was indeed derived from the name of his magic.

It was the greatest compliment paid him by the fanatical and intense fans he had among the gods, in honor of the way he transformed from a comical dark knight into a true warrior king of darkness.

"There are many tributes this time…but be at ease, I have plenty of slashes to dole out. This blade of mine shall mark your grave."

In the name of exterminating the whole army, the evilest fairy resumed the massacre.

"General Orcas! The enemy has appeared!" a soldier reported.

"What?! What scale and from which direction?!" Orcas roared out with a booming voice.

As the clamor of battle rang out all around the Sindh Expanse, General Orcas, the aged general who was a veteran of many battles against Shalzad, was at the very rear of the formation, leading the reserves. They had twenty thousand troops who were supposed to react as the battle developed and support the main divisions as needed. It was a position of significant importance in battle.

The enemy's tactician even saw through the existence of our reserve forces and had troops lying in wait.

He suspected that the composition of their formation had been leaked to the enemy, since other divisions had already encountered surprise attacks that had been devastating enough that the cries could be heard from beyond the dunes even before the reports arrived.

"A bombardment carried out by a single person" and "A single swordsman cutting down more than half a force of ten thousand" and other absurd reports were flying all around, so he knew that the battle was enshrouded by the fog of war. However, his suspicions were overturned when learned of his own situation.

"There is one person each to our north, south, east, and west, sir!"

".........Huh?"

"Ummm, that is...well, there is one person in each direction, sir. In front and behind, and left and right. There are four armored prums in total..."

The well-trained soldier was at a loss for word for once as he struggled to clarify his report.

Orcas sat atop his camel as he trained his eyes in the directions the solider indicated—and he saw them, just as reported. At the summit of the sand dunes in the cardinal directions around his force of twenty thousand, there stood four short prums wielding a spear, hammer, battle-ax, and greatsword respectively.

"Hu—...Ha-ha-ha-ha-ha-ha-ha-ha-ha! Has Shalzad lost its mind?! Just four people to face off against an army of twenty thousand?!"

Orcas could hardly believe his eyes as his battle-hardened body shook from laughter and several people around him also broke out into guffaws.

No matter how strong they are, we're a force of soldiers and mercenaries who have all received Falna. Even if they could take out one thousand each, three thousand more would easily overwhelm them. And they're prums! The weakest of all the demi-humans! What a joke!

"What of it?! Do they intend us to act as if we've been surrounded by a force of just four people?! Don't make me laugh, fools!"

A wave of scornful laughter spread from the tough old general to the surrounding troops. Needless to say, they had let their guard down.

—If there was any miscalculation in Orcas's analysis, it was that he had not known that his opponents, despite being prums, were considered possibly the strongest prums in the world, four of the precious few first-tier adventurers in the world, members of the *Freya Familia*.

© nilitsu

In other words, he was entirely wrong.

"Everyone's in position."

"Shall we?"

"Let's."

"Let's do this."

The Gulliver brothers were standing stock-still atop the sand dunes as they looked down on the Warsa army, their voices overlapping despite being so far away from each other, as if they were telepathic.

To the four of them, distance did not count for much. As long as they could see each other, it did not matter whether the enemy was just one or ten thousand, they would exterminate them with such tight coordination that did not allow even one soldier to escape.

Staring blankly down at the army below them roaring with laughter, they lowered their visors and leaned forward, seemingly pulled down by gravity as they dashed down the dunes. An instant later, cries and screams began ringing out from all directions at the same time.

In later years, it would come to be known as the Battle of the Sindh.

A battle told in countless bards' songs and children's plays about the prince of a country in ruins who, with the aid of eight anonymous heroes, foiled the plot of evil deities manipulating Warsa behind the scenes. There would be no end to scholars and historians attempting to determine what exactly happened that day.

And one particularly famous point of study shrouded somewhere between the myth and truth of the battle was regarding the birth of a revolutionary tactic.

It was the "groundbreaking encirclement and annihilation formation carried out by just four people."

It was a maneuver where just four people in total were positioned at the north, south, east, and west of a force of twenty thousand that was both incomprehensible and yet somehow powerful beyond belief—a maneuver that would shock later military scholars and tacticians.

Renowned military scholars howled at its mention, as if to declare "How is that possible, you imbecile?" But it was emblematic of the age of deities, and records indicated that it was, in fact, used to wipe Warsa's force of twenty thousand off the map.

Records of that unbelievable battle were left by a historian who was well-known in the desert realm, Orcas Gruen. He was one of the few survivors of the Battle of Sindh and the one general who saw firsthand what occurred that day, and when he described the battle in his autobiography, the next passage he wrote was: "My humblest apologies. I'm truly, truly sorry for looking down on you."

"General Jafar! Warsa's army has already begun the battle!"

"What?!"

As Hedin, Hegni, and the Gulliver brothers embarked on their respective rampages and the agonizing cries of Warsa's army echoed throughout the desert, the Shalzad army deployed all by itself in the Gazoob Wasteland finally realized what was going on.

Based on reports from scouts saying, "I don't really get what's going on, but Warsa's army is getting its ass handed to it," the army hurriedly advanced toward the Sindh Expanse.

"Well, by the time they get there it will already be over," Freya said.

She was sitting in a chair with her legs crossed on the deck of the Fazoul Trading Company's desert ship. The ship was being steered by merchant trainees, keeping a safe distance from the battlefield while still being able to observe what was happening, as it leisurely cruised through the sand.

"Is this really okay, Lady Freya? Letting Lady Ali...Prince Aram move separately?" a stout, toned man asked.

"There's no helping it, since she said she wanted to see the battle with her own eyes. And if she is to be king, that sentiment is entirely reasonable," Freya responded.

Ali was currently watching the battle from an even closer position with the bare minimum accompaniment from the trading company.

Freya was more worried about her being attacked by monsters than soldiers, but figured it should be fine.

With the overwhelming battle going on around them, the monsters would be cowering in fear and not attacking humans. A smile crossed Freya's face as she imagined the look on Ali's face as she watched the battle.

"...Speaking of, though...who are you?" Freya asked, turning to the tall, handsome man who was waiting at her side as if it were the most obvious thing in the world.

She had been wondering about him for a while, but he had preternaturally adopted the role of her attendant so well she had not really had a chance to ask. The brown-skinned man responded naturally.

"I'm Bofman, milady."

NO WAY! Freya thought in her heart, forgetting her character for a moment.

The self-proclaimed Bofman was not a fattened blob of flesh but a well-sculpted mass of muscle. He had a short mustache, but beneath his brown skin, he had the physical structure of a slightly smaller Ottar.

Freya's wide-eyed gaze conveyed the question *What happened during that one night?*

"Last night I received a strict punishment from Messrs. Ottar, Allen, Hedin, Hegni, and Gulliver and was made aware how unsightly I truly was...Muscle is righteousness." The self-proclaimed Bofman averted his eyes as he responded.

But his answer was incomprehensible to Freya. It was not just his appearance; even his tone had changed. Such a dramatic transformation in the course of a single night shocked even a goddess.

"...Why don't you come to my room tonight?" Freya suggested.

"No, a lowly beast such as I am not worthy to be summoned by you, Lady Freya."

However, a gravelly, handsome voice politely rejected her. She wondered why she felt like she had been defeated. Freya was a bit annoyed by that and made a mental note to torment Ottar later.

"...Lady Freya, that is..."

Bofman and the rest of the crew all looked in the same direction. When Freya also glanced over, she spotted an air current rising into the sky, creating a sand tornado—

"A…a sandstorm…"

A fiendish vortex filled the sky as the soldiers of Warsa trembled in fear. The powerful wind whipping the sand into the air swallowed up the soldiers running for their lives one after the other as their screams were swept up into the storm.

Warsa's fourth division, ten thousand soldiers, fell into a panic at the inexplicable phenomenon occurring before their eyes.

"Wh-what is that?! Magic?!"

No. It was the aftereffects of someone sprinting. A preposterous, inhuman, almost supersonic movement kicked up a wind that scattered sand through the air. It was nothing more than a side effect.

The unit commander who cried out saw the single flash of a silver spear come from inside the depths of that evil storm for just a second before it pierced his chest.

"*Gaaaaaah?!*"

Paying no heed to the soldier who collapsed with blood pouring from his chest, the fighting cat kept sprinting.

"Tch, just like in Sand Land, huh? This always happens in sandy terrain."

Despite having already lost count of how many enemies he had killed, Allen did not slow his spear in the least. As he ran around in every direction at top speed, leaving only death in his wake, his passing created a tremendous wind, giving birth to a sandstorm that swallowed up an entire division of Warsa troops. He continued striking down his targets at an ever-faster rate as they fell into a panic.

The fastest in Orario.

Allen was faster than every other adventurer, and he ran riot around the battlefield, kicking up an enormous plumes of dust like a blindingly fast chariot. To the soldiers, it was like a natural disaster or a gigantic monster attacking. Their taste for battle vanished, but Allen did not allow even one who turned their back to escape.

There were no calls of surrender. No one would think to wave the white flag in the face of a storm. Because of the sand, no one could even see Allen as every last one of them fell to his silver spear without exception.

"Ha-haaaaaaaa!"

At least that was how it should have been.

Someone charged into the wall of sand, broke through, and swung dual swords down at Allen. Allen considered parrying with his spear for a moment—but quickly decided to avoid the blades instead. His superhuman dynamic vision noticed that the blades were a suspicious red and blue color.

And, as if announcing he was correct to jump back, a stream of flames and a blast of frost erupted from the blades. The combination of searing flames and ice that froze even the desert scattered the sandstorm. Allen stopped moving when he landed on the ground, observing the enemy that had been able to attempt an attack on him while he was moving.

"You're the one! You're the guy trying to disrupt my lord Resheph's plan!"

It was a lean and tall male elf. He was untanned with long black hair, wearing a cloak over his otherwise bare upper body. His face and chest were covered in warpaint-like tattoos, but he did not seem to be a proper warrior, instead giving off a bit of an ominous air.

"I am Lord Resheph's greatest follower, the leader of his familia, Seal!"

"...Do all the servants of that Resheph or whatever have the same bad habit of introducing themselves?"

The man who called himself Seal did not pay Allen's gaze any heed as his delightedly clanged his magic swords together.

"You're strong, aren't you?! I can tell just by looking! What was with that speed?! Are you by any chance a warrior from outside the desert, like us? No, wait! Is there any chance that you might be an adventurer from Orario?!"

Perhaps getting excited in the heat of the moment on the battlefield, or perhaps losing himself in joy at the appearance of an overwhelmingly powerful warrior, the elf twisted his face in a way that disfigured his features as he shouted, guessing at Allen's true identity.

Resheph Familia's leader spoke in a grating voice that served only to increase Allen's irritation even as the strange man's smile deepened.

"Even I, a kavir, can't hope to win against you! No chance at all! Ha-ha-ha-ha-ha-ha! Scary, scary! Aaaaah, what a fearsome warrior!"

Despite recognizing the difference in their strength, Seal could not stop laughing. Meanwhile, Allen had moved beyond displeasure and was ready to commit murder. Just when he had decided it was enough and was about to run down the elf—Seal noticed his ferocious hostility and quickly began to move.

"At this rate, I'll be killed! So I'll just have to show you my invincible warrior-killer technique!"

And he followed that up with a hair-raising chant.

"Run wild! Wind of pestilence!"

Allen gazed in surprise for a second when he realized it was not magic but a curse as Seal revealed his unerring technique.

"Hal Reshef!"

A bewitching light shimmered in Seal's eyes. Even Allen, whose legs could allow him to completely evade a barrage of attacks and the full brunt of an area of effect spell, could not evade a ray of light that worked on eye contact.

Allen immediately covered his eyes with one arm after the flash of dim, dark-purple light, as he stood there scolding himself for being careless. It was uncommon for curses to do direct damage like attack magics, so he did not move as he tried to determine the attributes of the curse afflicting him.

There were no abnormalities in his extremities, and he could not verify any kind of status ailments. Even if his magic or skills were sealed, it was irrelevant, since he did not need anything other than his raw strength to crush them. There were no obvious impediments to his five senses. Based on the quick double check he performed, Allen suspected it might be a counterattack sort of curse. The sort that inflicted whatever damage the cursed person dealt back onto them.

Having figured out from Seal's speech that he was not the kind of person to fight directly, Allen made a frustrated noise as he looked back up.

"...?"

Seal had disappeared. And not just him. Allen could not see any of the other soldiers, either. There was only the blue sky, the expanse of sand, and the murderous heat of the sun beating down on him.

Allen's thoughts immediately jumped to the idea he was hallucinating, but he quickly rejected that hypothesis. The corpses of the soldiers that Allen had killed were still visible, and the blood on the sand was still there, too. And most of all, Allen's keen nose could still sense countless soldiers in the surroundings.

—Concealment? Did he drop a pain-in-the-ass illusion on me?

Allen's brow furrowed as he looked on dubiously, preparing to follow his nose to slam his spear home, but—

"Big Brother."

That girl's voice stopped him in his tracks.

"—"

On his right, a girl suddenly appeared, tears in her eyes as she stretched out her hand toward him. The way she struggled to walk over to him was as if she had just suffered horrific injuries.

It was a catgirl wearing her battle gear, an adventurer like Allen. She had a gold shoulder piece on the opposite shoulder from Allen and brown fur. She did not have it with her there, but Allen knew that she carried a golden spear as well.

The fearsome fighting cat Allen forgot his annoyance and hostility, his eyes going wide as he stood there.

"Please wait, Big Brother...Don't leave me behind!"

Without a doubt, it was Allen Fromel's little sister, Ahnya.

It worked! I'll be taking some more of that sweet, sweet high-rank excelia!

Seal was sure of his victory.

He had changed locations, lowering his body and camouflaging himself against the sand using his cloak, as he licked his lips while watching Allen stand there stock-still.

He, of course, could not see Allen's little sister. The person facing Allen was an assassin from *Resheph Familia* with a poison dagger in one hand hidden behind his back.

Hal Reshef. As Allen surmised, it was an illusionary curse. Seal, the caster of the curse, had no way of knowing who the victim was seeing, but knew it was that individual's most beloved person. That was the effect of Seal's curse, *Hal Reshef.* It revived the traumatic memories deep in his target's heart, a curse that brought forth a heartrendingly foul pestilence.

Seal had used that power to lay low countless warriors stronger than himself. Given the nature of statuses and leveling up, it was essentially a rule that those who had accomplished great feats had also paid some sort of price. Whether their dark past involved a comrade, family, or a lover, they were all a perfect fit for Seal's curse. No matter how strong someone was, they would be shaken by the appearance of the person most precious to them and replay some tragic memory in their mind, leaving a fatal opening for Seal to exploit.

It's all thanks to this curse that I've gotten to Level Four.

Seal had no doubt that he was the weakest Level 4 in the world. Up against a strong opponent, he could only gain excelia by catching them off guard with tricks like that. His techniques and tactics were mediocre, and his abilities were all at the lowest levels. The adventure he had embarked upon was equivalent to the labor of gradually whittling down a rampaging wild bull. He was not really a warrior at all. He was a hexer.

However, Seal also had no doubt that he was the strongest. At the very least as long as he wasn't fighting a monster. He was the strongest in the world when it came to fighting other people. There was nothing fake about the most beloved person Allen was seeing at that very moment. It was projected from within him and was without doubt the person he truly loved above all else. Their shape, voice, scent, feel—all of it was real. They were reflections of his own memories, and no one would be able to doubt what had been engraved deep in their own heart.

Of course not. How could anyone raise a hand against their most beloved? The trauma every victim of Seal's curse saw was like a crossroad in life where the path had been chosen long ago and could not be rejected or denied now.

My lackey's dagger is coated in a powerful poison, a drop item smuggled out of the Labyrinth City...You won't be able to defend against it no matter how strong you are.

There was a chance that when Allen was stabbed he might kill the lackey in confusion, but that was fine. Seal had plenty of pawns capable of playing the role of a victim's most beloved. Allen could not see them currently because of the curse, but all the scared soldiers watching from the surroundings would do just fine. The world Allen currently saw was a mixture of illusion and reality, and until Seal released the curse, he would never break from the nightmare of seeing his most beloved.

"So, how will you scream for me?"

Seal watched with a sadistic grin.

"..."

Allen looked down silently. The assassin moved closer, step by step. The man who appeared nothing like the adventurer's little sister to Seal slowly lowered his arm. The voice tearfully calling for her big brother rang in his cat ears. And the moment his sister was right before his eyes—the moment the assassin's blade could finally reach him...

Allen swung his silver spear with all his might, turning his little sister into a broken lump of flesh.

"——What?!"

Time froze for Seal and for all the members of *Resheph Familia* who were familiar with his ability. The soldiers of Warsa were struck by a pure terror. Having killed his little sister with his own hands, Allen *snapped* like never before.

"You showed me a real pain in the ass..."

His chilling voice revealed that his normally restrained wrath had broken free. His voice was brimming with murderous rage, causing Seal to break into a cold sweat as he reflexively leaped backward.

Whipping around faster than the wind, the fighting cat locked his eyes onto Seal.

He should only be able to see his most beloved person—how did he recognize me?!

Seal dropped all pretenses as he screamed:

"Someone stop hiiiiiiiiiiiiiiiiiiiiiiiiiiiiiiiiiiiiiiiiiiiiiim!"

Resheph Familia and the soldiers reflexively obeyed his order. The soldiers all looked like Allen's most-beloved person as they barreled down on him. In Allen's eyes, they looked exactly like his sister in her adventurer's equipment; like his sister wearing her uniform for the restaurant; like his sister from days long past when she was young.

And not realizing the fuel he was adding to the flames of Allen's wrath, Seal watched what happened next. The cat's body blurred as he dodged and slaughtered every last one of the little sisters charging at him.

"Wh-what are youuuuuuuuuuuuuuuuuuuuuuuuuuuuuuuuu?!"

His spear pierced and its shaft smashed as he unleashed a flurry of blows to take the sisters apart. As Allen kicked up a storm wiping out all the enemy troops, Seal could not stop himself from screaming as he raised his twin blades. While the grunts were holding the cat back, he frantically readied himself to finish the adventurer with his magic swords.

However, the cat's wrath had crossed its boiling point. Allen leaped away from the remains of his most-beloved lying scattered around the ground. The dune he had been standing on exploded from the force of his leap as he unleashed his strongest charge, passing by Seal, who was swinging his twin blades down.

"What?!"

A ray of light flashed past right as Seal's arms swung down through the air. But his arms had both disappeared below the elbows. He froze when the magic swords he had been holding fell to the ground behind him, sticking out of the sand.

"*AAAAAAAAAAAAAAAAAAAAAAAAAAAAAAAAAAAAAAAAA AAAAARGH?!*"

An ear-splitting wail reverberated across the sands.

The shock of losing both his arms to Allen's silver spear, the light-speed movement that was impossible to sense, the burning pain in both his arms, and the sense of inescapable bloodlust that he never before felt—all of it ate away at Seal's mind, warping the elf's features as tears and beads of sweat coated his face, like he had lost all hold on his senses.

"Hey, asshole."

The sound of the man's voice behind him was more chilling, more terrifying than anything Seal had ever felt. Unable to breathe, Seal struggled to fill his lungs as Allen's subzero voice continued.

"You look just like some dumbass I hate more than anything in this world, too."

Liar, liar, liar! What you're seeing is the person you love the most! The irreplaceable other half of your soul! It can't be the person you hate the most!

—But why, then? Why can he so mercilessly and calmly swing his spear at his most beloved—?

—What the hell is he seeing with those eyes of his?!

"Undo this curse now. If you don't, I'll murder you. Slowly and painfully."

"O-okay! I got it! I'll do it! So don't kill me!"

Allen threatened Seal with a low, quiet, murderous voice as the bawling elf just about wet himself while intoning the curse removal.

"Be gooone, epidemic calamityyy!...It's gone! It's gone! You're greatest love is gone!!! So! So please don't!"

Announcing that the curse was removed, Seal begged for his life, half crying, half laughing.

Three seconds.

Allen gritted his teeth as tight as he could——and then swung his spear down with one hand, splitting Seal straight down the middle.

"You didn't undo anythiiiiiiiiiiiiiiiiiiiiiiiiiiiiiiiiiiiiiiiiiiiiiiiiiiiiiing!"

His howl thundered across the plains. Allen's eyes still saw his little sister, still saw that idiot, that disgrace.

His rage that had long since passed its boiling point and finally reached its critical point. He instantly cut down Seal, who had lost his reason and had not been able to control his magic well enough to undo his own curse. Now the elf's horrific corpse lay on the sand.

When Seal had failed to undo the curse, Allen had thought it would end once the caster was dead, but even after cutting him in half, her face was still all he could see. The effect continued even after the caster was unconscious or even dead—meaning it was the type of curse that would only disappear after a set amount of time had passed.

Allen's fur stood on end in rage. Sensing the danger, the soldiers, who all looked like his little sister, cried out in terror as they tried to run away from Allen's silver spear.

Don't fuck with me. I won't allow it. I won't forgive anyone masquerading as that nitwit.

Allen would never accept that that was his truth. Because of that, there was only one thing left to do.

"—I'm gonna slaughter every last one of them."

Ghastly was the only word to describe what followed.

Generally speaking, it was impossible for an army to be entirely wiped out. Once a force took greater than 30 percent losses, the battle would usually be over. However, the division that Allen had targeted was slaughtered to the last man by the fighting cat who

© nilitsu

enthralled to his rage. In order to erase the scene that so disgusted him, Allen summoned forth dozens of sandstorms, manifestations of his wrath.

"Whoa, whoa, they got Seal?!"

The transport and logistics squad. The true final line of Warsa's army.

Inside a tent that had been set up there, even Resheph could not hide his surprise at the reports flying in and the accelerating disappearances of children who had received his blessings.

"Y-yes, sir! And the other elite members of your followers are being defeated across all fronts! Our forces are not being allowed to retreat or even be routed. The only division still capable of fighting is Gorza's main division!"

"What? There are only eight of them, right? Are you freaking kidding me?" Resheph groaned, struggling to believe the reports he was hearing.

"I'm not freaking kidding you, sir!"

Even a god like him could not see through what was happening on the battlefield out there. But that did not stop him from breaking into a smile.

"Damn, I'd rather my premonition wasn't right, but it looks like I'm gonna have to use my trump card. ☆"

Standing up as the soldier looked at him in confusion, Resheph left the tent. He headed toward the part of the camp where supplies were being kept. There was a strange sight to behold there. It was a gigantic cargo container that would never be mistaken for carrying weapons or rations in it. It required several hundred people to carry it, and it contained the ace up Resheph's sleeve.

"Iza, send this to the middle of the battlefield. Don't worry, as long as you have this magic item I got from those Evils guys, it will do as you say. Probably."

Calling out to the lone tamer among his followers, he handed over a crimson whip with jewels in the end of it. At his command, the tamer swung the whip and a roar shook the ground. The giant cargo crate shattered as the troops around it drew back. A giant shadow that terrified even the tamer moved to the command of the whip and started advancing toward the battlefield.

"Ha-ha-ha-ha-ha-ha! You always gotta save your trump card for the very end. ☆"

The god's laughter rang out as everyone in the transport unit was frozen in place. Resheph turned around to head back to his tent, content that all that was left was for his trump card to take care of all those getting in his way. But as he departed, he paused for a second and turned to one of the messengers.

"Oh yeah, we got any word about who the enemy is? If they could kill Seal and the others that easily, then it's gotta be someone from Orario, I'd imagine."

"Y-yes, sir...the second and third divisions were assaulted by an elf and a dark elf respectively..."

"Uh-huh, uh-huh."

"And the fourth division and reserve forces were cornered by a catman and four prums..."

"Uh-huh......hmm?"

"And the central division is being approached by a large boaz man..."

" ... "

There, for the first time, Resheph's composure finally cracked.

A flurry of sand shot into the air. The Warsa general Gorza looked on with a trembling gaze as the resulting cloud grew big enough to block out the sun.

"What is he...?!"

The man held an unbelievably large sword. After he utterly smashed both wings and the central unit, he calmly strolled through the path he had created. The man did not needlessly kill anyone. He only turned his blade on those who approached him, using his over-whelming physical strength to crush them.

He was a boaz.

"We can't even stop his advance…?! It's just one man!" Gorza spat out as he watched through binoculars from far at the back of the main force.

The absurd reports he had just been getting from the various divisions being destroyed had sounded like lies, but at this point he had no choice but to believe them. The enemy really was attempting to eradicate an army of eighty thousand with just eight people. But Gorza could not give up. If they could not take Shalzad even after bringing in an outside power, a pestilence, then his position and his patron god's authority would plummet.

Even if it was just petty pride, if he could not at least take out a single enemy warrior—

"…?"

All of a sudden, a shadow appeared. He wondered if a cloud had floated across the sun, but that was not it. It was a gigantic monster whose head stretched up toward the sky.

"What?!"

More precisely, it was an enormous serpent. The gigantic monster had appeared behind Gorza, from the direction of the supply lines.

"I-it can't be…a basilisk?!"

It was a name that every resident of the desert realm knew from bedtime stories. A feared and despised creature.

A basilisk.

It had the imposing figure of a serpent, but it was also unmistakably a member of the dragon family, the strongest species of monsters. The giant serpent breathed fire while spreading a paralyzing toxin that seemed to petrify those afflicted by it. In ancient times, basilisks had destroyed countless cities and spread such devastation around the world that anecdotes about the menace of basilisks were still told all around present-day Kaios.

Appearing behind the main force, the monster trampled the soldiers in its path. More and more people cried out and abandoned

© nilitsu

their positions to run away. This clash had long since ceased to be a battle between humans. Gorza and his aide-de-camp desperately took refuge to avoid being consumed by the chaos.

This was Resheph's trump card. The unleashed basilisk had already killed the tamer. It had not been controlled by the whip, perhaps because the collar placed around one of its fangs—which was as large as a grown man—might not have been a finished product. Either way, the monster had crushed the annoying man yelling orders at it with its giant tail.

The basilisk swung its thick neck, as if only humoring the dead tamer's final words, and focused its gaze on Ottar.

"*OOOOOOOOOOOOOOOOOOOOOOOOOOOOOOOOOOOO!*"

Its body was over twenty meders long.

It tore through the sea of sand and charged straight at Ottar. It was an assault intended to crush anything in its way, a lethal technique that would leave nothing in its wake.

To take it on, Ottar, who had until that moment only been holding his sword with one hand, finally wielded it using both hands.

And then—

—he split the giant serpent's body with a single slash.

"_____"

There was a loud noise as the two pieces of the serpent's body fell to the ground and a curtain of sand flew into the air. And there was an enormous, deep slash left in the sand where Ottar's attack had split the ground. The desert fell silent.

His swing had caused a tremor that shook the entire battlefield. It had reached not just the Warsa forces or Shalzad's army but even Ali, who was watching from afar.

While the soldiers of Warsa were frozen in place, the curtain of floating sand gradually cleared, and their dusty faces turned pale as they stared, speechless.

The basilisk had been split perfectly down the middle and was lying dead on the sand. And in the middle of its corpse stood the boaz warrior still holding his sword where he had swung it down. The man who had unleashed that tremendous slash slowly released his stance and put the sword back on his shoulder as he had been carrying it before.

"Raise the white flag."

"What…?"

"We're surrendering."

Gorza lowered his binoculars as he gave that simple order to the soldiers close by. Ignoring their confusion, the commander looked off into the distance as he cast aside his fighting resolve.

"There's no way we can match a monster like that."

"A wise general…it would be a shame to kill him."

Seeing the dozens of white flags being waved, Ottar thrust his giant sword into the ground. His rust-colored eyes narrowed as he spoke.

"Hedin, I'm not going to kill them all. I want to give this potential a chance to grow."

The strongest adventurer left those words to the wind after destroying the enemy's will to fight with a single strike instead of rampaging through countless soldiers.

The Battle of the Sindh ended with the warrior's single blow.

"Prince! Prince Aram! General Jafar has rushed to your side!"

An old general and the troops he led approached Ali, who was standing atop a high sand dune overlooking the battlefield. Behind the general was the Shalzad army marching beneath the battle flag of the moon and jasmine.

"Your cunning in preparing a preemptive surprise attack is nothing less than spectacular! Allow us to join in as well! We shall crush the villains of Warsa! Where is the enemy?"

The old general Jafar was beside himself in joy at the prince's growth, and the soldiers behind him raised a hot-blooded battle cry. But in response, Ali just continued to stare into the distance, absorbed in the scene in front of her.

"I-it's over..." Ali said, looking on in shock as she slowly raised a hand and pointed to the results.

"Huh?"

"It's...it's really over..."

Countless Warsa soldiers were collapsed all across the giant desert that lay before them. The tiny shadows at the edge of the horizon were all the same. The corpses crumpled atop one another, and the horrifically broken weapons and armor all combined to form tens of thousands of gravestones. The atrocious *Resheph Familia* members had all been killed. The wind was gradually burying their leader Seal's corpse under the sea of sand.

The main force commanded by Gorza, which had surrendered, was bound with ropes and being led away by nervous Fazoul Trading Company merchants who had stuffed themselves into armor. Jafar and his troops froze at the sight, their jaws dropping.

"The giant walls surrounding Orario..." Ali caught her breath as she subconsciously started speaking. "They aren't for protecting their city from outside attack, are they?...They're for keeping the adventurers locked away inside...?"

Ali was sure of it. And she was correct. That was why the Labyrinth City hated allowing its assets to leave the city. Part of it was to keep other influential groups from gaining power, but the true reason was to keep the powerful upper-tier adventurers from being let loose upon the world.

If Orario unleashed their adventurers, it might lead to genocide. That thought was precisely what they wanted to keep the rest of the world from thinking.

Ironically, all of their precaution was to prevent the world from knowing that adventurers were just as much monsters as the calamities they were fighting.

In the ancient times, people had built a fortress to keep the monsters from flowing out of the giant hole and spreading across the land, a predecessor to the current city walls. However, Ali realized that the modern wall also served as a cage to keep the adventurers locked in after witnessing that battle.

The victors standing atop the sand dune numbered just eight. A boaz, a catman, a dark elf, a white elf, and four prums.

Ali was struck with awe again at the overwhelming victory that the adventurers had achieved. The battle that decided the fate of Shalzad and Warsa had been brought to an end by just those eight followers.

The sun hung low, nearing the horizon as the sky gradually darkened.

The natural results after a battle were occurring in the Sindh Expanse. The soldiers of Shalzad, who were disappointed at not getting to fight, looked like they were in a dream as they carried away the utterly ravaged corpses of the Warsa soldiers who had caused them so much suffering. They still had not cleared away all the dead bodies.

Resheph had disappeared in the chaos, running away somewhere. The being who had sparked the flames of war himself had not been captured, but the goddess had merely said, "Was there even a god called that? Whatever, just leave it be. He's not worth the effort," as if she was incapable of caring less.

The war was over. It was honestly debatable whether it could even be called a war, but either way, the fighting was done. The invaders had been removed—the girl's oasis country was liberated.

"Ahhh, Solshana…! I've returned!"

Leaving the cleanup work to the soldiers, Ali and the generals headed back to the capital first to report the destruction of Warsa and the return of peace to their people as soon as possible.

There was a white marble palace and a castle town around it. The beautiful cityscape had been wrecked during Warsa's invasion and the defenses had been mercilessly destroyed, but inside the walls, the citizens who had been persecuted so badly raised a thunderous, rolling cheer. And the voices that reached Ali's band were hailing a hero's triumphal return. It was a bit uncomfortable for the generals who had not done anything, but for Ali, it was a cheerful moment.

The capital she had fled so pitifully. The homeland she was finally returning to. Her eyes began to fill with tears.

"...Freya!"

As the generals began to dismount from their camels, Ali turned back and ran.

The goddess and her eight followers were standing with their backs to the red sky.

Ali ran to the familia that had saved her.

"You have my eternal gratitude! Thanks to you, peace has returned to Shalzad!"

"It has."

"I could never have done this myself! Neither returning to my homeland nor returning the smiles to my people's faces!"

"Indeed."

"Please accept my thanks! Though it may have been nothing more than a whim to you...I was saved by you!"

"I've been accepting it for a while now."

No matter how many times she shouted her thanks, Freya's responses were calm and collected. And having shouted too much, Ali was gasping for breath as she quietly tried to calm her breathing and locked eyes with the goddess's silver gaze.

Time did not wait for her as the sun continued to set. Their shadows grew. Long, shimmering shadows stretched out into the sea of sand. The girl's shadow flickered in the desert wind, trembling faintly. As if she were fighting something within herself.

"...Freya...I..."

Lit by the sunset, she was struck by a feeling as if she were gradually becoming just Ali and not Aram. The feeling of losing the mask and armor of a king, her feelings being exposed. It had not even been two weeks, but the time she had spent with Freya seemed to hit her all at once. The anger, sadness, and despair. Each and every word the goddess had spoken during that time echoed in her heart. A maddening, indescribable thing was clawing at Ali.

Freya was just looking at her, making no attempt to say anything. Ali was currently being faced with a choice. The goddess and her followers before her. And the magnificent palace and her people, her country, behind her. As if the sunset was telling her to choose, forward or backward.

"..."

Ali glanced at the catman. Allen seemed about to say something, but in the end, he said nothing. She could feel his gaze telling her, *Make up your own damn mind.*

"...Prince Aram?"

Jafar and the others finally noticed Ali and turned around.

It'd be fine, wouldn't it? Just take her hand.

No, of course it wouldn't be fine to cast my country aside.

But what I truly want is—

Desire and conflict. A taboo agony afflicted the last remnants of her rationality. And having lost Aram's armor, the naked Ali could not resist the impulse. She could not reject the irreplaceable time she had spent with the goddess.

I'm sorry you were not born a man. I could not even grant you happiness as a woman—

The words her mother had left her. That Ali would not be able to find happiness as she was.

If it were me, I would fulfill your every need, whether as a man or a woman...

The words of the goddess whose figure overlapped with her mother. Her bold claim that she could grant Ali happiness.

For the first and final time in her life, Ali, who was unable to be fulfilled as either a man or a woman, wanted to scream out her selfish desires.

Just as she was about to stretch out her trembling hand—

*   *   *

"I don't need you."

The goddess's voice stopped her.

"Eh…?"

"I said I don't need you, Ali."

Time froze for Ali as Freya repeated herself. Not understanding what was happening, the girl froze.

"It was a miscalculation on my part. You aren't suitable to be my Odr."

The goddess's eyes narrowed coolly, as if measuring the brilliance of the girl's wavering heart.

Ali's face filled with despair. The pain of being cast away rippled through her like cracks opening up in her body. The disappointment from the goddess, the one being in the world she did not want to disappoint, seared her heart, causing tears to well up in her amethyst eyes.

Wait. Please. Don't go.

While those voiceless shouts filled her throat, the goddess started to turn away.

"So go forth and live as a king."

"_____"

Ali's eyes opened wide. And what she saw was not disappointment or scorn on the goddess's face but a smile lit by the setting sun. And just like that, as if it were nothing, Freya turned away and started walking. And her eight followers followed after her. There was no farewell. No promise to meet again. No good-bye. The goddess just passed from Ali's sight like a breeze.

The desert wind blew, and hair fluttered as a lone tear trickled down a single cheek.

"Are you sure, milady?" Ottar asked.

"Yes," Freya responded as she continued walking. "She can't set aside her country. Even if she did what I wanted, her radiance would be gone."

Freya had seen Ali's conflict. Not only that, she had not allowed the girl to choose. She had pushed Ali away herself.

"The reason she could resist my beauty was because she was a king. What captivated me about her was the brilliance she had as she tried to behave as a king. If she stopped being that, then that brilliance would become something boring…would degrade to something no different from anyone else."

An Ali who was not a king was just a girl like any other. Just an unpolished gem that might as well be a stone. Because Freya could not attain her, she could become a glimmering jewel whose brilliance Freya could respect and enjoy from afar. So Freya would respect that beautiful radiance rather than try to keep it for herself.

"I got a little bit attached, but…using that excuse to please myself and rob her of her potential would be wrong."

She looked back over her shoulder just once. The girl was still standing there, her eyes not looking away at all despite how far they had gotten. However, finally, she raised her arm and rubbed her eyes. And as if conveying her determination, she turned her back on Freya and started walking. Toward the people waiting for their king. Toward the desert kingdom.

Freya smiled one more time, like a mother watching over her child.

"Sorry, Allen. I wasted all your effort."

"…I don't know to what you might be referring. Did you perhaps imagine something?" Allen responded indignantly.

"Hee-hee. Sure. Let's call it that," Freya said, giggling softly.

Ottar and the other followers glanced back at the girl just one time. Hedin looked back the longest, but finally, even he turned his back. As followers who had sworn their loyalty to their goddess, they would accompany her. Freya stopped at the top of a high sand dune with them at her side as she announced her farewell to the desert realm.

"So, shall we go back to boring Orario, a place more intense than any other?"

The series of battles involving Shalzad and Warsa and later Israfan would later come to be known as the Calamity of the Hot Sands.

From the impossible-seeming start of losing its capital, the Kingdom of Shalzad faced a threat to its very existence, and having survived that, it started developing at a pace that left neighboring countries in awe. And it went without saying, of course, that the brilliance of the fifteenth king, King Aram Raza Shalzad, was crucial to those developments.

The Battle of the Sindh led to the decline of Warsa and neither they nor *Resheph Familia*—who had been active behind the scenes in the lead up to the battle—ever threatened Shalzad's peace again. Rumors spread from the Labyrinth City that their country was under the protection of a certain strongest familia, though those rumors were never confirmed or denied.

It is impossible to determine the truth of the matter, but a statue to the eight gallant heroes who were said to have saved the country was constructed in the central plaza of the reconstructed Solshana at King Aram's behest. And apparently there was quite a debate about whether or not those statues' faces resembled some certain adventurers.

And while the kingdom was developing, it was said that the muscular organization, the Fazoul Trading Company—which had apparently undergone a muscle revolution—was always there supporting it. Bofman Fazoul, who had worked so hard in the shadows during the war with Warsa to aid King Aram and continued to support the king afterward, was the man of the hour, and on the back of his ~~muscles~~ charisma, his trading company became extremely successful. The rebuilding of Leodo progressed, and having stepped away from the slave-trading business, the Fazoul Trading Company became famed for never losing out to armies in terms of military power—a rather dubious claim to fame.

Shalzad experienced a golden age thanks to the rule of King Aram.

The king was widely hailed as the greatest player of Halvan in the Kaios Desert, and he used his strategic prowess in political and military affairs as well, and when the time came to put up or shut up, history remembered him as always daringly stepping up to the table. It was said that the king experienced an awakening during the Calamity of the Hot Sands, though he had a playful side as well, and would steal away from his advisers to go play Halvan around town, and he was seen many times out walking around enjoying a kebab.

King Aram was a handsome man who was wise, indulged in many pleasures, and was always beloved by his people. He would later be known as King Aram the Wise. At the time, he was recorded as having said:

"In the midst of that turbulence, a silver light shone upon me.

"It resembled both the moonlight high in the night sky and the ripples on the surface of the oasis. That light delivered a revelation from the heavens. In order to never turn my back on the teachings that light granted me, I continued pushing forward so that I could hold my head high with pride. That was all."

He left a successor and continued to rule justly until the very end, and he was hailed by all for his enlightened rule. His reign and his immense efforts led to the first-ever great power being born in the central region of western Kaios.

"The Heroic King."

"He Who Rules the Board."

"Aram and the Eight Warriors."

He was known by many different names and his tale was passed down to later generations in anecdotes and children's stories.

And whether a certain beautiful goddess smiled when word of those feats reached her ears—the world may never know.

6

I guess there really isn't an Odr for me?

Freya had nothing but time on her hands after coming back from the Kaios Desert.

Ali had been fantastic. Despite her immaturity, she had overturned Freya's expectations, and the way she transformed to such a brilliant jewel had been enough to give Freya some hope.

But in the end, it was not her. She was not the one Freya was looking for. Her brilliance was a radiance intrinsic to her regal stature. If Freya tried to take her for herself, that radiance would disappear.

If she had made Ali hers then and there, she would have been reduced to nothing more than any other girl. Just another inconsequential person seeking nothing more than the goddess's love, just like everyone else. If that happened, Freya would soon bore of her and start looking for another encounter. That was why there wasn't anything she could do. But it was disappointing enough to cause a fair amount of sighing on the goddess's part.

Her aimless days continued as before.

The mortal realm was stimulating. That much was certainly true. A smile would cross her lips when she heard the stories the children wove for themselves, and she was happy to see her followers grow as well. But at the same time, it was true that something was missing for her. Some corner of her heart was still unsatisfied.

Despite the invitations of various deities, she did not make an appearance at the feast of gods or at Denatus, choosing instead to wallow in the poison of boredom.

I guess I really can't find my Odr in this mortal realm—but just as she was about to give up—

That was when she found that boy.

*   *   *

The glimmer of his soul was incredibly small. It paled in comparison to the brilliance of her followers. But it was clear. Entirely see-through. A color Freya had never before seen.

White? A snow white. No, it's translucent.

She had never seen a soul like that before in Orario. White hair like driven snow and rabbitlike rubellite red eyes. A human. Freya spent a lot of time observing the children of the city, but it was her first time seeing him. A new arrival to the city? A new adventurer starting out on his journey? No, none of that mattered—

—I want him.

That was what she thought the moment she saw him. It was a feeling she had not had for a while. Not since she had left Ali. A chill as her body trembled, a twinge in the pit of her stomach, an ecstatic sigh crossing her lips. The unseemly, childish desire to make him her own reared its head.

It was a purely divine sort of desire. Faced with the unknown, deities would never lose interest.

But on the other hand, another wish took root, like a pure bunch of flowers beginning to blossom.

What sort of color will it become? Perhaps it'll stay translucent and clear? And most importantly, can he fulfill my true wish?

Her lips spread into a smile that no one could see. She had only just seen the boy for the first time.

First I need to find out his name. And what familia he's in. If he's another god's follower, I'll probably steal him away someday. I should find out his relationship with his patron god.

She had messed up a bit with Ali. She had been in too much of a rush and ended up inspiring too much reverence in the girl. What she sought in her Odr was not a one-sided sort of a respect.

It was true that she had wanted Ali to shine all the brighter, to shine bright enough to make even a goddess like Freya long for her. But this time she would rein in that divine imperiousness a little. She decided to watch his development for a while first.

I probably won't be able to resist flirting a little bit, though. But getting to know him slowly, ever so slowly, will be fine. Just gradually shrink the distance.

All the effort that deities might consider unnecessary would absolutely be required in order to fulfill her true desire.

She smiled in her heart, where no one else could see. There was just a single thought in her mind that no one else could know.

—I hope you will be the one to become my Odr.

The Origin
of the Strongest

Familia Chronicle

chapter

2

1

His oldest memories were of a musty smell, a freezing cold that burned the skin, and a merciless, brutal dark night.

A deserted alley and a night sky streaked with lonely moonlight.

His stomach should have been empty, but it had passed its limit and no longer even grumbling for food. It was reduced to just sapping away his strength and body heat. Every part of him felt cold as ice, but this poor child had no way to realize how alone he was. It was an almost laughable.

He did not know why he was there. He did not even know who he was. He had no name. No family. He had been abandoned. He didn't think or suffer. He wasn't aware of anything.

There was no way a young child who was not even conscious of the passage of time would be able to escape that place.

He felt like his instinct to live had put up a bit of a fight at first, but even that ran out of strength soon enough. Ignorance robbed him of any chance at a livelihood and a consciousness without desire made him little more than a plant.

He was weak. Nothing more than a pitiful lump of meat that could do nothing but wait for death. But fate, or more specifically, a goddess, did not forsake him.

"Are you all alone?"

Long silver hair and matching jewellike eyes.

He should have just been waiting to die, but his eyes opened wide at the sight of that otherworldly embodiment of beauty as he was captivated by her. He stopped breathing and forgot how to speak. To this toddler's eyes, she looked like the manifestation of something that surpassed the natural laws of the world.

In an instant, the cruel, cold darkness fell away and a halo of silver light filled his faded-out vision.

Time had stopped for him as the silver-haired goddess's eyes narrowed.

"—So pure," she said as she held out her hand.

And the young child silently accepted it. She lifted him in her arms.

"What's your name?" she asked.

The child could not respond. He did not know his name or even his lineage. He was not even truly self-aware yet. Because of that, to his immature mind, the goddess lifting him up became the entirety of his world. She was everything to him.

"All right, then I'll give you a name."

Her smile at that moment was utterly cute, like an innocent young girl's, and even now that that child had grown up, he still remembered it.

"You will be Ottar."

The Warlord, Ottar. That was the day the current strongest adventurer of the Labyrinth City raised his first cry.

The sky was clear, and the Labyrinth City, Orario, was full of energy. A melting pot where travelers, merchants, and adventurers mingled together in a lively bustle.

And in the south of the city, at one corner of the shopping district, there was a certain place filled with a distinctly different kind of activity.

Folkvangr. The home of *Freya Familia*, the city's strongest faction. White and yellow rings of flowers bloomed in a beautiful field and an enormous manor—almost a temple or palace, even—had been built on the hill at the center of the estate. It was like a little world all its own, cut off from the rest of the town. It was a grand scene like a painting brought to life.

And all around that field, an intense death match was unfolding.

"I shall have Lady Freya's favor!"

"For milady! For her love!"

"*Ooooooooooooooooooooooooooooooooooooooooooooo!*"

Many of the familia members were crossing blades. The lowest-level members, Level 1s, and the largest group of the familia, the mid-tier Level 2s and 3s, as well as the strongest participating in the struggle, the Level 4s. Her followers were all fighting among one another. It was a death match to gain the goddess's favor, to be of some use to the goddess. The never-ending sounds of intense battle were at odds with the calm and clear blue sky.

And amid all that, Ottar was calmly walking through the giant field. He did not even glance at the blood and roars, walking confidently right next to the battling warriors.

There were none who tried to attack him. Or more to the point, none could. No matter how hot-blooded and passionate the members of *Freya Familia* might be, they had no interest in receiving even one of his fierce blows and losing the entire day to recovering. Once in the past, almost all of the familia had conspired together to attack him at the same time, but every last one of them had been beaten down.

When he first joined the familia, Ottar had also taken part in that baptism. There was a time when he had been crushed by earlier members of the familia who were long gone, when he had coughed up blood but still kept on fighting and fighting and fighting, all for the sake of being the goddess's strength.

It was a nostalgic memory, but at the same time it caused him to furrow his brow because of the annoyed glare and the pained "I'm getting really tired of having to heal people on death's door..." he got from the skilled healer Freya had brought in to the familia— *ahem*—because of the objections that he had gotten about it.

In his role as leader of the familia, as opposed to the worries of a simple warrior, the merciless combat among members of the familia was a massive headache. He had tried to hide it by maintaining a studied silence behind a stern face, but that only got him lambasted. "There's no point in trying to hide it behind that tough look…"

His qualities as a leader were assuredly lacking in comparison to a certain prum, but Ottar also had no intention of ending the trial by fire, either. It was what made *Freya Familia* what it was.

The desire to gain the goddess's favor, to become a better version of oneself that was suitable for the goddess—that thought was foundational to every one of her followers. In other words, it was all for Freya's sake. And because of that thought, they continued to fight, polishing themselves, ridding themselves of weakness, reaching for ever greater heights. And Ottar was no different. Not when he first joined, and not now.

Entering the manor at the top of the hill, Ottar headed straight to his patron goddess's room.

"Lady Freya, may I?"

For once, Freya was in their home and not occupying the upper floor of Babel. The silver-haired goddess was by herself, sitting in an elegant chair.

"Is there something you need, Ottar?" she asked as she glanced at him.

"I would like to take a short leave."

"Oh?" Freya stopped flipping the page of her book. Her eyes narrowed as he piqued her interest.

Ottar basically never asked to leave his post as Freya's attendant of his own volition. Other than the female attendants who waited on her hand and foot, being at her side was something that only one person was allowed to do. It could be said that the follower who had most gained her favor was the one who was allowed to become her attendant. It was the greatest honor available to members of *Freya Familia*.

So for the same Ottar who had sworn his loyalty to Freya, who continued to worship her and exert his all at her side, to ask to leave her side…patron goddess that she was, there was no way she would not be intrigued.

"Where do you plan to go?"

"The Dungeon."

The answer was plain and simple. And it seemed Freya had antic-ipated it, since she smiled without showing any surprise.

"Before this, you went on an expedition by yourself, going all the way to the forty-ninth floor, was it? You were quite ragged when you came back, as I recall. You don't imagine I'd allow a similar attempt, do you?"

In order to avoid becoming rusty, Ottar would work in some training from time to time. It had been a long time ago at this point, but for his last training session he had gone by himself on an expedi-tion into the Dungeon to reach the lowest floor he could alone.

His failure to finish off the floor boss Balror in Moitra Sands on the forty-ninth floor was still a shameful memory and a stain that he wanted to clear someday, but that was not his goal this time.

"The thirty-seventh floor's Monster Rex...I would like to defeat Udaeus."

That request was apparently not in the realm of what Freya was imagining, though. She was not particularly surprised, but her lips curled in amusement.

"When the sword princess defeated Udaeus, it had a certain sword equipped. I would like to obtain that."

Three months ago, Aiz Wallenstein's great achievement, defeating the floor boss of a deep level by herself, had made waves in the city. At the time, it had been the talk of the town, and Aiz had risen up to Level 6 herself off the back of it.

In all the histories of Orario, there were no records of Udaeus hav-ing a sword. The Guild's announcement based on Aiz's report was that it was possible that the drop item Udaeus Black Sword could spawn in the event of facing Udaeus one-on-one or possibly with a very low number of people.

Ottar was saying that he very much wanted to get his hands on that extremely rare item. As a Level 7, the strongest adventurer, there were very few weapons capable of withstanding his strength. Because of that, he wanted to acquire it.

"Liar."

However, Freya immediately rejected his excuse. Her silver eyes could see his true feelings.

"It inspired you, didn't it? Your heart lit up when you heard about her feat."

" … "

"You're always like that. Even having reached Level Seven, you're still not satisfied."

Ottar did not say anything. And Freya did not challenge that. The beautiful goddess smiled as she accepted her follower's request.

"Very well, you may go."

However, she placed a single condition on his journey.

"Make sure you come back strong enough for me to dream about."

Having been picked up by Freya, Ottar did not immediately join the ranks of the goddess's followers.

He only received her blessing several years later, after he had clearly established a sense of his self. Until then, Freya would take care of him from time to time—probably because there was something about his soul that caught her attention. But the toddler Freya had named Ottar did not cry or laugh. He merely trotted along behind the goddess without any trace of cuteness. Apparently even Freya had shrugged at his behavior, describing it as disappointing.

After receiving Freya's blessing, it was two years before Ottar rose to Level 2.

However, between when he received Falna and when he began fighting—when he first immersed himself in that never-ending struggle—there was actually a blank period, so in truth, it had only actually taken him one year to level up. Ottar could still be called a boy when he gradually began to stand out from the rest of the familia.

"*Uoooooooooooooooooooooooooooooooooo!*"

Ottar roared with a deep voice unbefitting his age and size as he underwent the familia's baptism.

The fierce internal conflict. The pinnacle of cutthroat death matches. He and the rest of Freya's followers fought on the fields of Folkvangr that were unchanged to this day. He swung a sword the length of his body, lashing out at people far older, larger, and most importantly, incomparably stronger, only to be blown away and left coughing up blood every day.

As Ottar remembered it, the baptism in those days was more intense than at any other time.

—*Why are you fighting?*

It was not a question that anyone ever asked him, nor one that he asked himself. He had no room for any shred of doubt. It was really quite simple: There was nothing else Ottar could do.

He had received a name, a blessing, food, clothes, a roof over his head, emotions, and warmth from Freya. She was everything to him. Taken to the extreme, from the day she picked him up, his entire world had been made whole through her existence alone.

With his unsociability and simplicity, he could not please Freya. There was nothing he could give her in return. So all he could do was strive for power. Strength. He had nothing but his strength. He could do nothing but strive to be stronger. Because Freya desired peerless brilliance.

The roots of the warrior who sought strength with a tireless, ceaseless devotion were exceedingly simple. His foundational memories were of that cold moonlit night when he encountered the goddess and of Folkvangr consumed by the Einherjar's savage, restless battle. The shimmering, twilight plains were like a beautiful, golden sea, despite the countless weapons sticking out of the ground.

"Not dead yet, are ya?"

"...Mia."

His body was battered and beaten, covered in wounds, and one eye was swollen shut as he lay facing the sky. This was back when he spent a lot of time seeing the darkness spreading through the sky from the east. It was a given that the only person who would bother to talk to Ottar was a certain dwarf.

Mia Grand. She was at least twenty years older than Ottar, one of the members of the familia before he joined. At the time, she had a more dwarflike stature, was cute and lovely, and—ga-ha-ha-ha. Anyway, she had a figure worthy of being called a follower of a goddess of beauty. However, despite appearances, her personality was both strong-willed and straightforward. Her presence in the familia was less a heroine and more a plucky mother figure.

She had apparently been asked by Freya to keep an eye on Ottar to make sure he did not die.

"A right pain in my ass," she would say as she grabbed the unmoving Ottar by the collar and dragged him to the manor.

Mia was special, even among their familia. She did not revere Freya. And Freya, for her part, treated Mia as almost an equal in some respects.

Apparently Mia had been working in a tavern in a certain part of town and been scouted by Freya and grudgingly dragged into the familia. She must have owed Freya for something, because she had thrown in her lot with the familia despite very obviously not being particularly interested in it.

With that sort of background, the one and only member of the familia who did not fight for the sake of Freya had a lot of enemies. But she silenced them all with a single fist.

There was no counting the number of times familia members had immediately pounced when she entered Folkvangr only to just as immediately get sent flying themselves. Given a chance, the mountain of people she could pile up was unbelievable.

She was just too strong. So much so it was inspiring. And Freya herself quite enjoyed Mia's actions. Ottar could not believe his eyes the time he saw Freya holding her stomach in pain from the laughter when she heard Mia's war stories.

"All right, hurry up and eat, you numbskulls!"

"""………Seconds, please.""""

And more than anything, the food Mia served was exquisite.

The familia members who had been fighting from dawn to dusk all gathered in the enormous Sessrúmnir hall at the center of the home and silently wolfed down Mia's cooking and booze. Whenever Ottar reminisced about back then, he found himself thinking that her food might as well have been the reason the members at the time were able to restore themselves in order to continue facing the most intense baptism in the history of the familia, and how unfortunate were the familia members nowadays who still had the unceasing death matches but did not have Mia's food.

Mia Grand was just plainly, simply, and overwhelmingly strong. She rose to the top as if it were the most obvious thing in the world. She was a being who existed in a realm far beyond where the Ottar of that time could even imagine.

Before anyone really noticed, Mia had easily become the head of the familia.

"What do I have to do in order to surpass you?" Ottar had asked her once, before he had even gone through puberty.

It was late at night, and he had not been able to return to the home because he had passed out in the field. Mia was out on the moon-lit plains, heating up a pot—apparently people not eating was the thing that most annoyed her—stirring up a stew with her ladle as he stared fixedly at her with his battered body.

The question from the boy who was still lacking in knowledge and experience, who could by no means be called a warrior yet, drew a single glance from Mia, who continued to prepare the food.

"Think."

"Think...?"

"Far as I'm concerned, I couldn't care less about gettin' stronger, but no matter what I'm doin' I always try to think about it. As best I can as a silly little dwarf, at least."

"..."

"Folks who can't think can't live. That's true no matter the time or the place, but it goes double for Orario nowadays with so many monsters all in one spot."

Mia's response was simple.

It was by no means the answer that Ottar was looking for at the time. However, Mia's simple advice took root deep in his heart.

"And if after thinkin' it through, you still can't understand somethin', then the first thing to do is ask. If you don't, you'll never learn anything. At least in my experience."

Mixing in some spices and then lifting the ladle to check the flavor, Mia grinned as she served up a wooden bowl filled to the brim with stew.

"Well, in the plainest sense, though…folks who don't eat won't ever get stronger or grow up."

Ottar quietly looked at the bowl she held out and silently accepted it. The rising steam warmed his eyes and nose as he helped himself to the fragrant stew.

That day, Ottar finished off the entire pot of stew by himself. And from that day on, he started eating so much that Freya's eyes went wide at the sight, all in order to develop a physique adequate for a heroic warrior.

"Mia, are you really going to leave the familia?"

"I'm talking about someday. Not now. Besides, that goddess won't totally throw me out on my ass. Though I'm sure I'll end up sighing in my mind when she comes a-callin'."

"…Don't go. I still haven't beaten you yet," Ottar asked with a subdued, deeper voice.

Around the time his voice had started to deepen, Ottar had already passed Mia in height.

He had heard from Freya that Mia would end up leaving the familia someday, but his desire to stop her from leaving was not because they were comrades. Yes, far from it. But she was still necessary in order to achieve the strength he could envision. He needed to surpass her no matter what.

"What's the point in gettin' hung up on me, idiot. Look at the world around ya. The only thing that's grown about you is that body of yours."

"…"

His relationship with Mia was a bit of an odd one. It could not really be called a maternal sort of relationship nor were they really equals as comrades in arms. Their connection did not really go beyond the realm of associates. Forced to describe it in words, it was probably more like an adult listening to a child's self-indulgent complaints.

As Ottar fell silent, Mia swung around, and a grin appeared on her beautiful and sweet face.

"Besides, there'll be swarms of folks chasing you after this, just like you're chasing after me."

Leaving the silver manor that resembled the moon, Ottar departed the familia's home to head toward the Dungeon and easily passed through the middle levels.

He had the greatsword that was his weapon, a lightweight armor that was a bit on the heavier side, and a knapsack filled with rations and water. That was the only equipment he brought with him.

The scene of the Warlord heading through the Dungeon caused many to fall back and open the way for him, and others got excited as they looked on from afar. It was rare for him to head into the depths of the Dungeon equipped for a stay in the labyrinth, since he was always attending to his patron goddess. Reports of "I saw Ottar!" became the talk of Rivira, the relay town on the eighteenth floor.

For better or worse, the appearance of the city's strongest being and adventurer caused the monsters to become restless, forcing them to clear out. The monsters that could not comprehend their difference in strength and just attacked on instinct crumbled to dust with a single blow from his sword, leaving behind a trail of ash in Ottar's wake.

Neither monsters nor people could stop his advance.

—At least that was how it should have been.

"..."

When he reached the water metropolis that started at the twenty-fifth floor, he ran down the Great Falls, the largest waterfall in the labyrinth that cut down to the twenty-seventh floor. After landing at the bottom, Ottar started to proceed to the passage to the twenty-eighth floor when he noticed a certain presence and silently turned around.

He was standing on the edge of the basin at the bottom of the falls when a catman wielding a silver spear appeared before him.

"Allen…"

And not just him. The four prums in full battle armor and a dark elf appeared, surrounding Ottar on the beach.

"…A message from Lady Freya?"

Had something happened aboveground, was the question implicit in Ottar's tone.

"You aren't that stupid, Ottar," Allen responded quietly.

It was rare for Allen's voice to be so soft, but his gaze was far from kind. His eyes were blazing with a thirst for battle unlike ever before.

"Hee-hee-hee-hee…If an even more refined blade is the paradise the world desires, then we too won't stop until we reach that same realm…"

Translation: If polishing oneself through combat is the tacit agreement of the familia, then it applies to us first-tier adventurers as well. Needless to say, Hegni had a more dangerous air about him than usual as well.

The intense intra-familia struggle was not something reserved for just the lower-level members. It was of course obvious that Allen and the other first-tier adventurers were also constantly reaching for ever greater heights out of their devotion to Freya. There was nothing strange about the fact that they would want to drag down Ottar, who was the strongest not just in the city but in the familia as well.

For the core of the familia, fighting aboveground—the day-to-day baptism of *Freya Familia*—was off-limits. It was a measure put in place to avoid provoking other factions unnecessarily.

However, Freya had never said anything about fighting in the Dungeon. And this time, unlike when he trained the minotaur previously, his trip to the Dungeon was not at Freya's behest for the purposes of conditioning a certain boy.

Because of that, they could fight.

"Wait. At least save it for after. Right now, I—"

"Silence, Ottar. As her followers, we're not content to always be scurrying around beneath your feet. That is unacceptable. We're going to defeat you and surpass you."

The prum Alfrik cut Ottar off, and his younger brothers chimed in, too, not taking kindly to him looking down on them from his position as a Level 7.

"Quit stalling, boar."

"You're a perfect-sized serving of experience."

"Yum, look at all that excelia."

"…" It was about time for even Ottar to get angry.

"Let's do this. Today's the day I'm gonna tear you down," Allen said.

The first-tier adventurers were raring for battle, and Ottar dropped his knapsack. His expression was unchanged. Anger, sadness, bitterness—none of those emotions were visible as he merely readied his weapon to respond to their challenge.

The cat, dark elf, and prums charged in all at once.

Turning back time a bit.

Ottar had trained his body and spirit through the daily baptisms, fostered a repertoire of techniques and tactics through a diligent study and consideration, and constructed a body of steel by eating an awe-inspiring amount of Mia's homemade food every day, transforming him into a powerful man.

At the age of seventeen, he had become the undisputed second-in-command of the familia. He was Level 5. However, more so than his own developments, what changed was his relation to his surroundings.

He had already met his fated rivals—perhaps inescapable acquaintances would be more accurate—the three leaders of *Loki Familia*, and they were already competing ruthlessly. At home, Hegni and Hedin, who would become core members in the future, joined *Freya Familia*. And then the Gulliver brothers. And finally Allen and his little sister. Chosen by the goddess, they demonstrated the capacity of heroes as they achieved level-ups at a similar or even faster rate than Ottar had.

Mia had already left the familia by that time. In the end, he was never able to settle things with her, but he understood what she had said before she left. Somewhere along the way, Ottar had gone from being the challenger to the goal.

Hegni and Hedin, the Gulliver brothers, and Allen were chasing after him like he was their mortal enemy. They were forging themselves for the goddess's sake just as he had in the past, racing toward greater heights, determined to overcome Ottar and teamwork be damned. It was so bad that once, when they had gone on an expedition to the deep floors, they ignored the monsters, and the eight of them started fighting one another instead. The expedition ended up being a failure, of course, and even Freya could not help sighing heavily at the result, so ever after, they all practiced self-restraint so that a similar situation would never happen again. But it was only ever that: self-restraint.

Orario was already in the depths of its darkest period, and he passed through the Labyrinth City's dark age with them. There were many meetings and farewells. All of the members of the familia from before Ottar joined had died. Allen's little sister had disappeared from his side. They had all been cast aside during the hero's trials.

That was how *Freya Familia*'s strongest core and greatest assets in battle were formed. Ottar and the current generation were without a doubt the strongest Einherjar in the familia's history.

And without realizing it, Ottar had become the head of the familia. Truly without realizing it. He threw himself into fighting so much that he was not even really aware of himself as the leader of the familia. However, even if his position changed, the path he was walking down did not. What he needed to accomplish was the same as it ever was.

He honestly, simple-mindedly, pathologically, even foolishly chased after ever greater strength. And Allen, the Gullivers, and Hegni and Hedin, they all ferociously chased after him. However, while he felt quite bad about it, more so than most anything else—they did not register in Ottar's eyes at all.

He showed them respect, but they were only ever presences behind Ottar. And his eyes were only ever focused on what was in front of him. On the age that had already passed.

One day, a dumbfounded young familia member, a healer who was entrusted with the cleanup after the daily baptism, who often looked exhausted, asked him, "What's even the point of getting stronger than you already are?"

It was a stupid question. A truly foolish thing to ask. But it would have been rude to point that out to her. Because she did not know any better.

Yes, everyone hailed Ottar as the pinnacle. They all feared him as the strongest. Not realizing that that name itself just spurred on his fighting spirit. Not realizing that he was seething, not seeing the magma-like emotions in the depths of his heart hidden behind his boulder-like, solid-steel exterior and unflappable demeanor.

Apparently someone once said that the life of a warlord is far harsher and far more dazzling than anyone else's.

Ottar's response was simply:

"Don't make me laugh."

Mia and his rivals—those three leaders—they were probably the only ones who understand how he felt.

"Damn it!" Allen's interspersed his deadly dance with vehement curses.

Ottar easily parried the silver spear thrusts aimed at his neck using his greatsword.

A hole had been opened in the wall of the waterfall basin. The aftershock of a magic blast had created a giant opening leading into the labyrinth right next to the Great Falls, so the first-tier adventurers had shifted their battle to a more expansive room—a broad crystal hill surrounded by a current of water. The clusters of crystals growing around the room flickered.

The six figures moved at a speed the average person could not hope to follow, their movements reflected in the room's many crystals. The poor monsters foolish enough to mistake them for prey were either knocked back the moment they entered the battlefield or else shredded to pieces.

"...Nrgh!"

And standing at the center of that broad hill, that island, was Ottar, fending off the others' attacks. The cat was moving fast enough to leave afterimages as he unleashed a rain of spear thrusts, the dark elf had already used *Dáinsleif* to transform into the king of battle and was splitting the ground with his intense slashes, and the four prum brothers were using their peerless teamwork to attack from any and all directions without pause. The boaz warrior was exposed to a fearsome torrent of blows from six first-tier adventurers.

However, it was Allen and the other attackers who could not conceal their irritation as they continued the assault.

The silver spear that barely registered to the eyes as a fleeting slash was deflected with a single arm's gauntlet, the black sword brimming with destructive power was swept aside by a single swing of his greatsword, and the four weapons flying in from the front, back, left, and right were knocked down by an arc drawn by that same greatsword.

The attackers scowled.

There were scratches here and there on Ottar's rocklike skin, but his body had not sustained any sort of real damage.

Allen leaped forward, ready to kill as Ottar fended them off with a single sword.

"You're too light. You should eat more, Allen."

"What are you, my mom? Fuck off and die!"

The intercepted spear, and Allen with it, were blown away like a feather in a gale. The cat howled in rage as he flew through the air, twisting his body to land on a crystal pillar only to leap off with so much force that cracks started to form on the crystal. But faced with a tremendous thrust that pierced through the atmosphere itself, Ottar dodged by merely twisting his body.

The silver spear split the air and pierced the hill, the force of the impact leaving a crater and sending fragments of crystal flying through the air. As the fragments fell, disrupting Ottar's field of view, a split second after the boaz warrior squinted his eyes, the Gulliver brothers attacked, not overlooking the smallest of openings.

"Don't block it!" "Don't deflect it!" "What's the point of a surprise attack?!" "Don't warp space-time with that muscle of yours!"

"I'm not doing anything like that."

Ottar ably defended against the simultaneous attack in an instant while responding sincerely to Grer's comment.

As the four brothers readied a combination attack from low to the ground, so low that Ottar's attacks could not even reach, the boaz lowered his hips in order to deal with all four of them.

"You rely too much on your height to attack from below. Take the top, too. If you don't, you won't be able to make full use of your stature."

"I see you've got it easy enough to be handing down advice!"

"Are you looking down at us, Ottar?!"

"Not in the least. Just that if you increase the height of your attacks, the range of patterns you can use will increase dramatically."

""""You've just made an enemy of every prum in the world.""""

"…My apologies."

All light disappeared from the brothers' eyes as a never-before-seen intent to kill came loose, causing Ottar to apologize genuinely.

The prums formed their sure-kill formation and charged from all four directions. Their desperation attacks from all directions were fierce enough to be able to threaten the warrior. Faced with an attack of rage that would kill him instantly if he made even a single mistake, Ottar made a split-second decision to stomp his left leg down. The resulting tremor demolished the hill and blew away the Gulliver brothers' small bodies.

"*By the power of the demon blade, bring eternal destruction.*"

And immediately afterward, a super-short cast cut in from the side.

"*Burn Dáin.*"

An eruption of flame poured from Hegni's outthrust right arm. It was a short-range explosive fire spell, but in exchange, it had been honed to have a destructive force capable of incinerating countless enemies within its area of effect. The black magic circle at Hegni's feat caused the crimson blaze to flash even brighter—but Ottar just swung his greatsword upward from below, with a full swing.

"*Oooooooooooooooooooooooooooooh!*"

"Ghhh!"

The sound of metal scraping against metal resounded, drowning out the giant waterfall's thunderous cascade. Ottar used the force of his swing to extinguish the blaze and then shifted the momentum of the blade for a second slash to greet the dark elf who had charged in behind his magic. The greatsword he had swung back down clashed against the dark sword's blade, blocking Hegni's two-stage attack.

"Incarnation of power...to think I would fail to cut down that giant frame with my secret technique. You truly are the being who stands at the pinnacle of the demon realm, Ottar!"

"Speak a language I understand, Hegni."

While they locked blades, Ottar exchanged words with Hegni, who was speaking with a different tone and glare than usual. He then swung his greatsword aside. Losing in power, Hegni leaped backward and landed on top of a cluster of crystals.

In the blast from the blaze, the front of Ottar's armor and his skin had been a bit charred, but he still had not taken any serious damage.

He had endured, not yielding in the slightest to the string of intense attacks.

The ultimate defense. Ottar was feared by most for the attacks he could unleash using his unnatural strength, but Allen and the others knew that his true claim to fame lay in his defense.

His defense was the summation of all the techniques and tactics he had built up over the years. An unwavering stout pair of legs, the defensive movement to deal with any attack with milin-level precision, and trained eyes capable of seeing through any and all techniques. All of that combined with his extreme endurance ability and he was capable of weathering attacks like an immovable fortress. As evidenced by the fact that he had not been forced from the center of the island throughout that entire onslaught.

The attackers voiced their frustration as they readied themselves to try to dismantle his perfect defense again.

In truth, there were six opponents. If the Gulliver brothers were not the only ones working together, if Allen and Hegni worked with the prums, then even Ottar would probably have been cornered. He would have been forced to use the ace up his sleeve. But they made no effort at all toward teamwork.

"Piss off, prums! Don't get in my way!"

"That's our line, kitty-cat." "Quit chasing your tail!" "You're the real brat here!" "Die in a fire!"

"Your squabbling is unsightly, warriors. You vex me! Begone from my sight!"

Allen lashed out at Dvalinn and Grer with his spear when they got in his way, Berling and Alfrik counterattacked, and Hegni tried to cut them all down, along with Ottar, using the far-reaching slash of his cursed blade.

Freya Familia's first-tier adventurers would accept nothing other than a one-on-one. They poured their all into defeating Ottar with their individual strengths. Because to do otherwise would not grant them a victory worthy of a follower of the goddess. None of them had a resolve so half-baked as to try to defeat the strongest through cooperation. And because of that, the fight turned into a battle royale. There were countless flashes of steel everywhere. Sparks and remnants of magic never stayed put for more than a split second. If any other adventurers saw what was happening, it would be a scene that crushed whatever pride they might have in their abilities. This was an intense battle where everyone was trying to strike one another down.

And amid that all, Ottar continued to defend and endure everything. Allen, who attacked with an unparalleled speed; the Gulliver brothers using their teamwork to the utmost; and Hegni, who unleashed incomparable slashes and magic—Ottar rejected it all with his greatsword.

"—I'm gonna run you down."

And then, Allen's desire to kill reached its limit and he lowered his body. What was coming next would be the fastest strike. The brothers' and Hegni's faces tensed as, for the first time, Ottar shifted to a stance to use his full strength to defend. If he did not defend the next attack perfectly, he would be killed. Allen was about to unleash his ultimate attack that would trample everything that stood before him.

As Allen's magic rose, Ottar readied himself to respond with his blade—but just before the attack came—

"Strike forever, indestructible lord of lightning."

Valiant Hildr. The spell's name resounded, accompanied by a thunderclap and a bright flash that lit up the battlefield.

"""!"""

The giant bolt of lightning caused not just Ottar and Allen but even the Gullivers and Hegni to widen their eyes in surprise and leap backward. The lightning split the battlefield down the middle and caused the water to boil as it easily cut through the crystal hill.

The island was half-destroyed, stormy waves rose, and water mixed with lightning scattered about the room. Ottar and the rest turned to look as an elf wielding a rhomphaia appeared through the hole they had opened earlier.

"Stop fighting, you fools."

Freya Familia's only other first-tier adventurer, Hedin, released his magic circle as he stepped into the room.

"What are you trying to pull, coming late to the party?!"

""""""What's with the 'stop fighting' bit, you smug elf?!""""""

"Fall back, rival of mine. As Allen said, one who would enter late has no right to call themselves a warrior and thus no standing to join this melee."

As they all responded in their own ways, Hedin sighed as if in his heart of hearts he could not be any more annoyed than he already was, eventually pulling a letter from his breast pocket.

"A dispatch from Lady Freya."

"!"

"It reads, 'Don't make problems for Ottar.' Would you like to confirm it was written in her hand?"

The letter Hedin held up fluttered slightly as they stared at it with wide eyes.

Ottar had guessed it while watching their exchange, but while Allen and the others had left first to challenge him, Hedin had received the order from Freya to stop the fight.

"He was granted permission to challenge the floor boss by Lady Freya herself. Not allowing him to do so would be equivalent to betraying her divine will. What are you idiots getting so worked up about?"

"""""""Ghhhhhh…!"""""""

"Learn something from the incident with the expedition. If you want to please Lady Freya, then at least think it through a bit first, fools."

Allen and the other attackers twisted up their faces as Hedin made a point of hammering on them for their intelligence, or rather, their lack of it. In fact, veins were starting to become visible on their temples, and they looked about ready to burst. And while they were at a loss for words, Hedin just snorted.

"…How did you know we were here?"

"With you sending tremors through the entire Water Metropolis, there's no way to not notice. The other adventurers all ran away thinking there might be a new species of monster that had appeared and started running wild."

When Hedin pointed out that the aftereffects of their battle had been felt even three floors away, there was not really much more to say. Hedin looked exasperated as he walked toward Ottar and tossed him an elixir.

"I know you don't need it, but I'm sure this was more exhausting for you than fighting Udaeus will be."

"My apologies, Hedin."

"...I would have liked to become a giant fool and strike you down, too, Ottar."

The elf furrowed his brow dramatically as he said that. As if, at times like this, in the depths of his heart, he was jealous of the fools he despised.

And just like that, battle between the first-tier adventurers came to an abrupt end due to their goddess's will. Allen and the others looked on with dissatisfaction as Ottar departed without saying anything. Emerging from the hole, he returned to the basin and headed down to the next floor.

In order to reach his target from there, it would take Ottar half a day. He had lost some time dealing with Allen and them, though, so he walked a little bit faster.

He crossed straight through the second safety point and passed through two more regions, leaving the lower floors behind and heading into the deep levels.

The thirty-seventh floor, the White Palace.

A region composed of just one floor, it was the final border set by the Guild, a true deadline. However, despite it being the most dangerous region of the Dungeon, there was still nothing that could stop his stroll. Lizardman elites, loup-garous, skull sheep, spartoi—they were all disintegrated by a single slash from his great-sword. Warrior- and undead-type monsters could not even slow his advance as he broke through them.

It was instant death on encounter.

Anyone who could not do at least that much would be unable to solo-play the depths of the Dungeon. But by that same logic, it meant that because Ottar could do that much, he could proceed through the deep floors by himself without having anyone worry about him and without having to borrow anyone's strength. Even overwhelming numbers were not enough to be a challenge for Ottar in this region of the Dungeon. In fact, dealing with magic stones that dropped in order to avoid a repeat of the terrible blood-drenched troll incident—where an enhanced species was born of stones left lying around—was the more time-consuming effort. He would carefully aim for the core with his attacks to turn basically the entire monster along with its core to ash, but the monsters that died in the shock wave of his slash had to have their magic stones crushed underfoot.

The marble labyrinth trembled as he dominated the dim darkness that was supposed to pressure him as he proceeded into the depths of the thirty-seventh floor.

And finally, he reached it.

"…It's been long enough to feel like it's been a while, huh?"

The throne room. The area at the center of the floor where the staircase to the next floor was, as well as where Ottar's target would appear.

He had stopped in front of a single extra-large room. Unlike the rest of the labyrinth up to that point, the phosphorescence was bright enough to see clearly there. Overhead, the ceiling was high enough to not be visible, just like the rest of the floor.

There were no traces of a monster there. It seemed as if it was just a wide-open space, but then there was a crackle.

"It's here…"

As if Ottar's arrival had been the catalyst, the cracks started running through the floor. The deep fissures radiating out from the center of the space were accompanied by a large tremor. It was as if the Dungeon itself were crying out as it gave birth to its child. The next second, an enormous pitch-black body broke through the ground. White marble scattered around as its full form appeared.

The skeleton king roared out.

"—OOOOOOOOOOOOOOOOOOOOOOOOOOOOOOOOOOO!"

The Monster Rex, Udaeus.

The pinnacle of the undead on this floor, it had an overwhelmingly imposing appearance, like a spartoi skeleton monster that had been scaled up. Its lower body was still buried in the ground as vermilion will-o'-the-wisp eyes set in deep black eye sockets focused on the intruder.

It had been exactly three months since Aiz had managed to defeat Udaeus by herself. The interval had passed, and an intruder had appeared to set foot in its room, so it had awakened.

The passage Ottar had entered through was sealed off by pila shooting up out of the ground like spears to block the passage. Until Udaeus was defeated, there was no retreating from that room. The floor master used this room as its execution ground.

However, Ottar never had any intention of retreating.

"I'll have you show me everything that the Sword Princess saw and overcame…"

The powerful and imposing warrior did not look the image of a grave robber, and he did not fall back in the slightest at the skeleton king's roar as he swung his own sword.

The early stages of the battle were entirely one-sided.

Ottar either evaded the pila that had previously been believed to be Udaeus's greatest weapon with a speed at odds with his enormous frame, or else he nullified them by striking the ground with his greatsword before they could burst out. He closed in to the enemy, which caused it to swing its giant right arm at a range when he entered close enough to be hit, but Ottar used his perfect defense to block the brutal attack, much to the floor boss's surprise. His log-like legs dug into the ground a bit as he slid ever so slightly while skillfully wielding his sword to shatter the crystal sphere joints linking together the bones. Udaeus screamed and a thunderous sound rang out from its right wrist upward as the arm fell to the floor.

"Weak."

The truth was that *Freya Familia* had already developed the most efficient way of dealing with Udaeus—though Ottar was basically the only person who could actually pull it off. But he did not use that method. If he defeated Udaeus without laying eyes on the giant black sword Aiz had seen, then he would not get another chance for three more months. Even Ottar had no desire to wait that long. Because of that, he was being careful not to accidentally defeat Udaeus as he cornered it.

The floor boss roared as it summoned spartoi around the room, but that, too, was nothing worth mentioning to Ottar. He crushed them in groups with a single slash or else used the pila shooting out of the floor to lure them to take each other out.

Level 7.

Able to maintain the advantage throughout the fight against the enemy that Aiz had been forced to break through her limits in order to defeat, Ottar had the bearing of one who was the apex of adventurers. His body was much smaller than that of the floor boss, but it possessed a status that easily surpassed the floor boss's. He was like a little giant that did not pale in comparison to a Monster Rex. And the way he repelled those giant arms with a single sword was a testament to that fact while simultaneously producing a mind-bending scene.

The girl who had solo-challenged Udaeus with her Level-6 potential despite only being a Level 5 was worthy of admiration. But if asked whether he could do the same, Ottar would not hesitate to answer that he could. At the very least he could against the Udaeus he knew. The one that did not wield a giant black sword.

Ottar, who had reached this pinnacle with just his own physical body, possessed a strength that was a plain and simple power. Unlike his prum captain rival, he did not have an overwhelming intelligence or instinct, nor the extreme magic of that high elf. And he did not combine the preeminent power and resilience of that old dwarf.

Ottar's true weapons were his body and his mentality. The combination of his unceasing effort and indefatigable conviction brought about a similar or even greater advantage than Aiz's wind. And more than anything, Ottar had a tremendous amount of experience far beyond what Aiz had. He had been through an unbelievable number of situations and overcome a mind-boggling number of predicaments. And he had even experienced the ultimate humiliation, pity. Those were the factors that separated his blade from hers. Those mud-splattered memories were what made Ottar as strong as he was, and a genius and talent combined with not even ten years' worth of hard work could not overcome it.

"_____Gh!"

"!"

As the pitch-black bones were gradually broken and cut away, Udaeus roared in a different tone, as if it had lost its temper. Ottar's eyes narrowed at the long-awaited precursor as it summoned what he had been waiting for.

It kept growing and growing and growing. A particularly large pilum appeared from the ground in front of Udaeus. It had a hilt. It had a six-meder-long blade. It was unmistakably an extremely thick longsword.

"So that's it."

The huge black sword that until that day had only been seen by two other adventurers. It looked smoother than if it had been carved from obsidian and it gave off an alluring light and destructive air. Ottar acknowledged that it was in the highest tier of nature weapons that monsters could wield as Udaeus raised the great black sword over its head.

The shoulder, elbow, and wrist. Each of its joints flashed like burning starts and for the first time in that fight, the adventurer's instincts, the warlord's warning bells, cried out—but Ottar did not attempt to evade the attack.

Instead, he planted both feet and readied his own greatsword. Despite recognizing that it was the enemy's ultimate attack, he chose to face it head-on. The skeleton king mercilessly swung his sword at the fool who would dare to challenge its attack. There was an eruption as the blow landed.

"Guhhhh—?!"

It was an explosion of the enormous amounts of magic poured into its joints combined with the monster's intense power. The two created a destructive ray of light, and that slash was the first thing that caused Ottar's body to move backward. His planted legs slid, leaving two giant gashes in the floor of the room. His breastplate and shoulder armor were entirely blown away by the force of the great black sword, and his body itself was lacerated by the violent force and burned by the high temperature of the magic light. The greatsword he had readied—the first-tier weapon forged by *Goibniu Familia*, cracked under the force of it all.

Looking up, the scene around the room was like a field that had been burned. All of the pila sticking out of the ground had disappeared and the ground inside the attack's area of effect had transformed into a distorted, burned-out empty lot. The spartoi who had been caught up in it were, of course, destroyed and the skeleton king wielding its ultimate weapon ruled over the battlefield with a demeanor of absolute supremacy.

Ottar's perfect defense had not been broken, but his body had not been able to endure the full brunt of it. It could not blunt the force entirely. Several bones had been damaged, but Ottar was most disappointed in his own powerlessness.

"...I'm still green."

Derision. An actual emotion appeared on Ottar's face for once as he felt a burning physical pain for the first time in a very long time.

—*He saw its ultimate attack.*

—*He experienced that taste again.*

—*So there was no way that Ottar—the strongest—could lose now.*

That confident analysis borrowed the voices of various people and deities as it transformed into an illusion ringing in the back of his mind. That vexing title echoed in his ears.

"...Who's the strongest? How could someone this weak be the strongest?"

The warrior's face was twisted. Quietly, deeply twisted.

The skeleton king looked at the battered man before him, unleashing a series of pila from the ground. Ottar made no effort to avoid the swarm charging at him. He did not dodge. His sides, shoulders, and cheeks bled, cut by the pila. Ottar's body was possessed by pain and self-deprecation and an all-consuming rage that transformed into passion. His rust-colored eyes stared sharply at the floor boss. They were looking beyond it, toward memories from the past.

Ottar was glaring at the true strongest, the ones who Ottar was still chasing after.

How weak. How feeble. You can never reach those heights with such a frail body.

Cursing his own weakness, he limply held his sword in his left hand as he clenched his right into a fist with all the strength he could muster.

And then, Ottar opened his mouth. To overcome the being before him. To overcome his memories of the past.

"Silver moon's mercy and the golden plains. I offer this body to the lord of battle."

A chant rang out. Udaeus reacted in surprise at the spell being spun from inside the forest of pila that looked like pitch-black gravestones.

"Charge bearing the goddess's will."

Udaeus unleashed a single pilum cloaked in a flash of light to interrupt Ottar's cast. As it closed in on his forehead, Ottar easily grabbed it with his right hand and crushed it. And then he finished his short-cast. His one and only magic.

"Hildis Vini."

Someone once said the life of a warlord is far harsher and far more brilliant than anyone else's.

Ridiculous. Ottar's life was far from brilliant. Quite the opposite, even. It was filled with dirt and mud, blood and humiliation. It was a series of defeats.

* * *

He had a talent. He had conviction, too. He undoubtedly possessed the potential of a hero. However, there existed monsters far greater than he in his surroundings.

The two greatest factions that, along with the Guild, were so integral to the city ever since its founding.

Zeus Familia and *Hera Familia*.

The thousand years of history—a thousand years of trial by fire—that those two familias had built up poured down on Ottar.

"Gaaaah—?!"

The very first defeat had been a single strike. A hand had clamped down on the top of his head and slammed him into the ground. The man who had shattered the stone pavement while knocking out the Level-3 Ottar had been one of the lowest members of *Zeus Familia*. He apologized for slighting the goddess and then left as if it were nothing.

The next defeat was a single flash. A knife strike that Ottar had not even been able to see had sent his body flying into a dilapidated old home. He only realized he was being petted right before he passed out. That time it had been a core member of *Hera Familia*, a girl even younger than he. The embodiment of talent the likes of which Ottar had never before seen shot him a single glance of utter disappointment before standing up and leaving.

They were the impetus for the most intense trial by fire in *Freya Familia*'s history that was occurring in Folkvangr. No, compared to their baptism, the combat that Ottar and his fellow adventurers underwent on those fields could not even be called that much. It was a charade.

The twin mountains standing before *Freya Familia*, blocking the way. The true embodiment of the strongest.

The followers who had offered themselves up to Freya became desperate in order to clear the stain on their mistress's honor, to bring glory to her. And that thousand-year wall took their lofty sense of duty and easily kicked it to the curb. Zeus's and Hera's followers did not even laugh at them. They just seemed utterly disinterested.

Long, long ago, before she had settled in Orario, Freya had apparently lost to Hera in a conflict. At the time, she had also lost many of her followers.

It was a shock to Ottar. For some reason it felt like his chest would split apart at the very thought. The idea that such dishonor would befall the woman so suited to sitting at the pinnacle of all.

"Apparently she had been asked to scout me by Zeus, in order to get me to help with their machia. For some reason even though she was the one who won, she got all huffy and let her hatred get the best of her...Basically, I got caught up in the farce of a relationship they've had since they were in the heavens."

Freya told him the story once on a whim while she was enjoying some wine in her room.

"I keep my promises, so for a time, I gave up on looking for my Odr, since the deal was that I would help them if I lost. It was my fault for accepting the challenge. Even though it meant inciting an Orario adventurer, I trusted my children too much and misread just how strong that one monster was."

It suited Freya most to be like a whimsical breeze. For her to be tied down was a betrayal of all that she represented. Standing there in confusion, Ottar had asked, "Are you okay with it like this?"

"There's nothing more pathetic than a vengeful goddess. So—after I drag her down from her throne, I intend to dump a glass of wine in her face. And I'll tell her, 'How dare you steal my property from me.'"

She swirled the glass of wine in her hand as she quietly, coolly smiled. Her eyes narrowed. There was a certain intense light in her gaze that even Ottar could see. He clenched his fists and swore to accomplish her will, to clear the blemish that she had received—In the end, Freya never realized her revenge because she lost interest, but that was a story for another day.

Freya was fated to be tied to Orario in order to fulfill the promise she had made. Given that, Ottar and the rest of the familia devoted themselves to turning the land where heroes were born into a throne for her.

And then they continued to lose.

No matter how much they struggled, they could not reach them. There was no end to it. Just how high was the summit that he was trying to reach? It was obvious, really. No matter how rigorous the peak someone climbed, no one thought they would reach the thunder flashing through the sky. And even if their hand did reach it, they would only end up being scorched by the lightning.

It was a hopelessly high summit that would break the will of any normal person, but Ottar did not give up on his goal. Sustaining himself with his indefatigable spirit and a never-ending stream of scorn for his own weakness, Ottar continued to seek strength.

"—Interesting."

He was lying collapsed on the ground as rain fell, but even still, Ottar glared with an unabated blaze in his eyes as he heard the follower of Zeus, the city's strongest—no the world's strongest adventurer, the Level-8 supreme.

"—In another ten years, maybe I'll make you my husband."

Seeing Ottar beaten into the ground in the blazing labyrinth and yet still not having his spirit broken, the follower of Hera, the world's scariest woman, the Level-9 empress, laughed.

They always let Ottar go. Those who turned against them for the sake of their masters would always be crushed, but they never delivered the finishing blow. In fact, just the opposite, they spurred the defeated on with humiliation, as if telling them to become even stronger.

Ottar did not bear a grudge against them. And of course he did not bear any hatred for Freya. No, his murderous intent was directed solely at himself.

How weak. How feeble. What can you hope to catch with such a weak body?

Ottar's ire and hatred of himself elevated an overwhelming determination and tireless quest for strength that spurred him on to greater heights.

That was how the heroic warrior began to take shape. The impetus for all of his level-ups after Level 5 were related to *Zeus Familia* or *Hera Familia*.

The first was fifteen years ago. And the second was seven years ago—

Ottar knew that it was not a fair fight. Scoffing at their own unsightliness after being defeated by the one-eyed dragon and cursing their lack of strength, they had started a fire under Ottar and the rest of the next generation who were frozen in shock, leaving everything to them.

"Surpass us, fledgling heroes."

The city's strongest, the only Level 7. The pinnacle. The Warlord, Ottar.

He had still not even caught up to those strongest adventurers before him. The pure warrior who had sworn his loyalty to the goddess, just as so many others had done, continued to fight as he set off for the pinnacle with a resolve greater than that of anyone else.

In order to become the strongest. In order to surpass them.

A breeze was blowing. A cool, gentle breeze filled with magic that grew into a soft zephyr filling that entire cavern of the labyrinth.

The giant room where the skeleton king lay in a pitiful pile of rubble.

"*Gu...Gaaagh...?!*"

Its right arm was gone, the left side of its head was smashed apart, its jawbone and ribs were broken, too. Having lost so many of its pitch-black bones, Udaeus was struggling to cry out from the lethal blow it had received when its eyes saw it.

The boaz who unleashed that peerless attack was calmly standing there. He glanced at his greatsword that had shattered entirely and then cast it aside.

Sticking out of the ground behind the floor master, knocked back in the final attack, was the great black sword, cracks running through it.

Having lost the king's blade, Udaeus seemed to have run out of strength and its flaming eyes were flickering like a candle in the wind before suddenly extinguishing. The countless bones before Ottar fell to the ground with a deafening clatter. And standing in the middle of the pile of bones was a glimmering giant purple magic stone.

"So you beat it, huh…"

Hearing those words, Ottar turned around. In the distance behind him, Allen and the other first-tier adventurers were standing there. The pila blocking the passage disappeared as the skeleton king collapsed, allowing them to enter the room.

Allen's words did not have any trace of doubt as to what the outcome would be, and Alfrik, Dvalinn, Berling, Grer, Hegni, and Hedin all fixed their gazes on the wounded Ottar.

Their eyes all said the same thing.

—*Someday, I'm going to defeat you and surpass you.*

And standing right beside them was Ottar. The younger Ottar who had attempted to defeat Mia, to defeat Zeus and Hera.

Ottar smiled. The corners of his mouth just curled up ever so slightly, so it could barely be called that, but it was a smile, nonetheless.

And, as if history were repeating itself, he said:

"What's the point in getting hung up on me, fools?"

The report that Udaeus had been defeated was calmly reported to the Guild by *Freya Familia*.

Who could have imagined a consecutive solo conquest? No one at the Guild and no adventurer would have ever dreamed it.

Some time later—

"I forgot to ask, but did you gain anything out of it?"

In the goddess's room in the manor.

Freya's eyes narrowed as she sat in her chair, looking at Ottar, who had returned after finishing his errand.

"I've reaffirmed my own immaturity…and just how far away the summit I'm aiming for is."

Standing before her, Ottar responded with the plain and simple truth. Hearing that, Freya let out a muffled giggle, as if she were struggling to hold it in.

"…What?"

"I mean, you went to the Dungeon in order to get stronger, and yet you came back saying 'I discovered my weakness.'"

That was the truth, though, so Ottar did not say anything in response.

As he stood there clumsily, one ear folded down, Freya's shoulders trembled from her giggles as she pressed her favorite again.

"Did you gain anything else?"

"…This item."

The errand he had finished—picking up the custom sword he had ordered from *Goibniu Familia*. He drew the sword from its sheath on his back.

It was a jet-black sword. The blade was enormous. Ottar was over two meders tall, but it matched his height. A first-tier blade made from the rare drop item Udaeus Black Sword. Ottar held it out flat across both hands and knelt on one knee like a knight as he presented it to her for examination.

"What is its name?"

"If it pleases you, I would like you decide that."

Ottar wished for Freya to have that honor.

Engraving his oath in the blade of the monster that had allowed him to reaffirm his weakness and receiving a name for the blade from the goddess would allow him to become even stronger.

And he would someday surpass that memory of the past.

Freya understood what Ottar was thinking and respected his wish. After thinking for a little while, she said:

"Very well, then—Supreme Black Sword." She smiled as she bestowed a name upon the sword. "I chose it in the hopes that you will someday be able to overcome the past darkness standing across your path."

"You have my gratitude."

He lowered his head deeply before standing up.

As the goddess watched, the warrior who still had not become the strongest lowered his eyes and swore an oath to that black blade.

—*I shall only chase strength, tirelessly and without end.*

Their Various Pasts

Familia Chronicle

chapter

3

1

Allen was always carrying his little sister. After they lost their parents. And after they lost their home. He stubbornly kept walking, carrying his crying sister.

They were strays. Powerless, mewling kittens. The scene around them as they walked was always one filled with ruins.

Later on, he would learn that that place where hollowed out husks and debris spread as far as the eye could see was called the Scrap Heap. That it was the remnants of what had once been the largest country on the continent, which had been destroyed in a single night. That it was not a place where people could live. That it had become inhabited by ferocious monsters.

It was just the other day that they had been living in peace, together with their parents whose faces he could not remember anymore, and yet before he knew it, their home had transformed into ruins. He remembered something shining. And their parents disappearing. And then they were all alone.

"Lost little stray kittens, where is your home?" a headless bronze statue of an animal person asked.

I don't know. I don't even know if a home for us exists. The birds flying in the sky won't tell me anything.

He just continued wandering through the never-ending world of ruins, protecting his little sister, searching for a peace that might not even exist.

The powerless kitten Allen had no choice but to become strong for the sake of his idiot sister. If he did not, he would just get tripped up by her and end up dying himself. Fearsome magic beasts ran rampant in their world. There were those with grotesque figures and fangs and claws as well as hideous humanoid figures. Countless times, Allen fought them. Countless times, Allen killed them. And countless times, Allen grabbed his sister's hand and ran away from them.

They were constantly pelted by rain. There was never a day where the ashen gray clouds covering the sky cleared up. There was never a day that they were not faced with the sight of blood. And there was never a day that his little sister stopped crying.

His sister, who was starved for familial love, got on Allen's nerves countless times. He was always getting annoyed by her feeble fingers clinging to his clothes. He had lost count of how many times he had considered just casting her aside. He did not know how many times he had thought of swinging his fist down to knock her hands away. And he could not remember the number of times he had started to leave her behind only to have his heart give in.

But still, despite all that, Allen continued to carry his little sister, coughing up blood as she slept in exhaustion from all her crying.

The turning point came two years after their home had been turned to a mountain of rubble, when Allen was six years old.

The wind blew. It was the breeze of a capricious goddess.

"Come with me."

The goddess looking down at the two kittens simply held out her hand. Her body was hidden behind a robe, but even then, she was beautiful.

His little sister was captivated by the goddess, but also scared of her. The kitten's instincts were crying out that she might lose something precious.

And Allen, captivated by those silver eyes, found himself comparing his little sister to the goddess standing before him.

A crybaby and irredeemable idiot who was painfully bad at singing, who constantly annoyed Allen, who was weak.

After looking at his teary-eyed sister—Allen took the goddess's hand.

2

There was nothing they wanted.

The brothers were all individually skilled enough that they could make a huge variety of things with their capable hands, and they used the excuse of being prums to give up on most things.

The four Gulliver brothers were born in an industrial city. Their parents died early, but with what knowledge the four of them could muster, it was possible, albeit difficult, to make a living.

Their faces were identical, and their personalities…well, they were pretty much the same, too. The eldest had it slightly worse perhaps, but it was not like they did not get along with each other.

In order to make a living, the Gulliver brothers naturally became craftsmen. They were always covered in soot, wearing aprons and thick gloves. When they walked home after going shopping at the end of the day, the four of them often looked up at the evening sky muddied by the black smoke rising from all the workshops' smokestacks large and small and thought, *That looks disgusting*.

Having become craftsmen, the four brothers were able to make most anything a client might order if they worked together— beautiful bracelets, splendid earrings, and even tasteful gold- and silverwork, too. They never realized it themselves, but they had started to become known as the greatest craftsman in the city, the phantom master craftsman Gulliver, as if they were all just one person.

There was a reason they were called "phantom," though. Some crazy human or goddess or—anyway, someone with their own dangerous ideas tried to kidnap Alfrik because he had a cute face or something, so after that they did their best not to go walking around outside. After all, if someone tried to kidnap Alfrik, then that meant the other brothers who all looked exactly the same might be targets, too. They started holing up in a workshop carved out of a cliff that was little more than just a cave. Even if they were prums, they still did not want to have anything stolen from them.

Their workshop in the cliff was always dim. Without their naturally good vision as prums, they would not have been able to live there at all.

However, the four brothers always knew what the others were thinking. When they called out to each other, it was mostly just grunts like "Hey" or "Uh" and the responses that came back were just as short, "Yeah" or "Sure" and the like. Nothing that could really be called a conversation. Horrifyingly (amazingly?), there were times where they would go a whole day without saying anything because of their mutual understanding.

They just quietly went about their lives, filling the orders that came from the dwarf master who was their intermediary. But of course, the better the craftsman, the farther the craftsman's name would spread. The name Gulliver started to make waves even in the surrounding cities. So if you take a long enough view of it, they had actually been the masters of their fate.

"Were you the ones who made this necklace?"

One day, a goddess visited their workshop carved into the cliff. She had happened across one of the master craftsman Gulliver's works by chance, taken an interest in its gorgeous handiwork, and tracked down the place where the phantom brothers lived.

The four brothers froze. They had literally never laid eyes on such a beautiful being before in their lives, but it was as much because she had appeared at their dirty workshop and home. They awkwardly prepared tea for the goddess, and the goddess giggled as she watched them stiffly move around the workshop.

While the four brothers sat in their chairs, engrossed by her beauty, the goddess explained why she was there.

She talked about how she had a residence in the Labyrinth City, but from time to time, she would leave the city and go out in search of encounters—it was not until later that they learned that what she was looking for from those encounters was talented people the likes of which could not be found in Orario, in order to find souls suitable to be her Einherjar. And this time, she had happened to come across one of the Gulliver brothers' works during her journey and had taken an interest in its creator because of its wonderful construction. To have such an appraisal from such a beautiful goddess was an honor, of course, but they were caught between confusion and a desire to dance for joy. And if one of them lost his head, the other three would, too. The goddess's eyes narrowed as she smiled at the sight of the amusing brothers' telepathic link working even in times like that. As if she were embracing the radiance of their souls.

"Do you not have any interest in the world outside?"

The four brothers glanced at one another before responding to the goddess's question.

"We do. And we've thought before that we would like to go on a trip outside."

"But we're just prums and not yet master craftsmen, either."

"If we just up and left, we could never make it up to our master, who has always found jobs for us."

"And our dwarf master would surely never give us permission to leave."

The dwarf master who had walled them off was not a very good person. Recognizing their talent, he kept them hidden away and treated them unfairly because they were prums. Unfortunately, perhaps because of their own low evaluation of themselves as prums, the Gulliver brothers did not realize just how small their world was and how unfairly they were being treated.

After they finished, a smile slowly spread across the goddess's face.

"I would like a necklace made by you. Could you please do that for me?"

They leaped to their feet, readily accepting her request. When asked how long they would need, they responded, filled with determination. *Five days*, they said. *No we'll get it done in four!*

After she left the workshop, the brothers held hands and danced a little rondo.

Someone wanted us specifically!

She thought so highly of our skill!

Not just anyone! A goddess as beautiful as that!

Who knew such a wonderful thing could happen!

The prums were not greedy. In fact, they were utterly unselfish. They were so pure that the goddess's praise alone satisfied them so much they might have died. That was why they did not realize that they were always being exploited by such a greedy person.

Left to themselves, they might have never stopped dancing, but once the eldest brother spoke up, they immediately started work on the necklace. They used the precious gold that they had been holding on to for a special item for the casting, and they concentrated and poured their all into a delicate design. Sure they were creating their ultimate masterpiece, they decided to name it Bringar.

Four days later.

They were in high spirits, but the one to visit their workshop was not the goddess but their dwarven master.

"You guys are free to go now."

Huh? Doubt was visible on their faces as a lecherous grin spread across the dwarf's face.

"That goddess offered me a better deal than keeping you. Four nights' worth, one for each of ya. Ha-ha-ha! I could die a happy dwarf now."

The goddess had approached the dwarf for negotiations. She had wanted them to be released. And what the rapacious dwarf had wanted in return was not money or prestige but the goddess herself.

At that time, the Gulliver brothers, all four of them, felt a knot forming in their stomachs. Their minds went blank as a single desire consumed them. Without exchanging any words or signaling anything to each other, they dragged the dwarf into their lair with perfect coordination and butchered him.

Four murderous impulses combined into one in order to erase the wretched scum that had defiled that beautiful goddess.

They raised a fearsome roar from their tiny bodies as they stabbed the dwarf, who should have been stronger than them, over and over and continued to pummel him with hammers and other smithing tools, paying no heed to the dwarf's pained cries as they allowed their rage to take control of them.

The prums certainly were unselfish. However, they were by no means harmless. Their small bodies bore a potential befitting brave warriors that only the goddess had noticed.

"Quit it, Alfrik!"

"How much more broken can he get?!"

"Even we're getting grossed out!"

"Shut up, idiots! I'll never forgive this scummy piece of shit! I'm gonna murder him! This isn't over until there's nothing left of him! Not even his soul! He still hasn't suffered nearly enough yet for what he did!"

""""S-sorry!""""

And in the midst of that fray, the rage of the eldest brother, Alfrik, was beyond control. They had always been together, but his younger brothers had never known just how intense his wrath could be until that day. He just kept tenaciously hacking away at the body of their master, who had long since succumbed to his horrific wounds. From that day on, the younger brothers swore to never truly enrage their older brother, who was normally left holding the short straw.

"You killed him?"

After it was all over and their fury had passed, the goddess appeared at their workshop, and seeing the walls of the cavern stained crimson red, she looked sad.

"Spending a night with a boring man is a cheap price to pay to get my hands on you."

And then, as the brothers hung their heads, the goddess smiled.

"Because what I really wanted...was you."

The brothers wept. They bawled shamefully, like children. It was something they had never felt since they had lost their parents: the love of another. The goddess's love was equal for the four of them and was such that she had not hesitated at offering herself in order to have them.

The Gulliver brothers swore allegiance to her. In order to repay the goddess's divine will that had spent four nights with that rotten filth for their sakes, they became her followers.

There was nothing that they desired.

But that day, a lust for her favor was born.

The prums who had been so unselfish became covetous, wishing for one single thing:

That one love, and nothing else.

3

Hegni was an incompetent king.

More precisely, he was a dark elf whose only talent was fighting.

In the age of gods, dark elves were rare. In the distant ancient times, when monsters were pouring out of the giant hole and spreading across the land, the dark elves had fought to protect their race's sacred peaks, the Alv Mountains. They were overrun by the countless grotesque beasts, causing their population to shrink dramatically. Meanwhile, the white elves, the lineage considered normal elves in current times, had been led down the Alv Mountains by their high elf at the time who had chosen not to sacrifice them to fight the monsters.

The dark elves cursed the white elves as cowards and disgraces and hoped to one day revive their dark tribe. They dreamed of the day the dark high elf, whose lineage was said to have continued, would rise up and lead them again. And for the sake of that dream, the dark elves—or rather a specific hardheaded group of dark elves who had holed up in a forest—were desperate to take out the white elves in the forest whose tribe was flourishing. Even though they were all still elves, despite the differences in magic and magical ability and skin color.

Hegni was not a high elf, but he was nonetheless chosen as the warrior king of the dark elves' capital. He was not good at dealing with other people. More to the point, he was scared of his fellow elves, who tried to force concepts like pride and self-respect on him in the name of some duty. He was a more sensitive and easily hurt elf by nature. All things being equal, he would have been tragically bullied by his fellow elves.

Fortunately, though—or perhaps unfortunately for him—he had a talent for battle. To an unimaginable degree, the arrows and magic of elves famed as the marksmen of the forest were useless against him. The white elves who faced him cowered while the dark elves who had him on their side were filled with delight.

And because of that, he was exploited.

His clan spent all their time warring with the nation of white elves that lived in the same forest as them. And whenever hostilities broke anew, Hegni was always forced to stand at the head of a host, leading the warriors into battle. If he did not manage to strike down enough enemies, they would hurl abuse at him. And he knew that in the village, there was no end to the sniping at him behind his back. Before he realized it, and rather fittingly considering his personality, Hegni started to feel that the gaze of others was the most terrifying thing in the world.

In the remote, far-off frontiers of the continent, there was a giant lake, and in the middle of it was a forested island of fairies: Heodenings. Unbeknownst to and closed off from the rest of the world, it contained two states, one of dark elves and one of white elves. Isolated from its surroundings, it was a place of continuous battle. The end result of fanatical self-obsession.

Hegni, who did not know where he was in what should have been a wide world, started to think of the mysterious giant forest where the sacred tree and every other tree covered the sky as a graveyard.

And at the same time, he started to despise himself for being so small and so foolish, for being unable to change anything.

And in the end, Hegni started to love the darkness, where he could not be seen by anyone other than himself. The darkness was his one true friend. Kneeling down at the roots of a big tree and letting his worn-down body be embraced by the darkness became a daily routine for him.

And one day, when he was exhausted after a particularly fierce battle, after abandoning himself to the darkness, in a dream or a hallucination, he met a certain witch.

"You've worn down your body and even your soul so much, and yet you don't try to change anything?"

Hegni hugged his knees tightly, looking away as he answered the witch's question.

"I can't change anything, because my determination is weak and I'm trash. I'm scared of all the eyes looking at me in disappointment and blame. I'm scared of being laughed at. I'm embarrassed to keep living. That's why, at the very least…I want to fight and die with my trusted sword."

There was a being who had caught Hegni's interest. The other king, who led the white elves he fought.

Unlike him, that king was handsome and gallant. He had golden hair and a sharp, piercing gaze. The difference between him and Hegni, who was an incompetent king, was like the difference between heaven and earth. The title of king had caused Hegni all sorts of pain, but that white elf who constantly strove to be a proper king was dazzling to him. It made him envious and jealous. Hegni, who was consumed by a sense of inferiority, wanted to win against that man. Even if it meant trading blows, he wanted to run him through with his sword.

After all the fighting that was the only thing left that he wanted.

"I see. Then I shall set you free. Once I do, maybe you'll be able to achieve your dream."

He felt like the witch smiled after she said that. But when Hegni looked up, she was no longer anywhere to be found. He decided that she must have been an illusion he had seen in his exhaustion.

The battle between the fairies that was the pinnacle of unsightliness intensified dramatically after that day. The arrogant pride of the fairies that was on display for all to see demonstrated their true repulsiveness.

—*It was probably inevitable that they would be destroyed by the goddess who so valued beauty.*

Hedin was a young, wise king.

But at the same time, he was a white elf who was an embodiment of the fairies' tendency to look down on everything other than themselves. He appeared intellectual, but his true nature was far more severe.

When enraged, his features warped unattractively, and he would slaughter those who defied him like a merciless tyrant.

Hedin was hailed as the brilliant king of the white elves.

Of course he was not actually a high elf. Hedin understood better than anyone that his title was just the royal fantasies of provincial elves living deep in the woods. But even if it just extended their foolish make-believe longer, once he had been anointed king, he fully understood that if he did not fulfill his duties, his incompetent people would die.

Because Hedin considered himself competent, he did not try to escape his duties as king. Running away would be the same as lowering himself to the level of those trifling fools he most despised. His pride would not allow that.

At present, the source of his concerns, or rather his annoyances, was the dark elves continuing to attack his city. They were true barbarians who lived in the same forest but could think of nothing more than eradicating their own fellow elves. Judging the conflict with them to be the most inefficient use of resources, he restrained the other white elves and sent out a peace envoy. However, the dark elves were single-minded in their response: "We shall reclaim our Hildr."

In the long history of these two elf tribes fighting each other, there had been a single period where they negotiated a temporary non-aggression pact. As proof of their commitment, the dark elves had handed over the holy woman Hildr, a miraculous healer. And Hedin was descended from her.

Even though terms like white and dark are thrown around, to begin with elves were all the same race. Their children's skin color was mixed. And since the dark elf lineage only entered the pool once, it naturally weakened, meaning Hedin had naturally inherited the traits of white elves most strongly. Hedin was Hildr's descendant and thus would forever have her blood. What the dark elves were demanding was nothing more and nothing less than to wring every last drop of blood out of him.

—*Fools.*

Hedin spat back in response. And the negotiations fell apart.

He was fed up with the daily battles. Those puppets of pride and duty seemed to take more joy in fighting one another than they did with dwarves who were supposed to be their natural enemy. They truly never bored of fighting. Because he was the king, Hedin took command in terrific fashion, and wielding the powerful magic that was his birthright, he annihilated the dark elves. He became a symbol of terror to the dark elves while being a powerful leader for the white elves.

While that never-ending battle was raging, ironically, Hedin's talent as well as that of the other king on the dark elves' side continued to grow. They became preeminent powers, despite being trapped in their narrow world. If someone from outside their world saw them, they would not believe that neither of them had received Falna. Their strengths became such that before they knew it, they could no longer be contained by the world that they were trapped in.

Stupid. Stupid. Stupid.

Muttering the same thing over and over in his mind, Hedin had pondered ripping off his crown and casting aside his country more than a few times. And he had lost count of the number of times his face had been warped by the reality that if he did that, his country would be destroyed, which would leave a blemish on his record—the equivalent of a defect in the world—that would last forever. Stuck in that hideous situation, Hedin had become a slave to his pride.

And one day, in the evening in the king's room, the great window open so he could see the sacred tree from it, Hedin, who had been drinking alone, met a certain witch, perhaps in a manifestation of an illusion brought about by his drunkenness.

"Despite understanding everything, you continue to be a slave to your country?"

Hedin downed his glass of wine and laughed mockingly at the witch's question.

"I called myself king. Even if it is a narrow, foolish little world, I will carry out my duty. No matter how fed up with it I am. If I cast it all aside, then I'd become something worse than an incompetent. If I have to choose between being a slave and being an incompetent, then I, Hedin, would choose the former. And besides, I've long since decided I would die on the battlefield."

There was a being who had caught Hedin's interest.

The other king among the dark elves who had transformed into a glistening blade. A victim of the vagaries of the world who, despite being king, did not, could not live up to his title. And despite all that, he was stronger than anyone. A single incomparable genius great enough to overcome a hundred incompetents by himself. Hedin utterly detested that bundle of contradictions, a disgraceful failure who was simultaneously peerlessly skilled. And at the same time, Hedin was filled with an intense competitiveness, not wanting to lose to that other king, who was the only other being in this world that Hedin had acknowledged.

Hedin, who was an embodiment of pride, wanted to win against the one man he judged capable of killing him. Even if it meant trading blows, he wanted to pierce that dark elf with his lightning.

If there were to be any way of saving this world, it would be by reaching a conclusion with him first. That was the only way.

"In that case, I'll release you from the yoke of being king. What happens after that is for you to decide."

The witch smiled and held out a glass of wine to him. Hedin's smile twisted as he took the glass and drank it dry.

When Hedin sobered up, she had disappeared. He wet his lips with water, thinking he had seen a foolish dream. From that day onward, despite being scared of him, the fairies' arrogance brought about by their king's power became unstoppable.

Incapable of loving one another they instead only scorned one another, revealing their incompetence for all to see.

—And because of that, it was only natural that the goddess would turn her back on a world without love.

The conflict between white elves and dark elves gradually devolved into a total war involving all their people. Other than children who did not know any better and had not yet been stained by anything, every last one of them picked up arms and joined the final battle as if it were a holy crusade. The drumbeat pushing for a final decisive clash that was building was abnormal, but neither Hegni nor Hedin made any effort to stop it. Both the kings and their countries felt that if they were going to be destroyed in this one battle then at least they could devote themselves to their desired battlefield.

In the middle of the mystical woods, the battle began on the border between the two countries. As was to be expected, the white elves with their skilled commander held the advantage throughout, but that only lasted until Hegni faced off against Hedin. After that, Hedin did not have the leeway to focus on anything other than his own fight and could no longer give orders, and as a result the armies' positions flipped. The dark elves had a greater military potential. That was the price the white elves paid for having continued to rely on Hedin's skilled command.

As the two kings' battle intensified, around them, one elf after another fell, and before they realized it, Hegni and Hedin were the only ones left standing on the battlefield.

Crimson bloomed, bloodshot eyes opened wide, and masks of rage covered their faces as their mortal combat unfolded. Despite the fact that the people and countries tying the two of them down were already gone, they pushed themselves to their limits because if nothing else, they would not allow themselves to lose to the elf standing before them.

And three days later, they still had not determined a victor.

Suddenly, the witch appeared.

"You can't reach a conclusion. Even though I listened to your wishes and decided to welcome whoever survived."

They were in the center of the island surrounded by a river of blood and the corpses of countless warriors. She sat down on one of the undirtied crystals right next to Hegni and Hedin, who were breathing raggedly, beaten and battered.

The two swung around in shock as she rested an elbow on either leg and rested her cheeks on her hands. The goddess's eyes narrowed.

"Sorry I destroyed your countries. They were just too unsightly."

At those words, time froze for the two of them. Hegni recognized it instinctively while at the same time, Hedin understood it logically. The drumbeat to war that had been building among the elves had been her doing. She had delivered revelations to the elves like an oracle, provoking their pride, and inciting them toward their own destruction. In that insular little world, if a deity really had appeared, then the elves would surely have believed her words and obeyed.

"A king who tyrannizes his people and a king abused by his country—which is more unsightly? At least in this case, I'd have to say the latter is the one that makes me want to sigh more.

"It's amazing you both managed to reach such extremes," she added.

Hegni and Hedin were in awe as they faced the goddess, who was like the accumulation of all the beauty in the world. However, she merely continued to smile. Indeed, there was even a glimpse of mercy on display as she continued, "I just had to free you from that never-ending curse."

She was truly both a witch and a goddess. While there were those who were saved by her love, there were also those whose destruction was brought about by that same love.

Two sides to the same coin. Free-spirited and cruel.

However, in the eyes of Hegni and Hedin, who had been stuck in that cage of eternal struggle, she seemed utterly sublime.

"If I'm being honest? I just couldn't bring myself to forgive the two countries that were holding back two so splendid as you, so I used some dirty methods to snatch you away."

The two kings gasped as the goddess spoke without any hint of concern. Everything that she said was true. The goddess who had spoken only the truth asked them one final question.

"I've taken possession of these children's souls, and I've broken the world that was tying you down. My intention was to take you back with me, but…what do you want?"

Both of their answers were obvious.

Hegni, who despised himself more than anything, was granted light by someone who accepted him as he was, more than anyone else ever had. In front of her, and only in front of her, he had no need to hide himself in the darkness.

And Hedin was set free from his duty by meeting someone more suited to rule than himself. He was finally allowed to be free.

The two of them were saved by that haughty and cruel goddess. And from that day on, Hegni's and Hedin's souls were stolen by the goddess.

4

Snow was falling.

Beautiful, cruel white fragments fell from the heavens, gradually burying the freezing body. It was all alone. It was cold.

There was no one who would hold it close nor anyone who would relieve its starvation. The indisputable reality was there in the freezing limbs. The unalterable truth was there in that squalid body.

Why am I so dirty? So poor? So empty? So cold? Those questions rose to the surface of an ashen heart for the thousandth time before disappearing.

What would I have to do for this body to stop being this body? While an ephemeral consciousness gradually faded, what little remained was genuinely pondering that question. And as that pondering continued, the consciousness decided to try to stop living.

And at that time—

"—Are you okay?"

A soothing soprano voice resounded in those frozen ears. The voice wrenched open eyelids that were threatening to fall, and the moment those eyes saw the owner of the voice, they widened. An outrageously beautiful, rich, satisfied, warm being was standing there. It was the first evidence that such a being could actually exist in this world.

"I was thinking of trying to help you…Is there anything you want?" the being standing there asked, as if she was just asking to amuse herself. Or perhaps, as if she could see the glimmer of a wish harbored in that body.

There is. Of course there is.

Finding out that such a beautiful, rich, satisfied, warm being existed, there was a single thing gripped that cold, empty, poor, dirty heart.

It was not merely envy or longing or jealousy—it was an all-consuming desire.

I want to become you. I want to quit being me and become the clean, warm you.

That rich being honestly had not expected that answer. Shocked, she laughed out loud.

"You want to become me? How ravenous can you be? There's never been a child who's said that before!"

There were those who had been saved by her love. And those who had sworn loyalty to her. But there had never once been a person who had wanted to become her. She laughed. The silver-haired goddess kept laughing. As if to demonstrate how unbelievably strange the request was. As if her interest had been piqued.

"All right, then, I'll give you—. In exchange, will you give me——?"

There was a slight nod in response.

And then, in that slum devoid of all hope, the goddess reached out her hand and asked:

"What is your name?"

The girl's lips twitched.

"—Syr."

There was an explosion accompanied by a terrible odor. There was an odd *thwump* as a puff of black smoke started to rise.

Faced with the explosive disaster rising from the pot, the girl tilted her head cutely and calmly extinguished the heat source before shaking her head. Her platinum hair that was tied back, swaying as she did.

"It feels like something is off..."

Inside a narrow kitchen. The girl was cooking in a room that resembled a certain tavern somewhere, as if it was constructed to be a replica inside the familia's home. Wherever her gaze might wander around the room, there were countless ingredients in pieces and in the pot as well as several other pans and utensils were charred.

"Like it's wrong...or like there's something...like I'm missing something...?"

Beside her, holding back her nausea with a hand to her mouth, was a female member of the familia, a girl of a similar age. Even hidden behind her long hair, her face was clearly beautiful, but currently it was twisted in grim agony. She was the poison tester—or rather, taste tester—for the experimental cooking that was being conducted here.

"Should I say that it was far, far better back when you prepared things that you didn't have to cook...or rather, I would greatly appreciate it if you could return to that...?"

"Awwww, you're so cruel, Helen! Even if it turned out like this, I am still trying my best, you know!"

"I fully recognize and understand that you are trying your best, but...!"

Helen shrank back a bit as the little girl threw up her hands in anger. Despite being clearly far stronger than the girl, she was careful not to be disrespectful. It could even be said that that was why she was suffering.

"The die is already cast! There's no choice left but to push on, break through my limits, and create the ultimate tasty dish!"

Taking the cookbook from the table, the girl reaffirmed her resolve and furiously started reading it as Helen paled in despair.

What did a person have to do in order to create such novel, strange, deviant dishes? There was no end to Helen's questions. She could do nothing but shudder and declare it the work of a god.

"I'm going to use the results of this training to make Bell happy!"

Helen hung her head in exhaustion.

The girl made another few dishes that Helen suffered through taste-testing, and then she put the best one into a basket.

Even understanding it was not entirely fair, Helen could not help resenting the boy whose stomach would just barely survive thanks to the sacrifices of her and other taste testers.

She did fully recognize that he would have to endure a fair amount of suffering, too, at least.

"All right, I'm headed out!"

"Ah! W-wait a minute! What about protection...!"

"I'll be fiiiine! After I head to the orphanage, I'm just going to the tavern!"

As the girl finished up her preparations quickly, Helen gave up and just let it go.

"Umm, please take care of yourself...L-Lady Syr..."

She paused for a bit, struggling with what to say before getting it out. And the girl, Syr, smiled.

"I will! See you later!"

© nilitsu

STATUS LEVEL

Lv.7	STRENGTH	DEFENSE	DEXTERITY	AGILITY	MAGIC
	S999	**S**999	**S**991	**S**989	**D**566
	HUNTER	IMMUNITY	MAGIC DEFENSE	FRACTURE	STURDY BODY
	E	**E**	**F**	**G**	**G**

MAGIC

HILDIS VINI	? ? ?

SKILL

VANA ANGATYR	• Active Trigger.
	• Bestial transformation. All stats increase dramatically.
	• Stamina and Mind are drained heavily when skill is active.
STULTUS OTTAR	• During battle, temporarily gain the ability Heal.
	• During battle, temporarily gain the ability Spirit Heal.
	• During battle, all abilities are enhanced.
	• The enhancement during battle is proportional to user's status.

EQUIPMENT
Supreme Black Sword

- A *Goibniu Familia* creation. 410,000,000 valis.

- A top-tier piece custom-made for Ottar and created from the Udaeus Black Sword drop item.

- The Udaeus Black Sword was melted down with adamantite and forged into ingots before being reworked into a greatsword.

- Due to the difficulty of making the sword, all of *Goibniu Familia*'s high smiths were enlisted for the task. According to the familia's master, it surpasses Urga.

- The massive black sword was plenty usable in its original state, but it became a weapon worthy of its name after being reworked into its current form.

OTTAR

BELONGS TO: *Freya Familia*
RACE: **Animal person (Boaz)**
JOB: **Adventurer**
DUNGEON RANGE:
Fifty-eighth floor
WEAPONS: **Greatsword,**
Battle-Ax, Hammer
CURRENT FUNDS:
237,700,000 valis

© nilitsu

AFTERWORD

Before writing.

Chief Editor: About how many pages do you think the manuscript will be this time?

Author: The desert story should be around 170 pages, so combined with the new shorts, it should be around 250 pages total?

Chief Editor: All right, let's go with that!

At the deadline.

Chief Editor: So, are you done?

Author: Yes, I've finished the 300 pages for the desert story!

Chief Editor: I have no words.

The page count keeps going up with each new book. This isn't funny anymore—at this rate, can I really call myself a light novel author? This is really, really, unbelievably bad. Are you going to write a 500-page first volume for a new series out of nowhere next, idiot? I had a looming sense of dread about the future that was waiting for me as I somehow managed to write the second volume of the *Chronicle* series. My apologies for the two-year-plus wait since the last one.

Even though there were so many more characters that needed to be depicted than there were in the first volume, and even though it was the Goddess of Beauty's familia, meaning everything they necessarily ended up with being super flashy—regardless of all those excuses, I really do think this was over-the-top. Never in my wildest dreams did I imagine that my pulse would be racing hardest while writing the afterword. I seriously think I might have to adopt a strict page limit so that the next volume is a light novel instead of a heavy one…!

True to the afterword in the last volume, this is a story about a certain goddess of beauty and her followers. When I submitted the manuscript I was worried about whether it would be acceptable, or whether this was going to be too much, since the stories involving this goddess inevitably ended up getting a little bit licentious, but since no one commented on it, I decided it was fine and had it published. Romance in the desert is an essential part of lots of Harlequin novels and whatnot, so forgive me!

Personally, I was really happy with how this book's guest heroine, the prince (not a typo), developed during the story. I think the short story "Ali and the 8 Followers" that was also published in *Gangan GA* is also that prince's story. When I wrote the climax, I felt a tightness in my chest and a marvelous sense of wonder.

And since it was about the strongest adventurers on par with the Sword Princess and her familia, as I already touched on before, I went way over the anticipated number of pages and received quite the scolding. The barn door's already wide open now, but their characters are just a little too unique, which both makes me very happy and means the struggle is never-ending.

The boar warrior and cat chariot have made a few appearances here and there in the main series, but I was oddly excited at how the white elf—who had been ominously in the background up until now—finally managed to step into the limelight. With regards to the four prums, I had a certain image of the brothers and just let it all sort of flow from there. Also, I finally got to write in the dark elf! Basically what I'm trying to say is I, the author, ended up liking the Goddess of Beauty's familia even more after finishing this volume.

On the one hand, setting this story in the desert was entirely about catering to my personal taste, but on the other hand, I had been trying to sprinkle various world view points in the books that have already been published, and I wanted a chance to expound on that a bit. The Chronicle series stories may end up being primarily stories set outside of the city. Perhaps I could use this series to gradually expand on the world beyond Orario.

The flashback stories also presented here are intended to reveal more about the setting in general and to hopefully entertain those who have invested so much time and effort into reading this series. I don't know whether I'll be successful, but sometime around when the main characters' story is finished, I would like to be able to tell the tale of Zeus and Hera.

Even the afterword is getting long now, so with my apologies, I'll move on to conveying my thanks.

To my editor, Matsumoto, chief editor Kitamura, and everyone else who was involved, I'm sorry for crashing into the deadline. And I'm extremely sorry to the illustrator, nilitsu, for causing problems because of that! I have nothing but gratitude for your providing such wonderful illustrations even as the manuscript delays drug on. To all the readers, I'm sorry for keeping you waiting so long for this second volume. To everyone who helped support me and to everyone who waited for me, I'm extremely grateful.

I was quite worried this time, since it was my first attempt at writing a story that heavily featured the desert, so I shamelessly had my fellow GA Bunko author Awamura Akamitsu read over the manuscript for me. Thank you for agreeing to help me and taking the time when you were so busy, and thank you for all of the helpful pointers you gave me. It really helped.

I think the next volume might be a story of a fox girl from the Far East.

I plan on involving the main series' cast for the first time. Additionally, a story about someone unexpected might be included, too. I hope you'll look forward to it.

Thank you for reading this far.

And with that, I will take my leave.

Fujino Omori